The Song of the Winns

The SPIES of GERANDER

·BOOK TWO·

BY FRANCES WATTS
illustrated by David Francis

RP|KIDS
PHILADELPHIA · LONDON

*For Mum, who always let me stay up
late to finish one more chapter*

Text copyright © 2013 by Frances Watts
Illustrations copyright © 2013 by David Francis

All rights reserved under the Pan-American and
International Copyright Conventions

First published in Australia by
HarperCollins*Publishers* Australia Pty Limited, 2011

First published in the United States by
Running Press Book Publishers, 2013

Printed in the United States

Books published by Running Press are available at special discounts
for bulk purchases in the United States by corporations, institutions,
and other organizations. For more information, please contact the Special
Markets Department at the Perseus Books Group, 2300 Chestnut Street,
Suite 200, Philadelphia, PA 19103, or call (800) 810-4145, ext. 5000,
or e-mail special.markets@perseusbooks.com.

ISBN 978-0-7624-4658-2

Library of Congress Control Number: 2012955521

E-book ISBN 978-0-7624-4838-8

9 8 7 6 5 4 3 2 1

Digit on the right indicates the number of this printing

Cover design by Frances J. Soo Ping Chow
Interior design by Frances J. Soo Ping Chow, based on
the original layout by Ingrid Kwong
Typography: Fairfield, HT Gelateria, Lady Rene, and Perpetua

This edition published by Running Press Kids
An Imprint of Running Press Book Publishers
A Member of the Perseus Books Group
2300 Chestnut Street
Philadelphia, PA 19103–4371

Visit us on the web!
www.runningpress.com/kids

1

The Lonely Road

The mozzarella was in an icy crevasse," said Uncle Ebenezer with a shiver, to demonstrate how cold the crevasse had been. The movement made his big belly wobble and his long shadow shimmied on the road stretching up between two high ridges of rock.

"An icy crevasse?" said Tibby Rose, who was beside him. "The mozzarella was in an icy crevasse? But why? How did it get there?"

Alistair, walking behind them with Aunt Beezer, had to laugh at his friend's perplexed tone. He and his brother and sister were used to their uncle's stories, but then the triplets had been living with their uncle and aunt for years, while Tibby had only just met Ebenezer and Beezer.

Uncle Ebenezer didn't seem inclined to answer Tibby Rose's questions. (They were the kind of questions Alistair himself used to ask once upon a time, but his uncle had never answered him either.) "I saw at once that the only way to reach the cheese was to abseil down. Fortunately, I had a length of rope with me, so I looped it around a tree."

Tibby Rose nodded approvingly. "A firm anchor is crucial," she agreed. Tibby was an expert in survival skills. She had been named after Charlotte Tibby—a great explorer—and had read all her namesake's books. (Her mother had added the name Rose because of Tibby's pink-tinted ginger fur.)

"I have an instinct for these things," Uncle Ebenezer admitted modestly, stroking his mustache. "I left my brother Rebus at the top of the crevasse—that's Alex, Alice, and Alistair's father"—he reminded Tibby—"and began my descent." He shivered again at the memory. "The deeper I went, the darker it grew. The crevasse was so narrow in places that my back brushed the wall behind me, and my feet were so cold where they touched the ice that they burned. I knew that if I stopped moving I would probably freeze to death, and the crevasse would become my icy tomb."

Even though it was summer, Alistair pulled his scarf tight around his neck as he imagined being surrounded by sheer walls of ice.

Ebenezer paused in his storytelling, and for a moment the only sound was the rustle of leaves in the trees lining their way, and the soft pad of their feet upon the road. Even Alice and Alex, walking behind Alistair, had stopped their customary bickering to listen.

"So what happened?" Tibby Rose demanded as the

silence lengthened.

"What happened?" repeated Uncle Ebenezer. "I'll tell you what happened—just as I was within a tail's length of the cheese, I heard a loud thump, so loud the ice around me shuddered."

"What was it?" Tibby gasped.

Ebenezer shook his head sorrowfully. "It was Rebus," he said. "I'd quite forgotten how my poor brother was scared of heights. He took one look into the ravine and grew so dizzy he passed out. Well of course with Rebus unconscious he wouldn't be able to pull me up once I'd reached the cheese—and I might die waiting for him to regain consciousness! There was only one thing to do: I would have to climb the rope myself. And for that, I would need both hands." He sighed. "So, leaving that poor mozzarella all alone at the bottom of the icy crevasse, I began to climb. Inch by determined inch I scaled that sheer ice wall until at last I reached the top. Then, with my final reserves of strength, I lifted up my unconscious brother, slung him over my shoulder and carried him home." All of Ebenezer's stories, Alistair noted, ended with him slinging Rebus over his shoulder and carrying him home.

Alistair felt a tremor in his chest as he thought of his father. It had been four years since the triplets had seen their parents—and for most of that time, they'd thought that Rebus and Emmeline were dead. . . .

"I can't believe Mom and Dad have really been alive this whole time," said Alex, as if his thoughts had been following the same line as Alistair's.

"Do you think they'll have changed?" Alice asked in a small voice.

Ebenezer, serious now, said, "Four years in an enemy prison would change anyone. But you know, my dear, I think we will all have to get used to a great many changes now. Why, look how much you four have been through in such a short time; I'm sure your experiences will have changed you in many ways."

"I'm even braver than I thought," Alex boasted.

Alistair wouldn't have put it in those words exactly, but he knew what his brother meant. He definitely felt more confident, and more capable, as a result of his and Tibby's hair-raising journey through Souris.

"I'm glad to hear it," said Ebenezer. "You may well have cause to be brave now that we have joined the resistance movement to fight for a Free and Independent Gerander—or rejoined, in the case of myself and Beezer."

"Do you think FIG will send us on spy missions, like the one Mom and Dad went on?" Alex asked eagerly.

"Well, I hope not like the one your parents went on," Ebenezer said, sounding alarmed. "Look how that turned out. But yes, it's possible you will be asked to undertake missions." He sighed heavily. "As members of FIG we will all be exposed to risks and dangers; your parents risked their lives to free our homeland, and any one of us may be called on to do the same. We are going to be living a very different life now: always on the move, always looking over our shoulders. It's not what I would have wished for you. After your parents died—after we thought they had died, I should say—Beezer and I were determined that you would have a normal, happy, safe childhood."

"Is that why you never told us about Gerander and FIG?" Alice asked.

"That's right," Beezer replied. "We weren't going to tell you until you were older; though now I think we might have been wrong to hide it from you."

Even after everything he and Tibby Rose had been through on their way back to Smiggins, Alistair still thought the biggest shock he had ever had was finding out that he and his brother and sister were actually Gerandan, and that his whole family had been involved in the struggle to free their homeland from the Sourian occupation. He felt as if he'd had a whole new identity thrust upon him. He didn't mind it exactly, but it certainly took some getting used to. It was amazing to think his parents and aunt and uncle had lived with a secret so big for so many years.

And now he was the one with a secret, Alistair reflected—he and Tibby Rose. He gripped the ends of his scarf. "How much farther do you think, Aunt Beezer?" He tried to keep the impatience from his voice. A secret FIG meeting was being held near the town of Stetson in the northwest of Shetlock, right near Shetlock's border with Gerander. They had left their home in Smiggins before dawn three days earlier, and had been walking long hours each day.

His aunt replied, "It can't be far now. I was hoping we'd get there before dark, but I'm not sure we will." She lifted her eyes to scan the sky. Alistair knew she was watching for night hunters. And it wasn't only night birds looking for prey they had to be wary of as the light faded on this lonely road. There was a strong possibility that two Sourian spies were on their trail. "Ebenezer, let's take another look at the map," she suggested.

While Uncle Ebenezer and Aunt Beezer murmured over the map, Alistair and Tibby Rose stood with Alice and Alex.

"We probably would have been there by now if Alex hadn't ordered the cheddar soufflé at that place where we stopped for lunch," Alice grumbled, casting an apprehensive look over her shoulder at the road behind them. "It said on the menu it would take them an extra twenty minutes to make."

"It was the specialty of the house," Alex argued.

Alistair suspected it was fear making Alice so sharp with their brother. Unlike him and Tibby Rose, Alice and Alex had actually encountered the Sourian spies, Horace and Sophia, first-hand, and had only narrowly escaped being killed.

"Not far now," Beezer reassured the triplets and their friend as they resumed walking.

Tibby Rose fell into step beside Alistair. "I can't believe how tiring all this walking is," she said. "I can't remember being this tired when we were traveling across Souris. But it was much easier when we didn't have to carry anything." She put her hands behind her back to ease the weight of the pack on her shoulders.

"For someone who ran away from home with nothing,

you certainly have managed to cram a lot into that rucksack," Alistair teased. "Though we didn't really do that much walking in Souris," he reminded his friend. "Most of the time we were paddling down a river, on the raft you made."

"And even when we weren't on the raft, we did a lot more running than walking," Tibby recalled ruefully. "It would have been so much easier if we could have used secret paths," she added in a low voice, glancing at Alistair's scarf.

Alistair's hands closed on the ends of his scarf once more as Tibby referred to the secret paths that crisscrossed Gerander. Was it really possible that his mother had knitted a map of the secret paths into the scarf she had given him just before she left on her last mission?

He was distracted from these thoughts when a swooping movement caught his eye. There was something circling above them in the sky!

"It's a hawk!" Uncle Ebenezer yelled.

"An eagle!" cried Aunt Beezer at the same time.

Ebenezer ran back toward Alistair and Tibby Rose. "Hurry, everyone!" he called. Taking Tibby Rose's hand he ran toward the shelter of the shrubs at the side of the road, pushing Alistair along ahead of him. Aunt Beezer ushered Alice and Alex ahead of her.

Alistair crouched in the bushes, his heart racing, as the shape wheeled around, then descended. It was heading straight toward them! A shadow swept across the bush where he was hiding and Alistair thought he heard a voice say, "Oh, I really don't feel well," followed by a terrifying screech. A screech that sounded very familiar to Alistair . . .

"That's not a hawk or an eagle," he shouted. "It's an owl!" And before his aunt or uncle could stop him, he darted out of the bushes.

2

FIG Headquarters

listair, come back!" called his uncle as Alistair stood in the middle of the road.

A giant owl swooped toward the ground, its talons outstretched. Alistair could just make out the shape of a mouse grasped in each talon.

"Oswald!" said Alistair, waving. "Over here."

The owl hovered inches above the ground, then carefully released its two passengers, who stumbled a moment before regaining their balance. In the twilight Alistair saw a tall lean mouse and a small slim one in shiny black boots. It was Feast Thompson and Slippers Pink.

"We'll walk from here," the slim mouse was telling the owl, "and meet up again later."

"Hi, Feast!" Alistair said as the owl soared into the darkening sky. "Hello, Slippers."

Feast Thompson and Slippers Pink turned at the

sound of his voice. Slippers, Alistair noticed, was looking distinctly queasy; she hated flying.

"Alistair! Tibby Rose!" Slippers rushed over and hugged first Alistair and then Tibby Rose, who had joined him.

By this time, the others had left the shelter of the bushes, and Alistair introduced Slippers Pink and Feast Thompson to his family.

"A pleasure to meet two of FIG's highest operatives," said Ebenezer.

"People only call us that because we spend so much time in the air," said Slippers, laughing.

The group continued up the road together. Slippers Pink, walking with Beezer, led the way, followed by Ebenezer and Feast Thompson.

"It's just around the next bend," Slippers was saying. "FIG has taken over the Stetson school for our headquarters while everyone's away for the summer. The principal is a supporter."

"And when summer's over?" Beezer asked. "Where will the headquarters be then?"

Slippers shrugged her slim shoulders. "On the move again, I suppose. Setting up camp in a cave in a remote valley for a month or two, if we're lucky. More often it's just a week or so in a forest clearing or in the scrub along a deserted stretch of coast. It's been wonderful having a real base for a while: proper beds and running water and a cafeteria. Of course, we're keeping a low profile; I doubt anyone in the village even suspects that there's anyone staying at the school."

Alex, who was walking with Alice in front of Alistair and Tibby Rose, groaned. "We're going to be hanging out at a school? Eating in the cafeteria?" Then he let out an ooph as Alice nudged him sharply in the ribs. "Hey, what did you do that for?" he demanded.

Alice hissed, "Because Feast Thompson and Slippers Pink have more important things to worry about than what the food is—"

But before she could finish her sentence they heard Feast Thompson say loudly, "I hope Tobias has found a good chef. Slippers and I have been traveling nonstop for the last couple of weeks, and I'd give anything to sit down to a big, hearty meal."

Alex didn't say anything, but Alistair saw him shoot a self-righteous look at Alice.

"Here's the turnoff," Slippers said, and at a fork in the road they turned left onto a narrow road winding up through an avenue of pine trees. "The school isn't actually in Stetson itself; it's on a hill above the town. It's great for security, because there's only one road in."

"Except if you arrive by owl," Feast pointed out.

After about ten minutes' walking, Alistair saw that up ahead the narrow road opened out onto a large flat plateau partially enclosed by a wall of rock. He could just make out clusters of dark shapes, which must be the school buildings. As they drew close two mice stepped out onto the road to block their way.

Slippers Pink and Feast Thompson moved forward.

"Hi, Flora," said Slippers to the tall blonde mouse. She

turned to the tall brown one. "Is that you, Maxwell? It's been ages."

"I've been undercover the last few months," the brown mouse said briefly. Alistair noticed that Slippers and Feast nodded but didn't ask any questions about where Maxwell had been or why.

"Who else have you got there?" Flora wanted to know, peering past Slippers and Feast to where Alistair and the others were standing a few feet away.

"We've got Ebenezer and Beezer from Smiggins, and their niece and nephews and a friend."

Max consulted a list, then said, "So that's Alex, Alice, Alistair, and Tibby Rose, right?" He checked off their names and said, "We've been expecting you."

Flora told Beezer and Ebenezer, "You can have adjoining rooms in the dormitory building for the next couple of nights. After that..." She shrugged. "We've just had word from one of our patrols that they've found a group of refugee families from Gerander hiding near the border. They'll be here within forty-eight hours, and it sounds like they might have been injured in the escape. We'll probably have to move you so they can have your rooms. You can bed down in the hall after that; plenty are."

"Of course," Ebenezer murmured. His expression had grown concerned at the mention of injured mice.

Flora continued, "You're in room 17. The dorm is in block 1, on the other side of the oval. I'd suggest you drop off your bags and then go straight to the hall, which is the building beside it. Tobias is going to say a few words before dinner." She indicated a building close by; its high windows were lit up. "That's the cafeteria there."

"Thank you," said Beezer. "Come on, everyone." She and Ebenezer began to lead the way across the grassy oval.

"What about Slippers and Feast?" Alistair said, hesitating. He couldn't wait to tell Slippers Pink and Feast Thompson the secret he'd discovered about his scarf, but he knew he had to wait until they were alone. When Slippers Pink had told them about the hidden paths through Gerander, she had made Alistair and Tibby Rose promise that they would never reveal the secret to anyone.

The tall dark brown mouse and smaller almond mouse exchanged a wry look. "If I know Tobias," said Slippers, "we probably won't be staying long."

"Long enough for dinner, though, I hope," said Feast.

"Come on, Alistair," Ebenezer called.

"Quick, tell her," Tibby Rose murmured in Alistair's ear.

"Slippers . . . ," Alistair began. His hesitant tone must have alerted her to the fact that he had something important to say, because Slippers said, "See you, Flora. Bye, Max," and moved to Alistair's side. She, Feast, Alistair, and Tibby Rose began to walk slowly across the oval, keeping some distance between themselves and the others. Alistair noticed several mice flitting around the edges of the oval, and heard the occasional hum of voices carrying on the gentle breeze.

"What is it, Alistair?" Slippers asked.

"I think—I think I know something about the paths of

Gerander," he said in a rush. "I think Mom might have knitted them into my scarf, like a map."

Alistair heard a sharp intake of breath, though he couldn't tell whether it came from Slippers or Feast.

But Slippers merely said, "Tobias will want to hear this too. Feast and I will set up a meeting." She touched Alistair lightly on the arm. "You go with your family. We'll see you in the hall in a few minutes." And then the two FIG operatives strode off into the night.

"Who's Tobias?" Tibby Rose asked, as she and Alistair jogged to catch up with the others, their rucksacks bouncing uncomfortably on their backs.

"I don't know," Alistair replied, following his brother and sister up the steps of a two-story brick building.

As they walked down the corridor they passed small huddles of mice, clustered in twos and threes and speaking in hushed voices. A few nodded to the newcomers but most were so engrossed in their conversations they merely stepped aside absentmindedly so that Alistair and his family could squeeze past.

The triplets and Tibby Rose barely had time to drop their bags on the floor of a small room with two sets of bunk beds before they were being hurried out of the dormitory block to the building next door and through the double doors at the rear of the hall.

The hall was a large unfurnished space with a high ceiling and wooden floors, and a stage facing the doors. Alistair noticed a stack of gym mats in an alcove and a few sporting pennants fixed high up on the walls, and guessed that it probably doubled as a gymnasium. The room would have seemed huge when it was empty, but tonight it was crammed with mice, some standing alone in somber silence, others talking excitedly in groups, their voices echoing off the bare surfaces. Where had they all come from? As overwhelming as it was to find himself surrounded by so many mice—more overwhelming for Tibby Rose, who had never been in such a crowd, he realized as he felt his friend press closer to his side—it was also exhilarating to think that they were all members of FIG, and all here to play a part in liberating Gerander.

Through the crush Alistair saw there were quite a few rucksacks shoved up against the walls, and he wondered what it would be like to sleep in this cavernous space, among strangers. For a moment he thought longingly of the apartment in Smiggins: his bed in the small room that had once been Beezer's study, the shelf full of books, the jumble of sporting equipment in the corner. But with the Sourians after them, it was no longer safe for them to stay there. All he owned now was what he could fit in his rucksack. Then he thought of the refugee families Flora had mentioned; if they had had to flee their homes suddenly, they'd be lucky to have that much.

The hubbub had risen to a deafening pitch when a mouse with fur the color of orange marmalade walked onto the stage at the front of the hall.

Alistair felt a hand on his back and turned to see that Feast had squeezed through the crowd to stand beside him. Slippers stood on the other side of Tibby Rose.

"That's Tobias," Feast Thompson whispered, nodding toward the marmalade mouse. "He's been running FIG ever since Zanzibar was captured."

"He's also Zanzibar's cousin," added Slippers Pink. "They spent a lot of time together when they were growing up in Gerander—in hiding, of course. The Sourians have never been content to let the rightful king of Gerander walk free."

The marmalade mouse held up a hand and the crowd fell silent. He began to speak with calm authority.

"Friends, it has been three generations since the earthquake that devastated our homeland."

A gentle sigh rippled through the crowd.

"And it has been three generations since the Sourian army poured over the border into Gerander to help in our recovery . . . and then refused to leave."

The gentle sigh became a hiss of disapproval.

Tobias's voice became louder as he continued, "Friends, for far too long our homeland has been occupied by the Sourian oppressors. Our people are prisoners in our own land!"

A wave of angry murmurs swept through the crowd now.

Tobias's voice carried above the murmurs. "Since FIG was founded, everyone here has made many sacrifices. There have been many setbacks and many tragedies in our struggle against a more powerful opponent. And frankly, we have had little cause for optimism. But these are extraordinary times, and the news I wish to share with you today is worthy of celebration—"

"Zanzibar is free!" came a voice from the back of the crowd, and a small cheer went up.

Tobias raised his hands and the hall fell quiet once more. "Worthy of celebration and cause for great concern," he finished. He paused then, as if expecting another outburst, but the hall full of mice was silent. "As those of you who have been engaged in surveillance work are aware, there has been unusual activity in Gerander of late. We have reason to believe that the Sourian army has been increasing troop numbers. No doubt they are worried about the consequences of Zanzibar's escape. No doubt they are worried that under Zanzibar's leadership, Gerandans will rise up and repel the Sourian invaders"—Tobias's voice grew louder, booming across the hall—"and Gerander will be a free and independent nation once more!"

"Hurrah!" The room rang with cheers and Alistair felt a thrill of excitement run through him.

"Where is Zanzibar now?" asked a broad brown mouse to Alistair's left. "Is he here?"

Tobias shook his head. "No, Zanzibar is not here. For security reasons, he has gone into hiding. But I have met with him, and we have put together a strategy. It is time for us to redouble our efforts. The Sourians seem to be planning some sort of crackdown, but Zanzibar is free and momentum is on our side: we must seize the opportunity and act! Starting tonight I will be handing out assignments—some of them very risky. But for now . . . welcome. Enjoy this time with your friends and colleagues before the hard work begins."

The marmalade mouse nodded once, then strode from the stage to thunderous applause.

No sooner had the applause died down than Alistair spied several mice striding toward the sides of the hall and hefting rucksacks onto their shoulders. It was obvious from their rapid movements and whispered conversations that they were about to embark on urgent missions.

"Rescue detail!" someone was bellowing above the buzz of talk. "Could everyone in the rescue detail please report to the library immediately? Your briefing starts in five minutes."

Mice were rushing in all directions, being summoned to one of the many meetings that seemed about to start or delivering messages or trying to find word of friends and relatives. Alistair and his family were caught up in the surge of mice flowing out of the hall and across the oval to the cafeteria. If the smells issuing from the long, low building were anything to go by, both Feast and Alex would be satisfied.

There was a bottleneck at the door, but once he was inside Alistair saw that the walls of the cafeteria were lined with tables groaning under the weight of pots and platters and trays and tureens of delicious food. There was even a dessert buffet, and it looked as though a few mice had skipped dinner altogether and were already helping themselves to generous portions of cake and pudding.

Alistair joined the line filing past an array of pastas and sauces, and piled a plate with spaghetti, which he topped with a generous sprinkling of Parmesan. Then he pushed his way through the crowd until he saw a long table around which his family and friends were gathering. He slipped into a spot saved for him between Feast Thompson and Slippers Pink. It was great to see them again; funny, too, to be meeting up with them so far away from the lonely cliff top on the Sourian Sea where he had last seen them. But there were so many mice assembled here for FIG's special meeting, he had the feeling that if he sat still long enough everyone he had ever met would walk by. There was, in fact, one mouse he was hoping to see: Timmy the Winns, a mysterious midnight blue mouse whom he and Tibby Rose had met on their journey through Souris. It was Timmy who'd first given Alistair the idea that there might be something special about his scarf.

"Is Timmy the Winns here?" he asked Feast Thompson.

Feast shrugged and looked around vaguely. "He'll be here somewhere. It's hard to spot anyone in this crowd, though."

Alistair thought that a midnight blue mouse would be sure to stand out, yet he hadn't caught so much as a glimpse of him. Or was it possible that Timmy wasn't blue anymore? After all, he and Tibby Rose had been a brownish purple when they'd met Timmy and his traveling companions—they'd dyed their fur with blackberry juice so the Sourians, who despised ginger mice as Gerandan spies, would stop chasing them—but now they were ginger.

As he scanned the crowd, Alistair's eyes met those of a white mouse at another table. The other mouse appeared to be looking directly at him. As he gazed back, Alistair couldn't read the white mouse's expression. It didn't seem hostile, nor did it seem friendly. It seemed merely alert and . . . speculative, Alistair thought. Then someone walked between them, and when Alistair was next able to see the white mouse, he was engaged in conversation with a scruffy brown mouse to his left.

"Slippers, do you know him?" Alistair indicated the white mouse who had been staring at him.

Slippers Pink looked over. "Hmm, yes," she said. "That's Solomon Honker. I wonder what he's up to?" But before Alistair could ask anymore questions about the white mouse, Slippers was saying, "Eat up. You too, Tibby Rose." Tibby was on Slippers's other side. "Tobias said he'd see us straight after dinner."

Alex was already getting up for a second helping at the dessert buffet by the time Alistair twirled the last piece of spaghetti around his fork.

Alistair and Tibby Rose stood too, but they followed Slippers and Feast right past the dessert table and out of the cafeteria. They walked across a cement play area on which Alistair could just make out the faded chalk squares of a handball court, and pushed their way past a small crowd of mice to slip through the door of a building marked SCHOOL OFFICE.

"What are they all waiting for?" Tibby Rose asked.

"They probably have meetings with Tobias too," Slippers explained as they strode along a corridor. "He's using the principal's office as his headquarters."

Suddenly a dark gray mouse with sharp features came out of an office and barred their way. "Pink, Thompson, what are you doing here? Who let these children in?" He scowled at Alistair and Tibby.

"Out of the way, Flanagan," Feast Thompson said brusquely. "Tobias invited us—and them."

"We'll see about that," the dark gray mouse muttered, and turned to rap on the door he had just closed behind him. When a voice called, "Enter!," he slipped into the office, leaving the others standing in the corridor.

"Who's he?" asked Alistair.

"Tobias's assistant," said Slippers Pink. "He's a bit . . . overprotective . . . when it comes to Tobias."

"Flanagan thinks he's the only one who should have access to Tobias," Feast elaborated, not bothering to hide the dislike in his voice.

They stood in silence as a murmured exchange went on behind the closed door, then Flanagan emerged and gestured to them. "Tobias will see you now," he said ungraciously.

The marmalade mouse sitting behind the principal's desk half stood as Alistair and the others entered the office. He was wearing a pair of wire-framed reading glasses, which he removed to reveal tired, red-rimmed eyes. While he had seemed vigorous and energetic when rallying the FIG members in the hall, up close his weariness was unmistakable.

"Have you got enough chairs? Just pull some over from the table there, will you, Feast?"

"You look completely worn out, Tobias," Slippers said as she lowered herself into a seat.

But Tobias waved away her concern. "I'm fine," he said, slumping back into his chair. "Just busy." He waved a hand at the piles of paper on his desk. "We've got a few operations on at the moment, and a few more in the planning. Speaking of which . . . " He leaned forward and turned a kindly look on Alistair and Tibby Rose. "What a pleasure to see a couple of young faces," he said. "I've got a son about your age who's spending summer vacation with a friend. I'm afraid he doesn't write nearly as often as I would like." He shook his head fondly at a framed photo of a miniature version of himself. "And speaking of young mice who worry their elders, you've had quite an adventure, I hear. All the way from Souris to Shetlock." If he was angry at them for running away from the house in Templeton where Tibby's Grandpa Nelson and Great-Aunt Harriet lived, he wasn't showing it. If anything, he sounded amused, Alistair thought.

"They certainly have," Slippers Pink agreed, sounding distinctly less amused. "But I think the information they have for us now might be worth all the trouble they caused me and Feast." She lifted the corner of her mouth in a smile. "Tell Tobias what you told us, Alistair."

Taking a deep breath, Alistair stood up, unwound his scarf from around his neck and laid it flat on Tobias's desk. He quickly explained how he and Tibby Rose had encountered the mysterious mouse named Timmy the Winns on their journey through Souris, and how Timmy had sung him a song about the Winns. Alistair hadn't known at the time where the Winns was—indeed, he'd known hardly anything about Gerander at all back then—but Timmy's song about the river had nonetheless sounded familiar. Alistair repeated the first verse now:

> "From rock to ridge to tunnel to tree
> The songs are there for you to see;
> Read the land and follow the signs,
> Read the river between the lines."

"I asked Timmy about the Winns, and he said . . ." Alistair thought for a minute as he tried to recall Timmy's exact words. "He said, 'It is the spine that knits our head to our feet.'

"And then we met you," Alistair said, looking now at Slippers Pink and Feast Thompson, "and you told us about the secret paths through Gerander that my mother knew, and it was almost like you expected me to know them too."

"I was hoping Emmeline might have told you," Slippers admitted. "But you hadn't heard of them."

"She'd never mentioned them," Alistair confirmed. "Then Tibby Rose and I met up with Alice and Alex, who were coming to find me. On the way back home to Smiggins, we stopped off in Stubbins to show Tibby the house where we used to live. And I was thinking about Mom and Dad, and about how Mom had given me this scarf the night before they left, and then I remembered a song she had sung. It was the same tune as Timmy the Winns's song." He recited the words:

> *"A burning tree*
> *A rock of gold*
> *A fracture in the mountain's fold,*
> *In the sun's last rays when the shadows grow long*
> *And the rustling reeds play the Winns's north song."*

As Alistair reached the end of the verse there was a knock on the door and the dark gray mouse entered.

"What is it, Flanagan?" Tobias asked absently, his gaze still fixed on Alistair's scarf.

"An urgent message has come for you. It's sealed, and it's marked for your eyes only."

Tobias put on his reading glasses and held out a hand for the envelope, but instead of giving it to him his secretary said, "Perhaps you'd better step outside to attend to it, sir." He didn't even glance at the four mice who sat between him and Tobias.

Tobias sighed. "Excuse me," he murmured. "I'd better see what this is about." He rose from his chair and left the room.

When he re-entered the office a few minutes later he seemed distracted. He stood by the door, his eyes drifting around the room before settling on the scarf spread out on the table. He stared at it as if transfixed, then, with an impatient noise, he crumpled the letter he was holding into a ball and lobbed it toward the wastepaper basket by his desk. "Nothing important," he said dismissively.

"Is it just my imagination, or is Flanagan even more paranoid than usual?" Slippers asked as Tobias slid back into his seat.

"We, ah . . ." The marmalade mouse paused. "There have been some security issues," he said finally.

Beside him, Alistair sensed a new alertness about Slippers Pink.

"Security issues?" she prompted.

Tobias pushed his glasses to the top of his head and pinched the bridge of his nose with one hand. "A leak."

"How high?" Feast asked immediately.

"High," said Tobias, then held up a hand to indicate that he didn't want to talk about it.

"But—" Slippers protested.

"My concern," Tobias said firmly. "Not yours. Now, where were we?"

"I was just explaining about my scarf," Alistair reminded him. "Timmy the Winns was looking at it just before he talked about the Winns knitting our head to our feet. I think he was trying to tell me something. And this blue stripe, it runs from the top to the bottom of the scarf. That could be like head to foot, couldn't it?"

Tobias ran a hand through the rumpled marmalade fur on his chin. "And you think the song Emmeline sang is another clue?"

"We think the song might be about particular landmarks pointing the way to a secret path," Tibby Rose said. "A rock of gold and a burning tree."

"And that the scarf might be a map," Alistair finished.

"And that we could use it to find the secret paths."

Tobias was nodding. "It's possible," he said. Then he sat up straighter. "Yes. It's definitely possible." He put his glasses back on and studied the scarf, its vivid colors and strange design. "And have you found these landmarks— the rock of gold and the burning tree—on the scarf?"

Tibby and Alistair exchanged excited glances. Tobias believed them!

Alistair pointed to the burst of orange he and Tibby had found. "That could be a burning tree."

"And this could be the golden rock," Tibby said, pointing to a patch of yellow near it.

Tobias peered intently at the rock and the tree, then traced the blue stripe of the river with his finger to the top of the scarf. "Up here," he said, "to the north, this looks like the source of the Winns." He rested his fingertips on a dark green oval and closed his eyes. "It's a magical place," he murmured. "A deep mountain spring. The old folk say it has healing properties."

"Have you been there?" Tibby asked.

"I have," said Tobias. "I spent many vacations in the area as a boy."

"It looks like the golden rock and burning tree aren't far from the source."

"Well, if we've got some landmarks to guide us, and know they're near the source of the river, the next step is obvious," said Feast. "Slippers and I should go to Gerander and find the secret paths."

Before Tobias could respond, Alistair said, "Tibby and

I want to go to Gerander too. I have to find my parents—unless you already have a plan to rescue them?" His heart started to beat faster in anticipation of the marmalade mouse's response.

Tobias shook his head slowly. "I'm afraid we've been finding it rather difficult to organize," he said heavily. "It is nearly impossible to travel through Gerander undetected."

"Not anymore!" Alistair said triumphantly. "The secret paths go all over Gerander, don't they? I bet we could use them to get to Atticus Island."

"Not so fast," Slippers Pink broke in. With an apologetic look at Alistair and Tibby Rose, she said to Tobias, "Feast and I, we're more than willing to go. But there's no way Alistair and Tibby Rose should be sent into Gerander. It's too dangerous."

Tobias was drumming his fingers on the table thoughtfully, and Alistair felt a spark of hope. Despite Slippers's objections, the marmalade mouse actually appeared to be considering his idea!

Tobias cleared his throat. "I'm afraid it's not that simple, Slippers," he said. "It's not just because they are hidden that the secret paths have remained a secret. You see, not everyone can read the signs. They are passed down within families, but not to every family member. Those who read the signs recognize others with the same ability, as Emmeline must have recognized the ability in Alistair when she gave him this scarf. I don't like it anymore than you do but, as dangerous as it may be for Alistair to join you on this mission, I think he is essential to its success. And after everything they've been through, I think Alistair and Tibby Rose should stay together."

"I couldn't go without Tibby," Alistair said. "I never would have made it out of Souris if not for her."

"We're agreed then," said Tobias. "Now, we have been able to find out a little more about the situation on Atticus Island from one of our members who was imprisoned there. I have a detailed description of where Emmeline and Rebus are being held." He rummaged through the scraps of paper littering his desk, finally alighting on one. "Here." He gave it to Slippers Pink, who promptly slipped it into one of her shiny black boots. "Oswald will help you, I presume?"

Slippers nodded once, her mouth set in a mutinous line. Alistair could tell she wasn't happy that Tobias had agreed to let him and Tibby Rose accompany her and Feast on the mission—even if there could be no mission without Alistair to find the secret paths.

"There's one more thing," Tobias said seriously. "You are not to talk about this mission to anyone. And I mean anyone. I'm afraid to say that includes your family, Alistair. We cannot afford any lapses in security, especially now. Once you have left, I will inform your family that you have been sent on an assignment."

There was a rap on the door and Tobias stood, which seemed to signal that their meeting was over, for Slippers Pink and Feast Thompson rose too.

"Will there be any reply to the message which came earlier?" Flanagan asked, craning his head around the door.

Again, he acted as if there were no one else in the room.

Tobias cast a resigned look at the wastepaper basket. "I'll deal with it myself, Flanagan."

As Flanagan withdrew, Alistair took the scarf from Tobias's desk and hastily wrapped it around his neck, then he and Tibby Rose followed Feast and Slippers to the door.

Tobias accompanied them; at the doorway he laid a warm hand on Alistair's shoulder. "Well done," he said. "Working out the clue Emmeline left in the scarf was very clever."

"I think Timmy the Winns worked it out before I did," Alistair confessed. Then, remembering that he still hadn't seen the midnight blue mouse, he asked, "Is Timmy here?"

A pained expression crossed Tobias's face. "No," he said quietly. "Timmy hasn't turned up."

"Hasn't turned up?" Slippers sounded surprised.

"Timmy is . . . missing," Tobias said unhappily. He shook his head. "We think the leak . . ." His voice trailed off.

"Timmy's missing?" Slippers's voice was shrill. "But if even Timmy's not safe, what about Zanzibar?"

"My concern," Tobias said firmly, just as he had earlier. "Not yours." Then he added more gently, "Don't worry, Zanzibar is safe." He ushered them into the corridor. "Good luck," he said. "All of you. . . . Flanagan? I'm ready for my next meeting now."

The dark gray mouse bustled past them into the principal's office, closing the door firmly behind him.

"Alistair, you had no business volunteering for this

mission," Slippers said crossly as they retraced their steps down the corridor.

"You heard what Tobias said, Slips," Feast Thompson countered. "There'd be no mission without him." As Slippers stalked ahead of them through the door into the cool night air, Feast turned to Alistair and Tibby Rose. "She's not really angry at you," he said in a low voice. "She's just worried."

They walked slowly across the playground, talking about the mission ahead.

"Oswald won't be able to carry us all, so we'll have to go in two trips. The obvious place to start is at the northernmost point of the Winns," Feast reasoned. "The source."

"Okay, but I do have one condition," Slippers said to Alistair and Tibby Rose. "Oswald will drop me and Feast at the source first. We'll check it out while he returns to fetch you two. If there is any sign of danger—no matter how small—I'm aborting the mission and Oswald flies you straight back here." She put her hands on her hips and looked at Alistair and Tibby Rose sternly. "Do you understand?"

The two ginger mice nodded.

Feast resumed his planning. "Os'll cross the Gerandan border just to the north of here, then follow the Winns as far as the Crankens, where the source is."

"The source is in the Crankens?" Alistair asked with a shiver. It was in the Cranken Alps that the Sourians had their notorious prison camp.

"In the foothills really," Slippers Pink explained, "not the mountains themselves. On the Gerandan side of the border, of course."

Feast continued, "Then we can walk south along the river until we find the landmarks from the song—and, hopefully, the secret paths." He looked at Alistair and Tibby Rose. "Os should be back to pick you up a couple of hours before dawn. You should try to catch some sleep in the meantime. I'll tell Oswald to tap on your window when he returns from the first drop. That's the signal for you two to head immediately to the oval. Os'll meet you there."

As Feast Thompson outlined the plan, Slippers Pink was staring into the sky with a slightly anxious expression on her face, rubbing the back of her neck absently.

"Watch her," Feast advised, gesturing at Slippers. "When she rubs her neck like that, it means something isn't right. She doesn't even know she's doing it half the time—but it never fails. It's like she's got a sixth sense for danger."

"Does that mean something could go wrong with the flight?" Alistair asked, feeling a prickle of apprehension raise the fur on the back of his own neck.

"Not necessarily," said Feast. "In this case it's probably just a fear of flying."

Slippers groaned. "For someone who doesn't like to fly, I seem to be doing an awful lot of it recently," she said.

"The weather's fine; I'm sure we'll have a smooth flight," Feast reassured her. "Okay, Slips, let's move. See you two at the source."

3

Night Flight

The crowd in the cafeteria had thinned by the time Alistair and Tibby Rose rejoined the others at the long table.

"There you are," Ebenezer said with obvious relief. "When you disappeared with Slippers Pink and Feast Thompson I thought they might have whisked you back to Souris." He chuckled.

"Where *did* they take you?" Alice asked curiously.

"We, ah, we went to meet Tobias," Alistair explained. Tibby Rose kicked him under the table, as if warning him not to reveal too much.

"You met Tobias?" Alex's mouth dropped open and the others were looking similarly astonished. "Why?"

It was a good question. Alistair tried desperately to think of something he could tell his family that wouldn't mean revealing their secret mission. Then he remembered how Tobias had greeted them. "He said it was a pleasure to see some younger faces," Alistair said casually. "Apparently he has a son about our age who's on vacation with a friend. I think he misses him. Hey, sis, can I finish your ice cream?" Alistair pointed to Alice's bowl to change the subject.

"I don't know why seeing your face would be a pleasure," Alex grumbled. "My face is much nicer. Tobias should've asked to meet me."

Fortunately Tibby Rose succeeded in distracting him with a question about which desserts he had tried from the buffet, and Alistair was able to finish his sister's ice cream in peace—though perhaps peace was the wrong word, since his thoughts were anything but peaceful. Timmy the Winns was missing. . . . He and Tibby Rose were about to go on a dangerous mission without telling anyone. . . . They were going to rescue his parents! Worry, guilt and anticipation tumbled around in his mind so that he barely tasted the dessert. He was glad when Ebenezer stood up and said, "Come on, you lot, we've had a big day. Let's get some sleep."

Alex started grumbling again as they walked across the dark oval toward the sleeping quarters. "I still don't get why you two met Tobias and we didn't."

"Maybe they reminded Tobias of his son because they're ginger," Alice suggested. "He has a lot of ginger in his fur, so his son might too."

"That must be it," Tibby Rose agreed. "We saw a photo of him and he looked just like his dad."

"So Alistair and Tibby Rose get special treatment

because of the color of their fur?" Alex complained.

Alistair had to laugh. "Makes a pleasant change from being abused and hunted because of it!" he said.

Soon they reached the small bedroom that the four young mice were sharing. "Let's unpack our rucksacks so we have a bit of room to move in here," Alice said.

Alistair and Tibby Rose exchanged glances.

"I'm really tired," Tibby said, yawning and stretching her arms above her head. "I might leave mine till morning."

"Me too," said Alistair quickly.

Alice shrugged. "Whatever. Bags this bunk." As the other three scrambled to claim their places, she wondered aloud, "What will happen tomorrow, do you think? Tobias was talking about having assignments for everyone. Do you think he meant us too?"

"I hope so," Alex said. He was lying in the bunk above Alice, his hands crossed under his head. "I hope it's something really dangerous and exciting."

Alistair didn't say anything; it was torture not being able to tell his brother and sister about his mission. He was thankful that Tibby Rose chose that moment to turn out the lights.

At a light tap on the window, Alistair opened his eyes. In the moonlight streaming through the window he saw that Tibby Rose was already awake, kneeling by the foot of the bed and tightening the straps on her rucksack.

Alistair slid soundlessly from the top bunk, though he couldn't suppress a soft thud as he landed on the floor. Alice sighed in her sleep and murmured something indistinct, but she didn't wake. Alex, in the bed above hers, was as solid and unmoving as a rock. Trumpet blasts from the room next door, interspersed with light whistles, told him that his aunt and uncle were also sound asleep. It seemed wrong to creep away without saying good-bye, and Alistair hesitated for a moment, but when he glanced at the door he saw Tibby Rose beckoning. With one last look at his sleeping siblings, Alistair secured his scarf around his neck, heaved his rucksack onto one shoulder, and followed Tibby out into the dark corridor lined with closed doors.

As they walked quickly toward the exit, a symphony of snores and snuffles, woofs and whiffles, toots and tweets reverberated through the still air of the dormitory block.

They stepped outside into a world bathed in moonlight. The rocks encircling the school and town loomed black and forbidding against a sky illuminated by stars, and the grass of the oval was silvery.

"Where's Oswald?" Alistair asked.

As if in answer to his question, he felt a sudden downward breeze as the giant owl swooped from a nearby tree and came to rest a few meters away.

"Ready?" the night bird asked in his deep voice.

The two mice moved so they were standing about a meter apart, rucksacks securely over their shoulders. Alistair clutched the ends of his scarf between his fingers.

Oswald flexed his wings then gave a couple of short

flutters, enough to propel him to hover just above their heads and slightly behind them. The downdraft ruffled the fur on Alistair's head and he was about to lift his hand to smooth it back when he felt the owl's talon close like a vice around him and he was immobilized. Inching his head to the left, he could just make out Tibby Rose, similarly imprisoned.

"Okay, Tib?" he called, but just then the owl began to flap his giant wings in great beats and Tibby's reply was lost in the rush of air past his ears.

Oswald must have been weary from his previous trip, because it took five beats of his wings before he was able to lift off, and his usually smooth climb seemed labored. At last, though, they were airborne, rising high into the starry sky. The buildings below grew small, the hall and the dormitory squatting on one side of the oval, the cafeteria and school office on the other. The town of Stetson itself was visible as a few lights twinkling at the foot of the great hill. And then, as they rose higher still, Alistair could see the rocks and hills surrounding Stetson in a protective embrace. He could also feel currents of air now, blowing hard against him.

Alistair would have thought there was no chance of sleep with the wind roaring in his ears and the slightly jerky movement that accompanied each powerful thrust of Oswald's wings, but to his surprise he was feeling rather drowsy. . . .

When he opened his eyes some time later it felt as if he was being smothered in a cold damp blanket. It took him a few seconds to understand that they must be flying through a cloud. He wanted to keep his eyes open until they had cleared the mist, but the moisture stung so he closed them again, rubbing his scarf between his fingers for comfort, trying to picture the colors and shapes, all of them bound together by the broad blue stripe that was, he now knew, the Winns. He let his thoughts drift lazily as he tried to imagine the great river that ran the whole length of Gerander from north to south. He could hardly believe that in a matter of hours he would be there, by the Winns, in his family's homeland. "*The Winns is a river, and more than that. It is the spine that knits our head to our feet. Its veins run through our country and its water runs through our veins.*"

For a moment the frigid air lost some of its chill as Alistair remembered sitting by a fire on the bank of another river, in Souris, with the mysterious midnight blue mouse who had spoken as if he knew Alistair. Where was Timmy the Winns now? he wondered. With a heavy feeling in his chest he considered the possibility that Timmy was a prisoner of the Sourians—perhaps he was even in the dreaded Crankens prison camp from which Zanzibar had so recently escaped. Timmy the Winns, who loved freedom more than anything.

"Wherever the Winns takes me, that's where I'll be,
For me and the Winns will always flow free."

That was what Timmy had sung by the fire that night in Souris. How surprised he'd be to know that Alistair was actually going to see the Winns. Or would he? Timmy never did seem surprised somehow. Like he hadn't been surprised to meet Alistair and Tibby Rose... Alistair stretched his toes closer to the fire, closer, closer—too close! They were burning!

Alistair awoke with a start. An icy wind was swirling around him and, as he squirmed a little within the owl's grasp, he realized that the burning in his toes was not from warmth, but from cold. And it was not only his toes: his ears, his nose, everywhere not enclosed by Oswald's talon was burning—except his tail, which was so numb with cold he couldn't feel it at all.

He wasn't sure how long he'd been asleep, but the sky to his right was now edged with the palest of yellows, a promise of dawn. He squinted at the shadowy landscape far below, but it was still too dark to make out any landmarks.

He closed his eyes again, and tried to think warming thoughts, imagining that he was back at the fireside of Timmy the Winns, or drinking Uncle Ebenezer's super-chocolatey hot cocoa with his brother and sister in front of a roaring fire in the apartment in Smiggins, but it was hard to lose himself in imaginings with the wind driving icy needles into his feet and tugging at his ears with icy fingers.

Alistair opened his eyes. The sky was now lit with the pale gray of dawn, and as he peered down he was startled to see a vista of white. Giant mountains reared and plunged in crests and troughs like a stormy sea far into the distance.

That was odd. Feast Thompson hadn't mentioned that they'd be flying over the mountains. The source of the Winns was in the foothills, Slippers had said.

"Whoa!" Alistair said aloud, as with a sudden whoomph they slewed sideways on a particularly strong gust of wind.

The owl doggedly resumed his course, flapping hard against the buffeting of the icy wind.

As his eyes traced the snowy peaks and steep, rocky dips, Alistair thought the mountains were very beautiful, in an awe-inspiring way. He was just glad he was able to admire them from a distance; there was no way he'd like to actually be down there in that frozen terrain.

He squeezed his eyes shut as another gust of wind hit him in the face so hard he couldn't draw a breath.

"Are you all right, Oswald?" he called as they listed farther to the right.

Alistair strained his ears, but the owl didn't respond. His talons seemed to be shuddering slightly, though, as if he was breathing hard.

The wind was coming very strongly from the west. Was it possible they'd been blown off course? As they were buffeted by another wild gust, Alistair turned his head to try to make eye contact with Tibby Rose, but Tibby's eyes were tightly shut. Alistair couldn't tell if she was sleeping.

Oswald continued to battle the freezing wind. Each

gust shocked the breath from Alistair's lungs, leaving him fighting for breath. He kept his eyes on the mountains below. It was now apparent that they were being pushed farther and farther to the east, and the wind was increasing in ferocity, whipping and whistling around the owl and his passengers in a near frenzy as they crested a mountain range and entered a long, wide valley. It seemed to Alistair that Oswald was tiring, that the beats of the owl's mighty wings were slowing. Alistair clutched his scarf, hoping desperately that Oswald had the strength to keep going.

Suddenly, above the shriek of the wind, Alistair heard an ear-splitting screech. He gasped as Oswald's talon suddenly squeezed tighter.

Alistair looked around wildly, but he couldn't see anything. He glanced over at Tibby Rose, and saw that her gaze was now raised upward. Alistair scanned the clear sky above until he finally spotted a dark shape circling high above. An eagle!

His whole body tensed as he watched the circling shadow, his heart pounding. Had they strayed into its territory, was that it? For several long minutes nothing happened, and Alistair began to relax. The eagle had obviously decided that they posed no threat, and hadn't meant to encroach on its territory. But then another bloodcurdling cry filled the air and it was diving, screaming toward them like an arrow.

"It's coming straight at us!" Alistair struggled against the restraint of Oswald's talon in panic as the eagle came closer, closer . . . Alistair could see the menace in the bird's hooded glare. Had it spied the mice trapped helpless in the owl's grip? He quivered at the sight of the raptor's cruel curved beak.

When it was barely a few meters above, the eagle veered away, soaring on the currents as they carried it higher until it was a distant shadow once more.

It was probably just trying to frighten them off, Alistair reassured himself.

But if that was the case, the eagle didn't seem content that the warning was heeded, for with another grating screech it dived again almost immediately, and this time its outstretched talons grazed Oswald's head. Oswald let out a belligerent hoot as he took evasive action, swooping and spinning—straight into the path of a second eagle!

Its wingspan was huge, blocking from view everything but its muscular brown-feathered legs, the giant talons flexed to grasp.

Alistair had always thought of Oswald as enormous, but the owl seemed small now and very vulnerable. As the second eagle's talons scraped his head, Oswald let out a strange, pained shriek and suddenly began to plummet.

"Oswald! Are you hurt?" Alistair cried as they began to lose altitude, but either the owl didn't hear him or couldn't answer.

Mountains rose to their left and right and Alistair could make out jagged clusters of rocks and clumps of stunted trees as they headed toward the valley floor, the snowy ground below rising and falling unevenly, patches of stark white fading into bruise-colored shadows. The shadows made Alistair think of the icy crevasse of Uncle Ebenezer's story, and he glanced at Tibby Rose to see her staring back at him, wide-eyed with alarm.

The eagles continued to swoop and dive, filling the air with their grating calls, and the owl continued to descend in a series of curves and loops that made Alistair's head and stomach spin so that now he could barely tell the snowy ground from the pale sky.

And then suddenly the owl's grip loosened and he was falling.

4

The Assignment

When Alice opened her eyes that morning the first thing she saw was the empty bunk bed.

"Alex," she said, propping herself up on one elbow and poking at the mattress above with her other hand, "where are Alistair and Tibby Rose?"

"Mmmph," her brother muttered into his pillow. Alice saw the mattress shift as he rolled over.

"How would I know?" Alex said sleepily.

With a surge of panic that she tried to quell, Alice was reminded of the last time she had woken to find Alistair missing. "Their rucksacks are gone too."

"They've probably gone for a walk, worry-whiskers," Alex said, as if he sensed his sister's unease. "Where else could they have gone?"

Sinking back onto the pillow, Alice considered what Alex had said. He was right, of course. There was nowhere else for them to go. "Maybe they got up early and have gone over to the cafeteria for breakfast already," she suggested.

"Breakfast?" Alex sounded alert now. "Do you think there'll be a buffet? What are we waiting for?"

He threw off the blankets and clambered down the ladder. "Come on, sis."

"Let's tell Aunt Beezer and Uncle Ebenezer where we're going," she suggested, pointing to her aunt and uncle's room. The door was slightly ajar and, when she stuck her head into their room, she saw that their bed was empty.

"They must have gone with Alistair and Tibby," she said. "I can't believe we slept through it all."

"Hurry," Alex urged. "What if we're the last ones there? What if there's only scraps left?"

The cafeteria was as crowded as it had been the night before, and filled with the clatter of cutlery and the babble of voices. "There's Alistair," Alice said, as a flash of ginger caught her eye. But as she drew closer she saw that it wasn't Alistair at all, that this ginger mouse was much paler than her brother. It occurred to Alice that she had never seen so many ginger mice in her life as she had seen in the last twelve hours. Alice was brown, like their mother, and Alex was white, like the triplets' father. Ebenezer's fur was tan, and Beezer's was creamy. She had seen every shade of black and brown and gray and white, sometimes all mixed up together, but for most of her life Alistair was the only ginger mouse she had ever known—until Alistair had introduced her to Tibby Rose.

But it seemed that several ginger mice belonged to FIG: pale ginger and dark ginger, reddish-ginger and orangey-ginger. But that made sense, she supposed, since ginger fur was only ever seen on Gerandan mice.

Alice trailed after her brother to the breakfast buffet—there was plenty of food left; they needn't have worried—and then to a long table where Beezer and Ebenezer sat facing each other.

"Where's your brother got to?" Beezer asked as Alex and Alice slid onto chairs beside their uncle.

Alice shrugged, and felt her earlier anxiety prickle her fur once more. "We thought we'd find Alistair and Tibby Rose here," she said. "Wherever they've gone, they've taken their rucksacks with them."

"I haven't seen Slippers Pink and Feast Thompson this morning either," her aunt noted.

Before they could speculate further, an officious-looking dark gray mouse with a clipboard approached them.

"Are you Alex and Alice?" he asked, and when they nodded said, "Tobias wants to see you now."

As Alice and Alex exchanged mystified looks, the dark gray mouse turned away.

"Ah, excuse me," Ebenezer said.

"What is it?" the mouse with the clipboard asked impatiently.

"You wouldn't happen to know where my other nephew and his friend are, would you?"

"Do I look like a nanny?" the dark gray mouse snapped.

"How should I know where they are?"

"I just thought, since they met with Tobias last night . . . ," Ebenezer said apologetically.

The dark gray mouse stilled. "Oh," he said. "Them." It seemed to Alice that he looked shifty now. He cleared his throat and turned to Alice and her brother. "What are you two waiting for?" he demanded. "Didn't I just tell you that Tobias is expecting you? Come on." And he rushed away.

"I think we'd better see what this is all about," Ebenezer said to Beezer, and they rose to accompany their niece and nephew.

"What do you think is going on?" Alice asked as they followed the dark gray mouse out of the hall and across the playground. Then, voicing her own fear, she said, "You don't think Alistair's been kidnapped, do you?"

Her uncle was looking extremely worried. "No, my dear, not that; I'm sure there's no way Sourian agents could reach him here. And kidnappers wouldn't take the rucksacks too." He looked at his wife. "It's not possible that they'd send him and Tibby Rose on assignment, is it? No, surely not. And anyway, Alistair wouldn't leave without saying good-bye."

By this time the dark gray mouse had led them into another building and down a corridor. He stopped by an open door and gestured to Ebenezer, Beezer, Alex, and Alice to enter.

Inside the office, Tobias was sitting behind a wooden desk. His brow was furrowed above a pair of reading glasses. He was scanning a piece of paper, watched by a mournful-looking white mouse with long, drooping whiskers.

"I've got Alice and Alex here," said the dark gray mouse.

"And their uncle and aunt," Ebenezer added firmly from behind them.

Tobias looked up at the dark gray mouse over the top of his glasses with a questioning frown.

"Emmeline and Rebus's children," the dark gray mouse reminded him.

Tobias's face cleared. "Of course," he said. "Alice and Alex. And Ebenezer and Beezer—it's been a while, hasn't it? It's good to see you again." He shot a look at the dark gray mouse still hovering in the doorway. "Thank you, Flanagan. That'll be all for now." He made a few notations on the piece of paper he'd been perusing then handed it to the white mouse, who squeezed past them and out the door.

Tobias nodded for the two young mice and their aunt and uncle to sit in the chairs grouped in front of the desk, then shuffled through a stack of folders by his left hand. "Ah yes," he said, extracting a folder. He opened it, quickly read the first page, then closed it again. "I have a very special assignment for you two." He was looking at Alice and her brother.

"Yes!" said Alex, to Alice's right.

"Oh no," said Ebenezer, to her left.

"Shhh . . . ," said Beezer gently, patting her husband's arm. "Let Tobias explain."

"Thank you, Beezer," said Tobias. "And let me say on behalf of FIG how pleased we are that you and Ebenezer have consented to join us once again."

"Naturally we want to do our bit," Ebenezer said, his voice gruff, though Alice thought he looked rather pleased. "We do worry about the children, though. Emmeline and Rebus left them in our care, you know, and—well there was that unfortunate incident with Alistair disappearing, and then these two running off. Now Alistair is missing again. Do you know anything about that?"

Tobias shifted in his seat. "Alistair and Tibby Rose have been sent on a very important mission."

Ebenezer stared at him in disbelief. "You have sent them on a mission?" he repeated slowly, as if he couldn't believe what he was hearing. "What kind of mission?"

Tobias looked uncomfortable. "You know the rules, Ebenezer. It's top secret, I'm afraid." He cleared his throat and looked from Ebenezer to Beezer. "It's been a pleasure to see you both, and I'll look forward to meeting with you each later to discuss your roles with FIG, but if you'll excuse us. . . ." His eyes slid toward the door. After several seconds, when it was clear that Ebenezer had no intention of leaving, Tobias raised his shoulders in a resigned shrug. "Ordinarily, an assignment such as this would be revealed only to those FIG members directly involved in its execution, but given your concerns—and that you are the children's guardians—I will include you in this briefing."

"Thank you," Ebenezer said. It seemed to Alice that he

was struggling to stay calm. "But to go back to this mission that Alistair and Tibby Rose are on, would you say it was a dangerous mission?" His voice was rising.

Tobias nodded his affirmation.

In the four years that the triplets had been living with Ebenezer and Beezer, Alice had hardly ever seen her ebullient uncle angry. But now his face reddened beneath his tan fur as he shouted, "Of all the reckless, irresponsible things to do! This is exactly why I left FIG in the first place. This careless endangerment of lives, this—this . . ." He seemed lost for words.

When he was sure that Ebenezer was finished, Tobias said, "I believe Emmeline and Rebus would approve."

"What about Zanzibar?" Ebenezer demanded. "Does Zanzibar know about this?"

Alice couldn't imagine why her uncle would think that a mouse as important as Zanzibar would be interested.

Beezer spoke up. "You were saying something about an assignment for Alice and Alex."

"That's right." Tobias sounded reluctant now. "The mission calls for young mice, you see."

"Young mice?!" Ebenezer jumped up and, leaning over the desk, roared, "No! Absolutely not! You need young mice for this assignment, you say? Send your own son then!"

At this, Tobias's calm deserted him. His expression darkened and he too jumped up, so that he stood nose to nose with Ebenezer. "You leave my son out of this!" he thundered, jabbing a finger at Ebenezer. "My boy . . ."

As suddenly as he had leaped up the marmalade mouse sank back into his chair. He seemed deflated, his eyes now indescribably sad. "We have all made sacrifices, Ebenezer. Every family. Not just yours. My wife . . ." He straightened. "But the needs of the many—"

"Outweigh the needs of the few," Ebenezer finished. He sat down heavily, looking contrite. "Of course," he said. "You're right." He sighed. "I just wanted to keep the family together."

Tobias was nodding sympathetically. "I do understand, my friend. Really I do. And I wouldn't ask Alice and Alex to undertake this assignment if there was any other way," the marmalade mouse went on. "I won't lie to you: if your niece and nephew accept this assignment they will be in danger."

"We'll do it!" Alex broke in.

Tobias gave him a stern look. "Young man, your enthusiasm is commendable—but foolhardiness is not. I'd recommend you wait to hear what the assignment is before you accept it."

Alex, abashed, hung his head.

"However, I believe that careful planning will ensure their safety," Tobias continued as if Alex hadn't interrupted. He opened the folder again, and spoke directly to Alice and Alex. "Now the assignment calls for you to go undercover."

"Undercover. . . . ," Alex breathed, but although he squirmed in his seat excitedly he restrained himself from further comment.

"I'm sure I don't need to remind you that everything I say now must be treated in the strictest of confidence," Tobias said to Beezer and Ebenezer. Then he glanced down at the file and back at the younger mice. "You will take on the identities of two Sourian orphans, and you will be sent to Gerander to work as servants in the palace in Cornoliana."

Alice gasped, as did her aunt and uncle. Even Alex, who had been so enthusiastic only moments before, looked paler than usual beneath his white fur. They were being asked to infiltrate the headquarters of the Sourian army in Gerander!

5

Crossing the Crankens

Alistair heard a cry—it might have been his own—and saw a flash of color; the ends of his scarf were streaming past his face as he tumbled, clutching at the air as if it could arrest his fall. The wind roared in his ears and caught in his chest, until suddenly he was sinking, engulfed by a sea of snow, and he couldn't see, couldn't hear, couldn't breathe as the cold filled his eyes, his nose, his mouth. He clawed desperately at the thick wet snow, not even sure which way was up, until a shock of chill air told him that his left arm was free. He scrabbled at the snow until he had dug a hole wide enough to let in a small burst of light and air—and sound, it seemed, as he heard a voice: Tibby's. She sounded like she was very far away.

"I'm over here!" he called, waving through the hole. His voice echoed around him in the dark, snowy cocoon and he realized his friend probably couldn't hear him.

He scraped at the hole some more until he was able to push his head through.

At first the light was so dazzling he couldn't see anything but glittering white, but as his eyes adjusted he found that he was looking at an expanse of snow lit by the sun, which had just cleared the jagged mountain range before him. At his back were more mountains, their craggy peaks and sheer rock faces swept with a blanket of snow. He was in a narrow valley between them, a sea of white dotted with the occasional clump of tall thin pine trees or an eruption of snow-encrusted boulders. He looked from left to right, hoping to see the pink-tinted ginger fur of Tibby Rose, but nothing moved.

Alistair struggled to pull himself out of the bank of snow he had landed in, hampered by the rucksack on his back. When at last he was free he lay panting in the snow for a few seconds, then rose unsteadily to his feet. "Ugh!" He was completely coated in white. Even his scarf was white. He brushed the snow from his fur, then began to trudge through the heavy knee-deep snow along the base of the slope, frustrated by the slowness of his pace. "Tibby!" he called. "Tibby Rose!" He was sure he'd heard her voice, but there was no answering call. Perhaps she'd fallen into a snow drift, like he had, and couldn't get out. He felt a quiver of fear in his belly. How long could a mouse survive buried in snow? Or maybe she wasn't here at all, and he'd only imagined the sound of her voice. Maybe she'd been snatched by one of the eagles. His heart began to pound crazily as he tilted his head to scan the sky.

Nothing. Where was she?!

"Tibby!" he cried desperately.

He had almost reached a rocky outcrop when suddenly his legs began to sink. The snow beneath him was caving in. Half falling, half leaping he managed to grasp the sharp edge of a rock. As he heaved himself onto it, he thought he glimpsed a flash of ginger on the other side. He scrambled over, scraping his hands and knees. Tibby Rose was lying on her back, eyes closed, unmoving. "Tibby!" Alistair bellowed, sliding down the rock to land beside the prone body. "Tibby Rose!"

Breathing hard, Alistair put his ear to Tibby's chest, but could hear nothing over the thumping of his own heart.

Impatiently, he took Tibby's wrist in his hand. Her pulse was steady, and when he put his ear to her chest once more her heartbeat was strong.

Alistair leaned back against the rock, his shoulders sagging with relief.

He heard a muffled squeak and, leaning forward again, saw Tibby blinking against the glare of the sun.

"What . . . ," she gasped. "What happened?" She struggled to sit up, but Alistair gently pushed her back down.

"You fell," he said simply. "You've been unconscious. Try not to move too quickly. Are you hurt?"

"My head, a little."

Alistair rummaged in his rucksack for a bottle of water, then held it to Tibby's mouth. She sipped, then asked urgently, "Are you all right?" Once Alistair had reassured her that he was fine, she closed her eyes. Then she opened them again. "Oswald," she said weakly. "Is he . . . ?"

Alistair started guiltily. He hadn't once thought about the injured owl.

"I don't know, Tib. I haven't seen him or the eagles since we fell."

"Poor Oswald." Tibby sighed. "The eagles wouldn't— they wouldn't kill him, would they?"

Alistair shook his head. He didn't know. With a pang he thought of all the owl had done for him, the distances he had flown. Oswald might be grumpy, but he was generous too. And not once had Alistair said thank you.

Finally he cleared his throat and said, "Where do you think we are?"

"The wind was blowing pretty fiercely from the west," Tibby offered. She sat up slowly, turning her head to face Alistair, a look of pain crossing her face as she did so. "I'd say we were blown off course to the east."

Alistair tried to picture their original course, north-west toward the source of the Winns. If they had ended up due east of there, that would mean . . .

"So we're in the Crankens," Tibby stated matter-of-factly. "But where in the Crankens is anyone's guess."

Alistair gulped. "What side of the border do you think we're on: Gerander or Souris?" He had rather hoped never to see Souris again.

"It doesn't make much difference," Tibby Rose pointed out. "Whether we're in Souris or Gerander, if the Queen's Guards spot us we've had it."

She was right, of course, but Alistair thought he would still rather be in Gerander.

"So we need to head west," Tibby continued.

"I don't know if it's really safe for you to move around, Tib," he said. "What if you've got a concussion? We should just wait here for rescue." A thought struck him. "But unless Oswald comes back . . ." He let the sentence trail off, then finished, "We have no way of letting anyone know where we are or what's happened."

"I'll be okay," said Tibby. "I've got a bit of a headache, but my vision isn't blurry or anything." Her eyes lit up. "Anyway, the explorer Charlotte Tibby found herself in much tighter spots than this. She was crossing the Crankens when she became lost in a blizzard. Then she fell and broke her leg. She survived alone for three weeks before finding her way out."

"So would I be right in guessing you know something about surviving in the snow?"

"Everything that Charlotte Tibby wrote about it," Tibby Rose agreed. She seemed almost excited by the opportunity to test her survival skills in a new terrain. Alistair hoped her optimism was genuine, and not a symptom of concussion. Personally, he was feeling rather anxious about being lost in the Crankens. He hoped it wouldn't take them three weeks to find their way out again. Not with his parents on Atticus Island . . .

"Come on, we should start walking. Where's my rucksack?" Tibby looked all around before realizing she was sitting on it.

"Let me carry that for a while, Tib," Alistair offered.

"Thanks," said Tibby. "Help me up."

Alistair gripped her wrists and pulled her to her feet. When he let go of her she wobbled unsteadily for a moment, then fell back down onto her bottom.

"Oh," she said. "That didn't work very well. I'm still a bit dizzy. Hang on a minute and I'll try again."

"I don't think you're well enough to walk, Tibby," Alistair said, slinging his own rucksack over one shoulder and Tibby's over the other.

"But we can't stay here," Tibby argued. "It's too exposed. At the very least, we need to find shelter."

Tibby was right, Alistair knew; they did need to find shelter—from the weather and from predators. He could piggyback her, he supposed, but it would be pretty hard going when he was already carrying two rucksacks. Perhaps if he dragged the rucksacks behind him? Or dragged Tibby Rose behind him. Hmm, that wasn't such a bad idea. . . .

"Tibby, can you tell me how to build a sled?"

"A sled?" said Tibby. "Let's see . . . two forked branches . . . cross beams . . . Yes," she decided. "If you can find the right kind of trees. You'd better take my rucksack. There should be a pocketknife in the front compartment, and you'll need some thin cord. Oh, and the rope."

Alistair concentrated as his friend described how to build a basic sled, then he set off toward a stand of slender saplings. They looked perfect.

Using the knife—which he recognized as Uncle

Ebenezer's—he sawed away at first one long slender forked branch, and then another. Then he cut away one side of each fork to leave two curved sticks. These would be the runners. He placed them side by side on the ground so that the curves pointed skyward. Now for the cross beams. He cut three short pieces and, spacing them evenly along the runners, lashed them in place with the cord.

By the time he was done, it looked just like a real sled.

He added some diagonals for strength, then pulled a coil of rope from Tibby's rucksack, which was starting to look decidedly emptier now. He tied each end of the rope to the front-most cross beam, so he could pull the sled along.

When he returned to where Tibby sat, dragging the sled behind him, she was pleased with the results. "It's very well made," she said, admiring the curved runners.

"Hop on, Tib," he suggested. "Let's give it a test run."

Tibby sat on the sled with the two rucksacks on her lap, and Alistair began to pull.

"Ouch!" he cried, as he tried a turn and had his tail squashed by a runner. "I'll have to remember to keep my tail up."

It was hard work tromping through the snow, but the sled slid smoothly along behind him.

"This is the way to travel," called Tibby. "Let's not bother with looking for shelter now. We can start trying to find our way out of here. We'll just make sure to find somewhere to stop for the night before the sun sets. The valley runs northwest," she observed, "so let's follow it as far as we can."

As the sun beat down, Alistair found that it was possible to be boiling hot from the exertion of pulling the sled while his toes and ears and tails were numb with cold.

By the time the sun was directly overhead, its rays on the snow were blinding and Alistair was finding it hard to focus. Not that there was much to focus on: snow, snow, and more snow. If only there was something to look at, he thought, he wouldn't be so aware of the weight of the sled, or the heaviness of his steps as they crunched through the snow.

His legs were tired and his arms were aching by the time Tibby said, "Do you want some water?"

"Yes, please," he said. He dropped the rope and rolled his shoulders, then did some arm stretches.

"I wish we had some food too." Tibby looked upset. "I can't believe I set off without packing supplies. What a stupid mistake."

"But we didn't exactly have time to ask for supplies last night," Alistair reasoned. "I just presumed Slippers and Feast would take care of it. And we couldn't have known we'd end up in this situation."

"That's no excuse," his friend said. "Charlotte Tibby would never have set off so underprepared. And trying to find something to eat around here . . ." She gestured at their bleak surroundings.

"All the more reason to keep going," said Alistair. "Hey, are you sure you're not just faking that headache, Tibby?" he quipped, trying to change the subject; he hadn't really been aware of his hunger until they'd started talking about food. "I won't be angry if you say yes. Just get up and walk and we'll forget the whole thing."

Tibby smiled. "I am feeling much better," she agreed. "Maybe I could walk."

Alistair helped her to stand, and this time she was much steadier on her feet. They lashed the rucksacks to the sled and set off again, Tibby walking beside him.

Alistair found that the afternoon passed more pleasantly than the morning had. Pulling the sled was much less tiring with only the rucksacks for passengers, and the sun was warming his shoulders. But Tibby raised her hand to call a halt.

"If we were heading west now, that sun should be in our eyes. The valley must be curving around to the east." She turned to face the sun. "Looks like we're going to have to climb some mountains," she said with a sigh. "Pity."

Alistair followed the direction of her gaze. "We have to climb that?!" The mountain towering over them was huge. Its lower slopes were studded with trees and rocks, before rearing to a high pointed peak.

"Well, not all the way up." Tibby pointed to a dip between the mountain and its neighbor to the north. "We can pass between the peaks. At least we should get a better idea of where we are from up there."

"How long do you think it will take to reach the pass?" Alistair asked. He was feeling tired again just from looking at the mountain.

"I don't know," Tibby replied. "But I don't think we'll manage it today." She pointed to a dark patch about

63

a third of the way up the mountainside. "We could aim for that last stand of trees, and set ourselves up there for the night."

They began the uphill climb. The slope was gentle at first, and Alistair found it easy enough, though it was very uncomfortable walking into the sun. But as the afternoon wore on and the slope grew steeper, the sled grew heavier. At last it seemed to Alistair that although he pulled with all his might, they were barely moving.

When the first clouds passed across the sun, Alistair was glad not to have the glare in his eyes anymore. Then the clouds began to gather, more and more of them appearing over the mountain until the sky was much the same color as the ground. Soon the mountain peaks were no longer visible as the clouds began to sink. It gave Alistair the strange feeling of being imprisoned in the valley.

"I don't like this," Tibby muttered. "I don't like this at all."

A wind came howling down through the trees to whip Alistair's tail about his feet. Then snow began to fall, dashing across his face and body, stinging his ears and eyes and nose.

"It's a blizzard!" Tibby cried. "Keep going! We have to find shelter in the trees!"

Lower and lower the cloud descended, obscuring the trees, the rocks, shrinking the space around them. Alistair could no longer see the trees, and couldn't remember how far they had been from them. He concentrated on placing one foot in front of the other, step by interminable step, his head down. Without the sun, the temperature dropped rapidly, and the cold crept from his toes to his knees. He could hear Tibby, breathing hard beside him, but he could barely see her.

One foot in front of the other . . . The snow swirled and eddied around them. It coated his fur, collecting in icy clumps where his scarf circled his throat. His hands ached where they gripped the rope, his eyes streamed where the snow stung them, and his ears hurt from the roar of the wind. He was so cold his blood felt as though it was freezing in his veins; his very bones felt chilled. Alistair couldn't imagine ever being warm enough again.

One foot in front of the other . . . His hunger was growing sharper, a relentless nagging in his belly. Yet while the sensation in his stomach seemed to grow more intense, his thoughts grew dull and his limbs leaden. He longed to stop and rest, but they couldn't risk it. The temperature would drop even further as evening fell. If they didn't reach shelter soon, there was a very real chance they'd die of exposure out there on the freezing mountain.

One foot in front of the other . . . Each step was becoming more of an effort as their toes sank deeper into the snow. And still they hadn't found shelter. How could they even be sure they were going the right way? Alistair wondered. They couldn't follow the position of the sun, couldn't see the trees they were aiming for. They had only the relentless climb uphill to assure them they were on course.

Alistair still couldn't see the trees even when they finally reached them. The huge dark trunks had been buried in snow and the white-covered boughs were invisible through the dense white fog. It was only when the sound of the wind grew muffled, and the snow was no longer driving into his face, that he realized shelter was close at hand.

Tibby's voice sounded unaccustomedly loud as she said, "Let's stop here." Still breathing hard, she looked around. "We should be able to find space around the trunk of a tree where it's sheltered by a spreading branch. We'll need to dig a bit though. How about—ouch!"

Alistair dropped the rope of the sled and rushed toward the sound of her voice. "What's wrong?"

"It's nothing," she said. "I just walked into this big rock. Hey . . ." She was feeling in front of her with her hands. "There's an overhang. We can just crawl under here—it should give us enough protection."

She sounded so happy that for a moment Alistair felt happy too: they might be tired, hungry, and lost in a blizzard somewhere in the Crankens, but at least they were safe—for now.

6

The Sourian Orphans

"You can't be serious," Ebenezer said.

Tobias looked grave. "Desperate times call for desperate measures," he said. "In the current climate it's become almost impossible to infiltrate the palace. The Sourians have grown increasingly strict about security—which is one more reason why we believe they're up to something. But they'll be less likely to suspect children of being spies. That's where Alex and Alice come in."

"I don't know," said Ebenezer doubtfully.

Alice, who had kept quiet until now, spoke up for the first time. "Do you really think we would be useful?" she asked Tobias.

The marmalade mouse gazed at her steadily. "Your presence in the palace would be invaluable," he said. "We have had serious problems with intelligence-gathering since the Sourians tightened security. This could be our one chance to slip beneath the radar." He looked at Ebenezer. "Believe me," he said, "if there was another option, we'd take it. And I would never even have contemplated the idea if the stakes weren't so high."

"If it's that important," Alice said, turning to meet the eyes first of her brother, then of her aunt and uncle, "I say we should do it." Even as she said the words, she felt a tremor of fear in the pit of her stomach, but she tried to keep her expression businesslike and determined. Alex, too, looked uncommonly solemn.

Uncle Ebenezer swallowed once, then said in a pained but resigned voice, "I can see I'm outnumbered here. But please"—he fixed Tobias with an appealing look—"please do everything you can to keep them safe."

"I will," Tobias promised. "Now, while I've got you two here," he said, turning his attention to Beezer and Ebenezer, "I'd like to discuss your own assignments." He rifled through his stack of folders once more. "Beezer," he said, consulting one, "you're a math professor, as I recall."

"That's right," said Beezer.

"Excellent. I'm hoping you might agree to become one of our codebreakers. We haven't put much effort into codebreaking to date, but we're putting together a team under the leadership of Celestine."

"Celestine is here? I'd be honored to work with her!" Beezer exclaimed. "She's a professor of logic at the University of Grouch, in Souris," she explained to Alice and Alex. "Her work is amazing."

"Good," said Tobias with a satisfied nod. "In that

case, please report to room 3A tomorrow at nine a.m. Ebenezer . . ." The marmalade mouse pulled a third file from the stack. "Ah yes. Serena, who's been in charge of the kitchen for the last few weeks, has to return to her restaurant in Shudders. I remember that you trained as a chef. Would you take over from Serena?"

"Of course," Ebenezer replied.

"Excellent," said Tobias. "That's settled then." He raised his voice to call, "Flanagan?"

The dark gray mouse opened the door so promptly that Alice suspected he must have been standing with his ear pressed to it.

"Ah, Flanagan. Can you tell Solomon Honker to report to room 2B in ten minutes? He'll know what it's about." Tobias turned back to the four mice in front of him. "Alice and Alex, Solomon is in charge of your mission. And to begin with, he is going to help you to construct your new identities. You're to meet him in room 2B in ten minutes sharp. Anymore questions?"

Alice had a hundred, and she suspected the others did too, but Tobias looked so harried that she held her tongue.

When no one spoke up, Tobias inclined his head. "Good luck with your assignments then." His eyes dropped to the list in front of him. "Right, who's next . . . Skinny Jim. Flanagan, once you've spoken to Solomon go find Skinny Jim for me, would you?"

The dark gray mouse hurried from the room and Tobias began to flick through a new batch of files, making notes on a pad beside him.

Ebenezer, Beezer, Alex, and Alice quickly and quietly left the room.

"Phew," said Ebenezer. "I wouldn't like Tobias's job." Then he looked at Alex and Alice worriedly. "And I wouldn't want your job either: spying on the Sourians in their own headquarters in Gerander! Are you quite sure you want to do this? No one would blame you if you changed your minds."

"We're sure," Alice said, more bravely than she felt. "You heard what Tobias said: it might be the only way to find out what the Sourians are up to."

"I suppose I should get started on my own job," Ebenzer said. "I'd better go introduce myself to Serena and find out when she's leaving. I just hope I can rise to the challenge. It's a long time since I've cooked professionally."

"You'll be great, Uncle Ebenezer," said Alex loyally. "You're the best cook ever."

They accompanied Ebenezer to the cafeteria, where he disappeared into the kitchen.

"So Alistair and Tibby Rose did go on a mission," Alice said. "I wonder where?"

"I bet Oswald took them somewhere," said her brother. Alice knew he was envious of the fact that his less-adventurous brother had flown twice, while he had never left the ground.

"Aunt Beezer," said Alice, remembering a question that had occurred to her during their meeting with the marmalade mouse, "what happened to Tobias's wife?"

Beezer let out a heavy sigh. "Yes, I'd forgotten about

that; I think Ebenezer had too. Marina was a doctor, and a few years ago—not long after your parents, in fact—she crossed the border into Gerander on a mission to assess the medical and health-care situation. There'd been reports that Gerandans were barred from hospitals. She was discovered by the Queen's Guards and sent to Atticus Island. She died there."

Alice smothered her gasp as Alex asked, "What did she die of?"

Beezer shrugged. "Cold, hunger, disease . . . take your pick. It could have been any one of them."

"But Mom and Dad . . . ," Alice began.

"Have survived this long," Beezer said firmly. "Now you two had better hurry along. You don't want to be late for your first lesson."

"Lesson?" said Alex, following Alice out through the double doors at the back of the cafeteria. "What did she mean by 'lesson'?"

"I don't know," Alice shrugged. "I suppose we have to learn how to be undercover agents."

"We'll probably have lessons in self-defense," Alex said, striking a karate pose.

"Maybe," said Alice vaguely. She looked around at the other buildings grouped around the large green oval. "I think that's the library over there," she said, pointing to a large, low building to her left, "and block 1, next to the hall, is the dorm, so those buildings to the right must be blocks 2 and 3." She set off across the oval toward the two-story brick buildings on the far side.

"And I bet we'll learn the art of disguise," said Alex. "I could have a limp." He began to drag his right leg behind him.

"That would rule out any quick getaways," said Alice over her shoulder. "Hurry up."

"True," said Alex. "Perhaps we could wear mustaches."

Alice looked at him incredulously. "I'm a girl, Alex. Why would I wear a mustache?"

"It was just an idea," Alex said defensively.

"A stupid one," Alice muttered. "Come on, we're in here," and she climbed the three steps into block 2.

They walked up the corridor to the door marked 2B, and Alice knocked tentatively.

"Come in," a voice called.

Alice pushed open the door to find an ordinary classroom, much like the ones at their school back in Smiggins. There was a whiteboard at the front of the room, and four rows of desks facing it. There was a bank of windows down one side of the room, and the other side had windows looking onto the corridor. The back wall was covered in hand-drawn posters of cheeses of the different regions of Shetlock. (Alex, Alice noticed, was looking at these appreciatively.) A soft *thwack* drew her attention to the white mouse in a blue bow tie sitting at the teacher's desk next to the whiteboard, lightly tapping the desk with a long wooden ruler. She hadn't seen him at first, as he was almost dwarfed by two piles of folders stacked as high as his ears.

"Good afternoon," he said briskly. "You must be Raz

and Rita. I'm Solomon Honker—but you may call me 'sir.'" He stood up and Alice saw that although his top half was white, from the waist down he was a rusty orange. "Thank you for being so punctual. We have a lot of ground to cover and only a short time in which to cover it, so we'll need to begin immediately. I'm still finalizing the details of your transport into Gerander, but you will need to be ready to depart as soon as that's arranged."

"Sorry," Alex said, "I think there's been some mistake. My name's Al—"

Bang!

Alice jumped, startled, as Solomon Honker rapped his desk sharply with the ruler. "In this room, you are Raz"— he pointed the ruler at Alex—"and you're Rita," he told Alice. "Understand?"

The two young mice nodded mutely.

"Do you understand?" Solomon Honker repeated more loudly.

"Yes, sir," Alice squeaked.

"Good."

Solomon Honker waved his ruler at two desks in the center of the front row, and Alice and Alex hurried over.

"Raz?" Alex muttered in Alice's ear as they took their seats. "Raz? What kind of ridiculous name is Raz?"

"It's your name, young man," said Solomon Honker, who obviously had exceptional hearing. "And you'd better get used to it."

"Yes, sir," Alex said quickly.

"As I was saying, there's a lot to get through." Solomon

Honker tapped one towering pile of folders then the other. "You'll need to understand the political situation in Souris, Gerander, and Shetlock in order to grasp the context in which you'll be operating. You'll have to learn all about your new identities and cover stories, as well as the culture and geography of Souris and, in particular, Tornley, the town you come from."

"We come from Smiggins," Alex corrected him.

Bang! went the ruler.

"Young man," said Solomon Honker sternly, "I don't know how things are done in Shetlock, but in a Sourian classroom the pupils do—not—speak—without—first—raising—their—hand." Solomon Honker smacked the desk with his ruler in time with the words.

"But this is a Shetlock classroom," Alex objected.

"What is your name?" Solomon Honker demanded.

"Al—"

Bang!

"Raz," Alex said.

"And where are you from?"

"T-Tornley," Alex stammered. "In Souris."

"That's right," said Solomon Honker. "You are from Souris. And this is a Sourian classroom. The day after tomorrow, you must travel behind enemy lines as Sourian children. We have no time to waste with pointless questions and quibbling." He glared at Alex. "Do I make myself clear?"

Alex gulped. "Yes, sir."

"Then let's begin." Moving to the left of the whiteboard,

Solomon Honker tapped his ruler three times to indicate the three maps tacked to the wall. The first was a map of Shetlock, which was a common enough sight in a Shetlock classroom. To the right of this was a map of Souris, with a purple and silver flag in the top right-hand corner. They had studied Sourian history and geography at school, and Alice recognized the diamond shape of Shetlock's neighbor across the Sourian Sea. She knew that the capital, Grouch, was roughly in the middle, just south of the Eugenian mountain range. She turned her gaze to the third map. The long, thin strip of land was a mere fraction of the size of Souris. It had a coastline running down the western side along the Cannolian Ocean, and a small part of the eastern side abutted the westernmost curve of the Sourian Sea. Along the eastern side it bordered Souris—Alice could just make out the Cranken Alps in the northeast—and its southern tip bordered Shetlock. Although she had never seen it before, Alice knew this must be a map of Gerander. It was odd to think that she had lived all her life in a country bordering Gerander—it was closer even than Souris—yet knew nothing about the place. Staring at the sliver of land, Alice wondered why exactly the Sourians were determined to occupy such a small country.

Solomon Honker tapped the ruler on a large red dot in the west of Gerander. It was marked "Cornoliana." This, she supposed, was the Gerandan capital.

"Cornoliana," Solomon Honker said. "Does that name sound familiar? Think of your history classes."

Alex raised his hand. "Is it something to do with Queen Cornolia?"

"Who was . . . ?" prompted the rusty-orange and white mouse.

Alice raised her hand and said, "She was the Queen of Shetlock, ages and ages ago."

"Just the Queen of Shetlock?" queried the teacher.

"Oh!" Alex's hand shot up.

"Raz?"

"She was the Queen of Souris too. She was Queen Eugenia's great-grandmother. No, wait, her great-great-great . . ." He shook his head. "I can't remember."

But Solomon Honker was nodding. "Almost," he said. "Queen Cornolia, of the House of Cornolius, was the great-great-grandmother of Queen Eugenia. So she was the Queen of Souris and of Shetlock. But what do you make of this?" He tapped the red dot of Cornoliana again.

Why would Gerander have named its capital after the Queen of Shetlock and Souris? Alice wondered. Unless . . .

She thrust her hand into the air. "She was the Queen of Gerander too!"

"Correct." Solomon Honker tapped the ruler on the desk. "Queen Cornolia ruled all three kingdoms, though at the time they were all one kingdom called Greater Gerander. When Queen Cornolia died, Greater Gerander was divided into three lands, one for each of her children; they were triplets you see."

"Like us!" said Alex.

"Ah yes," said Solomon. "So you are. The young ginger

fellow with the scarf, he's your brother, isn't he?"

"That's Alistair," Alex confirmed. Alice wondered how Solomon knew their brother.

Bang!

The ruler crashed down on Alex's desk, and he jolted backward in his chair. Alice made a mental note not to get too comfortable around Solomon Honker, even when he appeared to be approachable.

"What's your name?" the teacher demanded.

"R-raz," said Alex.

"And are you a triplet, Raz?"

"I-I don't know," said Alex.

"You'll find out soon enough," said Solomon Honker. "Until then, don't assume."

"Yes, sir," Alex muttered. He looked almost frightened.

"Sir," said Alice, raising her hand to draw the teacher's attention away from her brother, "what will we be doing in Cornoliana?"

"If you listened to Tobias's speech last night, you'll remember him talking about unusual troop movements in Souris." He raised his eyebrows questioningly and his two pupils nodded.

"FIG is now focusing all its energies in two directions," he continued. "One, finding out what exactly the Sourians are up to, and two, preparing to organize Gerandans to rise against them."

"And you think that while we're in the palace we might hear something about the Sourians' plans," said Alice.

"Correct." The rusty-orange and white mouse nodded once, curtly. "And to be able to interpret the significance of what you hear, you need to understand something of Sourian politics. Let's start with General Ashwover, who is the top-ranking Sourian officer in Gerander. He effectively rules Gerander on Queen Eugenia's behalf, from the Sourian headquarters in the palace in Cornoliana. Queen Eugenia is directly descended from the House of Cornolius, remember, so she claims the right to the palace. Of course, she isn't the only heir to the throne of Cornolius. Can either of you tell me another one—someone who is directly descended from the triplet who inherited Gerander?"

Although they were still new to FIG, both young mice knew the answer to this question.

"Zanzibar!" they shouted in unison.

Solomon Honker smiled briefly. "Correct!" Then . . . *bang!* The ruler smacked down on Alice's desk. "But you will raise your hands before speaking and you will address me as 'sir.'"

By six o'clock, when Solomon Honker finally called a halt to the lesson, Alice thought her head would explode with all the information crammed in it. After a break for lunch, they'd spent the whole afternoon studying the history of the Sourian occupation of Gerander from the Sourian point of view, since that was what Raz and Rita would have learned.

"If I'd known that an undercover assignment would be worse than school I never would have volunteered," Alex groaned as they made their way to the cafeteria for dinner.

They found Beezer and Ebenezer already there. Ebenezer was his old cheerful self, Alice was pleased to see.

"I've been shadowing Serena this afternoon, learning the ordering system and so on," her uncle explained. "She'll be leaving the day after tomorrow. She's given me some of the recipes from her restaurant. I'm really looking forward to trying them out."

They had just carried their plates, piled high with cheesy crepes, to one of the long tables when an all-too-familiar figure came toward them.

"Oh no," groaned Alex under his breath.

"Why it's my two favorite pupils," Solomon Honker said.

"Hello, sir," they chorused politely.

Their teacher had exchanged his somber blue bow tie for a cheery candy-striped one. And that wasn't all that had changed. "What's all this 'sir' business?" he asked jovially. "We're not in the classroom now—call me Solomon Honker."

"Yes, Solomon Honker," Alex and Alice said obediently.

"Have you tried the Stetson Camembert yet?" he asked over his shoulder as he moved off toward the buffet. "It's delicious."

"Is that your teacher?" Beezer asked. "He seems nice."

"Nice?" Alex snorted. "What he was like just then—all cheerful and friendly—is the complete opposite of what he's like in the classroom. He kept yelling and banging our desks with a ruler." Alex slammed his fork onto the table, making them all jump. "He's like that mouse in the book that Alistair talks about. You know, the one with two completely different personalities."

"Dr. Jekyll and Mr. Hyde?" suggested Alice.

"Yeah, him," said Alex. "He even looks like two different mice, with his white top and his orange bottom. It's like two mice were cut in half and their tops and bottoms swapped."

"He's probably just playing a part," said Beezer. "Like you'll have to play a part when you're undercover. You'll be servants, remember—you'll have mice yelling at you and barking orders."

Alex looked more glum than ever. "So much for the exciting life of a spy. It looked like so much fun when Sophia and Horace were doing it. Remember, sis?"

Remember? Alice had no trouble remembering Sophia and Horace. It was forgetting them that was proving difficult. . . .

But if Alex was concerned about anything more than having orders barked at him, he didn't show it. He polished off his cheesy crepes with relish then, seeing that Alice was just pushing hers around her plate, said, "Don't you want yours, sis?" and scooped them off her plate without waiting for a reply.

Alice didn't even bother to protest.

That night, Alice's sleep was haunted with dreams. She was running down the shadowy corridors of the palace in Cornoliana, pursued by some nameless dreadful thing, and around every corner she turned she was confronted with Sophia and her partner, the doleful Horace. Sophia of the silvery fur was laughing her silvery laugh and saying, I will always be a step ahead of you. And then Alice saw the silvery flash of the knife in Sophia's hand and—

She awoke, panting. Sophia and Horace were nowhere near Cornoliana, she reminded herself. They were in Souris, or maybe Shetlock. Not Gerander. With the help of this calming thought, she breathed slow and deep and fell asleep again, then slept dreamlessly until she was woken by sunlight pouring through the window.

7

Never Vanquish'd

Huddled next to Tibby Rose under the overhang of the rock, Alistair drifted in and out of a restless doze; he had too many anxieties gnawing at his brain to allow him to really relax. The first, and most urgent, was the situation he and Tibby Rose were in: lost in an unforgiving terrain with no hope of rescue and no idea where they actually were. As the wind howled around their meager shelter, Alistair knew there was a very real possibility that they would not make it out of the Crankens alive. But if they didn't, who would rescue his parents? Alistair reached for the ends of his scarf, now encrusted in ice. The paths through Gerander would remain a secret as long as his scarf was lost in the Crankens. There would be no help for Emmeline and Rebus on Atticus Island, no safe passage through Gerander for FIG members. He tugged at his scarf and felt it tighten and rub around his neck, and remembered Slippers Pink rubbing her own neck as they'd said good-bye in Stetson just over twenty-four hours earlier. She had sensed something wasn't right. Was this what her "sixth sense for danger" had been warning her about? Were she and Feast Thompson waiting and worrying by the source of the Winns, wondering why Oswald hadn't yet delivered Alistair and Tibby Rose? Or were Slippers and Feast in trouble too? Had the Queen's Guards discovered them?

It was the longest night of Alistair's life. He could hardly wait to leave their lonely shelter and continue their journey, and as dawn broke he nudged Tibby Rose. She responded so quickly that he suspected she too had been awake. Neither of them mentioned the hunger clawing at them as they drank from their water bottles and brushed the snow from their fur before lashing their rucksacks back onto the sled.

"If you're better, maybe we don't need the sled anymore," Alistair suggested. He was still feeling the ache in his arms from the weight of it the day before.

Tibby said, "I think we should keep it. It might come in handy." Her tone was serious, and Alistair wondered if she was thinking of Charlotte Tibby's broken leg, and how easily something like that could happen to one of them. "I'll help you pull it, though."

They each took hold of the rope and together began to haul the sled up the long, steep incline.

"At least it's stopped snowing," Tibby remarked.

But the night's blizzard made their trudge up the never-ending slope even harder than it had been the day before, as with every step they sank into drifts of soft, knee-deep snow. For a long time they plodded on without speaking, all their concentration focused on the effort required by each step. The silence was broken by Tibby.

"Alistair, look." She was pointing to a dark smudge on the pristine expanse of white ahead.

Alistair, who had been keeping his head down to avoid the blinding light on the snow, lifted his gaze. His heart nearly stopped when he saw what Tibby had spotted. It was a large striped feather.

"It looks like an eagle feather," he said, swallowing, as they drew closer. He tilted his head back to peer at the clear sky. There was no sign of the storm of the day before in the sweep of blue. The icy peaks soaring above them glittered like crystals in the glare of the sun. Squinting against the dazzling light, Alistair searched anxiously for any hint of a giant raptor, but there was none.

Tibby picked up the feather and stroked it thoughtfully. "This might be just what we're looking for," she murmured.

Alistair looked at her. "You must be mad, Tib. The last thing we want to see now is an eagle." He shivered with the sudden memory of a grating screech followed by Oswald's cry of pain.

"I haven't forgotten what happened to Oswald," Tibby said softly, and Alistair noticed a slight tremble in her whiskers as she said the owl's name. "I only meant that feathers could be useful." She slipped the feather she was holding under the cord securing their rucksacks to the sled, and they resumed their silent course.

Reluctant though he was to see an eagle, looking for feathers distracted Alistair from their arduous trek, and he felt quite jubilant when he spied a second and then a third feather. By this time, the sun on his head and the hunger in his belly had combined to make him feel quite light-headed.

"Are you trying to collect enough to make a feather quilt?" he called when Tibby sprang forward with a happy cry to pick up a fourth feather.

"Better," said Tibby.

"Unless we can eat them it couldn't possibly be better than a feather quilt," Alistair said, thinking of the freezing night they had just passed.

"Okay, it's not quite as good as food," Tibby conceded, "but what I have in mind is more immediately useful than a feather quilt." She rummaged in her rucksack and pulled out some string, then ordered, "Now sit down and hold your feet up."

"What?!" Alistair didn't know whether to laugh or fear for his friend's sanity, but he did as he was told.

As Tibby proceeded to tie an eagle feather to each of his feet he really did start to wonder whether the knock on the head she'd received yesterday had affected her more than he knew.

"Tibby, are you sure you're all—"

"Just wait till you're standing up, Alistair," his friend said. "You won't think I'm crazy then." She grabbed him by the wrists and hauled him into standing position. "Now take a few steps."

Alistair took one hesitant step, then another. To his surprise, instead of sinking into the snow, he remained on top of it.

"Tib, how come I'm not sinking?" He gestured at his feet, then took another couple of steps. His gait was ungainly—he had to turn his feet out slightly so that the feathers didn't catch against each other—but walking like a duck was much better than wading through deep snow.

Tibby Rose was looking very pleased with herself. "They're like snowshoes. Instead of all your weight being concentrated on your foot it's distributed over a larger area. So instead of sinking into the snow you kind of float on it." Sitting down, she took the two remaining feathers and strapped them to her own feet. "So what do you think?"

"I think you're a genius," said Alistair fervently.

Now that it was easier to walk, Alistair's spirits lifted, and he felt that they were making good progress toward the top of the mountain. He tried to imagine what they would see when they reached the pass. Would they be able to see the Winns? Or, even better, a restaurant? That sounded like something Alex would wish for. Alistair rubbed his grumbling stomach and tried not to think about his brother and sister, and how they must have felt on seeing his empty bed the morning before.

It was early afternoon when, panting from the final steep climb, they reached the cleft between the mountains and gazed eagerly down the other side.

There was just a series of ridges rising and falling away into the distance like a rumpled sheet, dotted with pine trees. The deep trough between where they stood and the nearest ridge was quite densely forested, Alistair saw.

"The snow seems lighter down there," Tibby said, nodding toward the trees below. "I wonder if that means we're coming out of the mountains and into the foothills?"

"You mean we could be in Gerander?" Alistair said.

"We could be," Tibby said, "though we shouldn't get our hopes up." Despite her caution, Alistair noticed that she, too, sounded excited.

And it was impossible not to feel elated as they descended toward the trees and saw a large wooden chalet with three stories nestled in a clearing. The sign above the door read SOOTHING SPRINGS RETREAT.

"Soothing Springs," Alistair read aloud. "Remember what Tobias said? The source of the Winns is a deep mountain spring said to have healing properties. Tibby, we must be close! Let's go find out." He moved forward but was halted by a tug on his tail.

"We can't just knock on the door and ask the way to the Winns," Tibby argued. "That chalet could be full of Queen's Guards. We need a plan."

Alistair thought for a second. "We can pretend we wandered off from a picnic with our parents."

"A picnic?" said Tibby Rose doubtfully. "Up here?"

"How about we get a bit closer and observe it for a while?" Alistair suggested. "If we don't see any Queen's Guards we'll try the picnic story."

Tibby Rose shrugged. "Okay."

Taking care to stay concealed by the trees surrounding

the clearing, they edged closer to the chalet. After many minutes had passed without any sign of life at the front, they circled around to the back.

There was a wide veranda lined with French doors. Outside one pair of open doors, a beige mouse in striped pajamas was rocking peacefully in a chair and basking in the hot sun reflecting off the snow.

Alistair shot Tibby a questioning look. The chalet really did seem to be a health retreat, and there was not a red-coated Queen's Guard in sight.

Tibby answered his silent question with a nod, and the two ginger mice swiftly untied their snowshoes and left them with the sled in the shelter of the trees.

"Excuse me," Tibby called as they walked into the clearing, "could you tell us if the Winns is nearby? We were having a picnic with Mom and Dad and . . . we got lost." She ducked her head sheepishly.

The mouse planted his feet on the veranda to still his chair and gave a toothy, happy grin.

"Well, hello, little ginger friends!"

Alistair exchanged a relieved look with Tibby Rose. If this mouse thought of them as friends they definitely must be in Gerander—and the mouse in pajamas must be Gerandan.

As they moved closer to the veranda the mouse in the rocker fixed them with a bright inquisitive gaze. "What was that you wanted? The wings?"

"No," said Alistair. "Not wings—the Winns."

"Oh the Winns," said the beige mouse. "Hang on . . . I

know this one. . . . It's a banjo, right?"

"Er, no," said Alistair as Tibby let out a small giggle. "It's a—"

"Wait!" The beige mouse held up a hand. "Don't tell me. It's on the tip of my tongue. It's . . . one of those whirlamagigs that you put on your hat and it spins around!"

"No," Tibby Rose burst out. "It's a river. The Winns is a river."

"Oh, of course!" The beige mouse threw both hands in the air, then slapped his thighs. "The river. Yes, yes, I know all about it. It's on that thingamajig in my room. The whatsit that has all the places on it."

"A map?" said Alistair.

"Yes, yes, one of those. Come on in, I'll show it to you." He rose from the rocker and led the way through the open doors, beckoning to the two young mice to follow.

"This is great," Alistair said to Tibby. "We'll be able to see exactly where we are."

They entered a small bright room with a wooden bed, a wooden dresser, a wooden wardrobe, and wooden floors. The shutters were flung open, and light streamed through the window above the bed.

"You sit there and I'll find it," the beige mouse said, pointing to the bed.

Alistair and Tibby obediently perched on the bed while the mouse in pajamas started rummaging through a dresser drawer.

"No, that's not it. . . . No, not that. . . . Oh, here's something." He held up an apple, and Alistair fixed his eyes on it ravenously. "Is this what you're looking for?"

"No," said Tibby patiently, "you were going to show us a map."

The beige mouse looked momentarily perplexed. "Was I?"

The two young mice nodded.

"Maybe it's in here," said the beige mouse, hurrying over to the wardrobe. He had just opened the wardrobe door and peered inside when there was a tap on the door.

The beige mouse turned to look at Alistair and Tibby Rose in surprise. "Were you expecting someone?" he said.

"Shhh," whispered Alistair frantically. "Don't tell anyone we're here."

"Oh, I see," said the beige mouse. He put a finger to his lips and said in an exaggerated whisper, "It's a secret. Quick—in here." He gestured and the two young mice scampered into the wardrobe just as the door to the room opened. The beige mouse pushed the wardrobe door till it was almost shut. Alistair put an eye to the gap and saw a mouse in a starched white nurse's cap.

"Wilbur, who were you talking to?" she demanded.

"Two ginger mice, Matron," the beige mouse replied promptly, and Alistair let out a silent groan.

"Don't be ridiculous," said the matron. "You know there are no ginger mice in Souris."

Souris? Alistair felt Tibby's hand grab his arm.

"Oh, I know they weren't real," Wilbur was assuring the nurse. "They were very friendly, though," he added.

"That just proves it then, doesn't it?" said the matron.

"If they were ginger, they wouldn't be friendly; they'd be violent, dangerous rebels."

"I suppose so," said Wilbur doubtfully.

"You don't believe me?" said the matron. "You just walk across the border over the next ridge there and you'll see—you'll be set upon by violent ginger mice as sure as your name is Wilbur John Bullwinkle-Fotheringham the Third."

Wilbur peered nervously out the window as if expecting to see hordes of ginger mice. "Are you sure we're safe here?" he asked.

"There's nowhere safer," said the matron. "The Queen's Guards are ranged all along the border. Anyway, enough of this nonsense about ginger mice. It's time for you to take the waters."

"Of the Winns?"

"Don't be ridiculous, Wilbur. The Winns is in the valley on the other side of the ridge. The Gerandan side." She said "Gerandan" as if the word left a sour taste in her mouth.

"With the ginger mice?"

"That's right," said the matron. "Now let's take you to the lovely hot springs."

"Will I need my dressing gown?" asked Wilbur. He moved toward the wardrobe.

"No," the matron decided. "You'll be warm enough without it."

Alistair sagged against the back of the wardrobe in relief, then sat bolt upright as the wardrobe door was flung open and Wilbur gave them a toothy smile.

"Wilbur, what are you doing now?" asked the matron impatiently.

"I'm just saying good-bye to the two ginger mice in my wardrobe," Wilbur explained. "Good-bye, ginger mice."

Alistair and Tibby stared at him in terror, but the matron merely said firmly, "Come along now, Wilbur," and with one final cheery wave the beige mouse disappeared.

As soon as the door to the room shut behind Wilbur and the matron, Alistair and Tibby Rose crept out of the wardrobe. Pausing just long enough for Alistair to snatch the apple from the dresser, they dashed to the doors leading onto the veranda. Alistair craned his head around the corner.

"All clear, Tib," he said, and the two mice scurried back to the safety of the trees.

"So, good news and bad news," Alistair said when he had caught his breath. He handed the apple to Tibby Rose.

"The bad news," said Tibby, "is that we're in Souris." She took a big bite of the apple and handed it back.

Alistair bit into the apple, savoring the crispness of the flesh and the tart sweet juice. "But the good news is that Gerander is just on the other side of the next ridge, and the Winns is in the valley."

"But there's more bad news," Tibby remembered. "The matron said that the border is lined with Queen's Guards."

They sat in gloomy silence. Alistair tried to imagine he and Tibby waddling like ducks across the border with feathers tied to their feet, pursued by Queen's Guards. "We're too slow," he said. "We'll never be able to outrun the guards." He glanced at the feathers, lying atop the sled, and was struck by a thought.

"What about the sled?" he said. "That'll give us some speed."

"But when they see us they'll chase us on their own sleds," Tibby pointed out. "And their sleds are probably a lot faster than ours. I think we're better off trying to stay out of sight under the cover of the trees."

"Under the cover of the trees . . . ," Alistair repeated thoughtfully. Tibby's words had given him the germ of an idea.

"Uh-oh," said Tibby Rose. "I recognize that faraway look in your eyes. You're about to propose an idea based on some book you've read, aren't you?"

"Kind of," said Alistair. "Though it's a play, not a book, and I haven't read it myself. My teacher told us about it. We were talking about camouflage in nature, and somehow he ended up telling us the story of Macbeth and reading out some of his favorite passages."

"Hey, I've heard of *Macbeth*," said Tibby Rose. "That was one of Great-Aunt Harriet's favorite plays. It's by Shakespeare, isn't it?"

"That's right. Macbeth starts out this brave and noble mouse, but then he and his wife get greedy for power. So he murders the king and becomes king himself, yet instead of it making him happy he's tortured by guilt, but at the same time is desperate to stay in power. Anyway, these three witches who had predicted that he would be king tell him that . . ." Alistair paused. "How did it go? I think it was: 'Macbeth shall never vanquish'd be until Great Birnam wood to high Dunsinane hill shall come against him.' So you see, he thinks he's safe, because a forest can't get up and walk, can it?"

"No," said Tibby cautiously. "I wouldn't have thought so."

"But it did!" said Alistair. "Because the soldiers who marched on his castle each plucked a branch from a tree and held it in front of them as a disguise."

"So you're suggesting that we hold branches in front of us and walk across the border and the Queen's Guards will think we're trees?" Tibby sounded rather disbelieving, Alistair thought.

"That's right," said Alistair. "Except we don't walk—we sled."

"Um, Alistair, won't the Queen's Guards think it's a bit strange to see a tree sledding across the border?"

"By the time they've thought twice, we'll be gone," Alistair said.

Tibby shook her head slowly, but Alistair could see she was intrigued by the idea.

"I wonder how we'd go about it," she mused. "I suppose we could collect some saplings and any fallen branches and tie them upright to the corners of the sled, then fasten their tops together like a teepee."

"I'll get the pocketknife from your rucksack, shall I?" said Alistair.

Tibby smiled. "Oh, all right. I think it's a daft idea, but somehow your daft ideas have a way of working out."

An hour later, they were pulling what looked like a very strange tree through the forest toward the Gerandan border.

As they crested the ridge, the tree cover grew sparser, and Alistair's heartbeat started to accelerate. Queen's Guards were ranged all along the border, the matron at the Soothing Springs Retreat had said. But to Alistair's relief, the snowy slope stretching away before them was deserted. "Looks like we'll have an easy run down into the valley, Tib," he said.

The words had no sooner left his lips than an angry cry echoed across the mountaintop. "Oy! What do you think you're doing?"

A small band of red-coated mice had stepped out from a group of trees some distance to their left.

"Tibby, quick, onto the sled!"

Tibby Rose pushed through the slender trunks to take up a position sitting on her rucksack at the back of the sled and Alistair clambered after her to sit at the front, the rough bark scraping his limbs. It was dark and close inside their tree teepee, with a sharp smell of pine, and the needles scratched his face.

"Halt! In the name of Queen Eugenia I order you to halt!" The sound of their voices was muffled now, but a quick glance through the gaps in the branches told Alistair the guards were advancing quickly, seeming to glide effortlessly toward them. They were wearing skis, he realized.

"Hang on, Tib," said Alistair and, grasping the rope in both hands, he pushed off.

The sled was slow to move at first, and Alistair scrabbled desperately at the icy ground with his feet, trying to get traction. At last they began to gather speed until they were hurtling headlong down the mountain.

"Where are they, Tibby?" Alistair called over the rush of wind whistling through the branches. His hands held the rope tightly and his eyes were fixed on the slope ahead, watching for obstacles.

"We've lost them," reported Tibby.

"Yes!" cried Alistair. "Tibby Rose and Alistair shall never vanquish'd be!"

They careened down the slope, every bump threatening to dislodge them. "Lean hard right!" Alistair yelled, and they narrowly avoided colliding with a tree.

Then, as they plummeted into a dip and flew out the other side, he saw a blur of red through the branches. "Oh no!" he said as the blur came into focus. "There're two guards right in front of us!"

"Barrel straight through," Tibby advised breathlessly.

The sled sailed down the slope toward the two guards.

"Halt!" yelled the first guard.

"Get out of the way, you idiot!" his partner called, yanking him back by his red coat. "It's a runaway tree!"

Then the vista was white once more and the only sound was the *whoosh* of the wind. They flew down a steep icy funnel lined on either side with towering trees, then shot out onto a wide slope that flattened out for fifty meters or so before dropping away again. The sled slowed to a stop.

"We'll have to pull it across this bit," Alistair said urgently, and he and Tibby struggled free of the branches' prickly embrace.

"Wait," said Tibby, as Alistair was preparing to climb back into position at the front of the sled. "I've got a better idea. What if we push the sled off without us? If the Queen's Guards are following the tracks of the sled's runners they'll go that way. . . . " Tibby pointed down the slope. "We'll go this way." She indicated the forest to their right.

Following Tibby's lead, Alistair hastily untied his feather snowshoes and rucksack from the sled and slung the latter over his shoulder. Then together they pushed the sled, still bearing its tree teepee, down the slope. Alistair felt a pang of regret as it sailed out of sight.

"Now we'll get rid of the evidence." Using one of her feathers like a broom, Tibby began to sweep away their footsteps. Then she walked backward into the trees, brushing away her footsteps as she went.

Alistair copied her, walking backward until they were well hidden by the trees.

Tibby put a finger to her lips. "Let's watch and see."

They didn't have long to wait. Only minutes later three red-clad figures shot past them as swiftly as arrows.

Alistair turned to his friend. "Brilliant, Tibby! That's bought us some time." But Tibby Rose appeared to be shaking uncontrollably.

"Tibby, what's wrong?" Alistair asked, then he saw that

she was convulsed in giggles. "It's a runaway tree!" she gasped, and they both collapsed to the ground in laughter. The cold of the snow was like a balm on Alistair's skin after the irritation of the pine needles and for a few minutes he enjoyed the relief that came with laughter, the feeling of all tension dropping away. But all too soon the reality of their situation came back into focus. At the speed the Queen's Guards were traveling, it wouldn't be long before they caught up with the sled and found it empty. And then they would come looking for the two ginger mice who had crossed the border. . . . His concern must have shown in his eyes, because when Tibby met his gaze her laughter faded and she stood up. Without a word, they turned and headed deeper into the forest.

They walked for hours through the trees, Alistair in the lead and, although several times they heard voices in the distance, they didn't encounter anymore Sourian patrols. The two young mice tried to keep their own conversation to a minimum, speaking only in low murmurs. As they hiked farther down into the valley, the snow became patchy, giving way to meadows of soft green grass. They came across blueberry bushes, and then a patch of small, sweet wild strawberries, which they fell on ravenously. Tibby Rose paused periodically to gather mushrooms, which she wrapped in a handkerchief and stowed in her rucksack. "I'm not going to get caught short of food again," she vowed.

The hardships they had endured seemed a million miles away now, with the golden light of the afternoon sun making the flowers of the wild rhododendron bushes glow a vivid scarlet against the dark green foliage, and the air full of the sweet scent of meadow flowers. Yet even though the conditions had improved, Alistair grew more and more exhausted. His eyes felt gritty and bleary. His legs, his arms, even his tail seemed heavy, the scarf around his neck weighed his head down so that he could hardly lift it. Now that the adrenaline was draining from his body, Alistair felt wearier than he ever had in his life.

When he judged that more than an hour had passed without any sight or sound of Queen's Guards, Alistair said, "It's going to be dark soon, Tib. Why don't we try to find somewhere to stop for the night? We can get some sleep, then start out early tomorrow to look for the source of the Winns."

Tibby, he saw when he turned, was in mid-yawn. "That's the best idea I've ever heard," she said.

It was in the sun's dying rays that they stumbled into a secluded clearing. A mix of spruce and pine trees were etched in black against a deep blue evening sky, and Alistair felt needles from the trees under his feet and heard the burble of a spring he could barely see. "This is perfect," he said, his eyelids already closing in anticipation. He shrugged the rucksack off his shoulders and helped Tibby off with hers, then sank with a groan onto a bed of needles. Tibby flopped onto the ground beside him.

"I could sleep for a thousand years," she murmured sleepily.

Alistair had just muttered his agreement when he was

seized roughly. His heart seemed to explode in shock and he could barely draw the breath to shout a warning to his friend.

"Tibby!" he yelled. But it was too late. Opening his eyes he saw a dark shape looming over his friend, about to pounce.

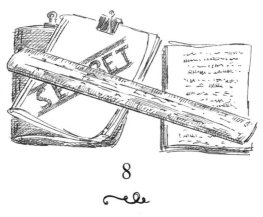

8

Departure

Even the thought that he was playing a part didn't make Solomon Honker any less intimidating. As Alex and Alice entered the classroom and sat at their desks, he didn't betray the slightest hint of the cheery mouse of the night before, not by so much as a wink or a twinkle in the eye.

"It's time to focus on your new identities," he said without even bothering to greet them. With a nod he indicated the folders standing ready on their desks, and Alice opened the topmost file, lowered her head and began to read the story of Raz and Rita of Tornley.

Rita and Raz were the children of Jez and Webbley, though they never saw much of their father, for Jez was a Queen's Guard. He had been sent to the Gerander–Souris border in the Cranken Alps, and only came home on leave infrequently.

"Ha, look at his big ears!" Alex held up a photo and gave

a snort of laughter.

"That is your dead father you're talking about, young man," Solomon Honker reprimanded him. "Show some respect."

When the children were six, Jez had been stabbed and killed by a gang of Gerandan rebels trying to storm the border.

"Oh," Alice cried out involuntarily. "Their father was killed by Gerandans!"

"Don't believe everything you read," Solomon Honker told her. "He was actually part of a patrol that lost their way in the mountains and fell into a ravine. It just makes a better story for the folks back home if he died a hero fighting the evil Gerandans."

Somewhat relieved, Alice resumed her reading.

Now a widow, Webbley took in washing and ironing. Six years after her husband's death, she fell ill and died. Her orphaned children, Raz and Rita, were passed from neighbors to relatives, but no one wanted to care for them full time. At last, someone had the idea of making them the responsibility of the Sourian army. Their father had given his life in service of his country, after all—let the army work out what to do with his children. And so jobs had been found for them at the palace in Cornoliana.

Alice shook her head. "Poor Rita and Raz," she said. "What a miserable life they had."

"Before you get too sentimental," Solomon Honker said, "there's something you should know."

"What's that, sir?" asked Alice.

Her teacher lowered his white head very close to hers. "They hated Gerandans," he hissed.

Startled, Alice leaned back in her chair, but Solomon Honker leaned too. "And guess what that means?"

"I . . . I don't know, sir," said Alice.

"It means, Rita of Tornley, that you hate Gerandans too."

Not for the first time, Alice had a sense of how difficult their undercover operation was going to be. Being Rita meant being completely unlike herself—and being it so completely and convincingly as to fool everyone she encountered. And Alice had never been a very good actor. . . . She hadn't really questioned it before, but now she wondered why, exactly, Tobias had selected her and Alex for this very dangerous operation. Was it really just because they were the same age as Raz and Rita? It seemed beyond strange that FIG would pick two young mice at random and send them on a mission on which so much depended. Her musing was interrupted by her brother's voice.

"What happened to the real Raz and Rita?" Alex asked.

"Killed in a house fire," said Solomon Honker briefly.

Once they had absorbed all the available material on the short lives of Raz and Rita, their teacher instructed them to open the file marked "Tornley—General."

"Do you think we'll ever stop reading about our undercover mission and actually go on it?" Alex muttered under his breath as they plowed through a stack of reading material about life in Tornley. Flicking through the sheaves of paper, Alice noticed a map of the town, a section on rivers and streams (including which were best for swimming), a description of the school Raz and Rita had used to attend, pictures of their neighbors, lists of—

"This afternoon," said Solomon Honker from his desk at the front of the room.

Startled, the two young mice looked up.

"Excuse me, sir?"

"You depart this afternoon, right after lunch, so if I were you I'd try to get through as much of that information as I could."

"Yes!" crowed Alex, who obviously wasn't concerned about details like neighbors and swimming streams.

This afternoon? Suddenly Alice felt woefully unprepared. How would she ever fool anyone that she came from Tornley? With a sense of panic, she picked up a page describing the best-known landmarks of Tornley and began to read.

"How are we getting across the border?" Alex asked Solomon Honker.

"You'll see," their teacher replied.

"Will we have to slip across in the dead of night?"

"You'll see."

"Will we be in disguise?"

Their teacher shook his head.

"Will we fly by owl?" Alex asked hopefully.

"Oswald's busy."

"Do you know an eagle?"

"Young man," said Solomon Honker, finally losing patience, "if your preparation is not complete, I will be forced to tell Tobias that the operation must be canceled and you won't be going anywhere at all."

Alex hastily bent his head over the pages.

For the next hour there was no other sound than the rustle of papers, then Solomon Honker rose from his chair and crossed the room to stand before his pupils.

"Let us see how much you've retained. What is the favorite pastime of the children of Tornley on a hot summer's night?"

Alice, glad that he had opened with a question she could remember the answer to, put up her hand. "We go out to the cave on Whistler's Road and scare the fireflies."

"Good, Rita. Now where did you—"

"How do we scare them?" interrupted Alex. "Do we sneak up behind them and yell 'Boo!'?" He laughed at his own joke.

Solomon Honker tapped Alex's desk with his ruler and Alex fixed a serious look on his face.

"Where did you go swimming?"

"That's easy-cheesy," said Alex. "Roxby Dam. I did the biggest dive bombs of any mouse there."

Alice nudged her brother sharply with her elbow. "Alex—er, Raz," Alice quickly corrected herself as she saw the ruler in Solomon Honker's hand twitch. "Stop joking around and concentrate. This is serious."

She glanced up at Solomon Honker. "I think Raz meant Roxenby Dam," she said. "Didn't you, Raz?"

Alex shrugged. "Whatever. But I still did the biggest dive bombs."

The rusty-orange and white mouse just sighed and said, "At least Raz is bringing a certain authenticity to the role. That can be helpful." He smoothed his bow tie as if to calm himself, then asked, "And when is market day?"

"Wednesday," replied Alice promptly.

"What kind of cheese do they sell there?" Alex butted in.

"Raz, I hardly think anyone will want to know about the cheeses of Tornley," his sister objected.

"I would," Alex persisted stubbornly.

Before Alice could point out that not everyone was as obsessed with cheese as Alex, Solomon Honker said, "Mozzarella."

"Excuse me, sir?" said Alice.

"Tornley is famous for its mozzarella."

"Thank you, sir," said Alex, giving his sister a smug look.

The morning wore on in the same way, with Solomon Honker giving them piles of information to read and memorize. As well as the lives of Raz and Rita and life in Tornley, they studied the geography of Gerander, the ranks of Queen's Guards in the Sourian army, and the differences between Sourian and Gerandan cuisine. Alex acquitted himself very well in this last category, though as Solomon Honker reminded them, "All you need to do is say that Sourian food is delicious and Gerandan food tastes like dirt and you'll be believable."

At last, their teacher tapped his desk three times with his ruler and said, "Well, that's all we have time for. I just hope it's enough." Alice was slightly alarmed to see the worried look creasing Solomon Honker's white brow.

Tentatively she raised her hand and asked the question that had been bothering her all morning.

"Sir, what will the Sourians do if they catch us spying on them?"

Silence filled the room as Solomon Honker gently laid down his ruler. Just when Alice was starting to think he hadn't heard her question, he said quietly, "Don't get caught." Alice felt the fear that had been nibbling at the edges of her mind settle like a stone in her chest.

Solomon Honker glanced at his watch and said, "You'd better get along and have some lunch. I'll meet you by the cafeteria steps in one hour."

As they hurried across the oval (Alex was determined not to miss out on the Camembert this time), Alice anxiously tried to recall their lessons of the morning. So much depended on what they had learned, but her brain felt empty.

"Alex, what were the names of our neighbors in Tornley?"

Alex just shrugged. "Who cares? They didn't offer to take us in when our parents died, did they? Come on, sis."

Although this wasn't the answer she'd been hoping for, Alice found herself comforted by her brother's breezy confidence. Solomon Honker was right: Raz mightn't have all the answers, but in a way that would make his performance quite convincing. After all, Alex wasn't very good at answers either, and she never questioned it, just accepted that he was a bit careless with details.

The cafeteria was crowded and noisy, with a long line winding back from the buffet.

"Oh no," groaned Alex. "I'll never get to try the Stetson Camembert at this rate."

Alice scanned the room for their aunt and uncle. There were so many mice bustling about with trays of food and sheaves of papers that it took her several minutes to spot them. They were seated near the edge of the room, and Alice saw her aunt shake her head as a dark brown mouse approached with a tray of food, obviously hoping to sit there.

She waved madly in their direction until Uncle Ebenezer spotted her. He stood up, beckoning. "I've already got your lunch," he called.

Alice and Alex pushed through the crowd to the table and slumped into the two empty seats.

"Uncle Ebenezer, you're my hero!" Alex exclaimed. One of the trays was piled high with cheeses of all descriptions, including a large wedge of Stetson Camembert.

"Ah, well, I don't know when you'll be back in Shetlock, so I thought I'd get you a sampler of our best cheeses. See this hard one here? It's from the slopes of Mount Sharpnest. . . ."

As her uncle and brother talked cheese, Alice stared at

the salad sandwich her uncle had thoughtfully selected for her. Fear had filled the place in her stomach where hunger should be. She pushed the plate away.

"How was your first morning as a codebreaker, Aunt Beezer?" she asked.

Her aunt beamed. "Fascinating," she said. "It's going to be very challenging, but I'll be working with some of the finest mathematical brains of Shetlock and Souris. And how was your morning?" Aunt Beezer's smile dimmed and her eyes were troubled. "Tobias sent a message to say that you're leaving this afternoon. Do you feel ready?" She glanced at Alice's uneaten sandwich.

Alice lifted a shoulder and gave a wan smile. "I guess so. Solomon Honker was very thorough. But I do feel a bit . . . a bit scared," she confessed.

"I'm not surprised," Beezer said. "Alice, you don't have to do this, you know. No one would think any less of you if you decided to pull out of the mission."

For a moment Alice was tempted. Yes, she and Alex could pull out (for surely they wouldn't send Raz without his twin). FIG could find another way. But then she remembered what Tobias said: there was no other option. And she knew that if she didn't do everything she could to help free Gerander, she could never live with herself.

She looked at her aunt and forced a smile. "All that is necessary for evil to triumph is for good mice to do nothing," she said.

Beezer smiled back; Alice was quoting one of Uncle Ebenezer's favorite sayings.

"We'll be fine," Alice continued. Adopting her brother's breezy manner, she added, "We can outwit any Sourian." (Except Sophia and Horace, she amended privately, with a quiver.)

When Alex had devoured the last of his cheese platter, Alice pushed her chair back from the table. "I think it's time," she said.

Together the four of them skirted the hall until they were standing on the steps of the cafeteria. When Alice saw Solomon Honker striding toward them she wondered if he was still their stern teacher or had once more become the friendly mouse they had encountered briefly the night before.

"You're ready?" he asked his pupils. "Good." He tapped the air with a white envelope he held. His manner was serious, but not stern. It occurred to Alice that perhaps they hadn't even met the real Solomon Honker yet. Maybe they had only seen him playing roles, like she and Alex were about to play roles. It was an interesting thought, one she filed away for future consideration.

"Would you like to come see them off?" Solomon Honker was asking Ebenezer and Beezer, who nodded gratefully.

Their teacher led them to the long tree-lined road they'd come up when they had first approached the school.

"Where are we going?" asked Alex as they started down the road.

But Solomon Honker merely raised a finger in a "You'll

see" gesture and, pushing back branches, turned down a secluded path partially obscured by shrubs. Exchanging mystified looks, his pupils and their aunt and uncle followed.

9

The River's Source

As Alistair was dragged to his feet he thrashed against the grip restraining him, kicking out with his legs and squirming in his captor's arms.

"Alistair, stop, it's okay." The voice was familiar and Alistair paused in confusion. "It's me: Feast Thompson."

Feast Thompson? As a wave of relief surged through him, Alistair's legs grew weak and he sagged against the FIG operative. He peered into the gloom and saw that Tibby Rose was hugging the slim form bending over her. "Is that you, S-Slippers? Are we . . . are we near the source?" His throat felt thick with emotion as it began to sink in that he and Tibby were safe—well, as safe as they could be on the run in Gerander.

Slippers Pink lifted her head. Her eyes shone in the dim light. "It's me, Alistair," she said softly, as if she, too, was finding it hard to speak. "And the source of the Winns isn't far away."

"What happened to you two?" asked Feast urgently. "Why did you arrive on foot? Where's Oswald?"

Tibby made a small, unhappy sound and Alistair's voice was low as he said, "So you haven't seen Oswald?"

"Not since he dropped us off here nearly forty-eight hours ago," said Slippers. "We didn't know if the mission had been aborted, or if something terrible had happened, or . . ." She shook her head.

"Something terrible did happen," Alistair told them, and he described the eagles' attack. He heard Slippers's sharp intake of breath when he recalled how Oswald had dropped them in the icy reaches of the Crankens. "And we have no idea what happened to him after that," he finished, feeling once more a pang of guilt and sadness as he contemplated the brave owl's fate.

"Oh, poor Os." Slippers put her hands to her mouth, clearly distressed. "I think we'd all better sit down to hear the rest," she said. "Feast, some hot tea is called for."

Slippers Pink fetched the pair's rucksack from a thicket of bushes on the other side of the clearing as Feast Thompson hobbled toward the trees.

"What happened to Feast?" Tibby gasped. "Is he hurt?"

"He twisted an ankle when we landed the other night," Slippers said.

Alistair and Tibby rushed to help Feast forage for kindling among the trees surrounding the clearing, and soon a small fire glowed within a circle of rocks. Slippers filled the pot from the spring and set it in the embers, then threw a handful of needles into the simmering water.

"Spruce tea," she said. "Full of vitamin C."

Soon they were each sipping at a tin mug of hot liquid.

"So what happened next?" Slippers prompted as Alistair breathed in the mild scent.

Tibby took up the story, explaining how she had hit her head and Alistair had pulled her on the sled he had built, all the way up to their narrow escape from the Queen's Guards on the same sled just a few hours before.

"That was very good thinking," Slippers said as they related how they had covered their tracks and fled into the forest while the guards went after the sled. "But," she added, "the Sourians now know that two ginger mice have crossed the border. We'll have to be extracautious."

"We're always extracautious, Slips," Feast pointed out. "But I agree that the sooner we find those secret paths and put some distance between us and the guards who are looking for Alistair and Tibby Rose, the better. Before anything else, though, these two need some sleep."

Alistair woke to sunlight filtering through the leaves and sat up immediately. The others still slumbered on beside him: Tibby, curled into a ball around her rucksack; Slippers Pink, her shiny black boots lined up neatly at her gingery pink feet; and Feast Thompson, stretched out on his back, one hand clutching a stout walking stick Tibby Rose had found for him when looking for kindling the night before. Alistair stood up and walked to the edge of the copse of trees. He knew it was useless trying to go back to sleep. Not with the fluttering of anticipation he felt.

He gazed down the slope into the valley below, still in shadow. Somewhere down there was the Winns. That was where their mission would finally begin, where they could finally start to solve the mystery encoded in his scarf. There, he hoped, he would find the first of the secret paths that crisscrossed Gerander—and might one day be used to set her free. Unbidden, the melancholy refrain sung by Timmy the Winns floated into his mind, and he sang it under his breath:

> *"Wherever the Winns takes me, that's where I'll be,*
> *For me and the Winns will always flow free."*

But however much Alistair wished to see the Winns flow free, more than anything he wished to see his parents freed. As the sun cleared the trees above him to send the first rays of light into the valley below, he glanced behind him impatiently.

They had a light but nourishing breakfast of berries and nuts, then the four mice walked in single file along a path, which led downhill from the clearing and meandered through flower-strewn meadows before re-entering a forest of oak and chestnut trees.

After a few minutes' walking, Slippers Pink, who was in front, stopped. "Here's the source of the Winns," she said quietly, reverence in her tone.

Alistair moved forward. There, in the center of a cool green glade, was a pool. The silence was absolute except for the whisper of leaves in the trees above and a single note of birdsong. Alistair perched on a rock and gazed into the pool's depths. The water, which was the deep green of moss, was clear and clean and fathomlessly deep. When he put a hand in, it was as cold as ice.

Just below the pool, water sprang from a rock and trickled down the hillside. Alistair stared at in wonder. It was hard to believe that this would become Gerander's principal river.

They followed a path alongside the trickle, which had become a stream by the time they passed a small stone cottage. Tucked into the green hillside, it looked as worn and weathered as the rock itself. Though they proceeded warily, there were no signs of life as they hurried past. Vestiges of crumbling stone walls were visible here and there among rampant weeds, and the trees nearby were groaning with fruit. What had once been a well-tended garden had grown wild.

They walked further into the valley, with the river, now broad and lined with reeds, on their left, and a high, forested ridge to their right. Across the river was a dense canopy of plane trees. Apart from the distant clatter of cicadas, the landscape through which they walked seemed to be deserted.

"But we mustn't relax," Slippers Pink warned. "The Queen's Guards have set up checkpoints along all the roads of Gerander, and patrols are roaming the countryside too."

Slowly, so that Feast and his injured ankle could keep up, they followed the river for several miles, but by lunchtime, when the path ahead entered an avenue of plane trees, they hadn't seen any landmarks to match those they had found on Alistair's scarf.

While Slippers Pink and Feast Thompson produced the makings of simple cheese sandwiches from their rucksack, Alistair and Tibby Rose sat on a rock and studied Alistair's scarf.

"We must have come too far," Tibby said. "I'm sure we passed this bend in the river ages ago." With her finger she traced a small curve in the stripe of blue bisecting the scarf. It was definitely below the burst of orange and speck of yellow they'd shown Tobias back in Stetson. "We'll have to go back."

And so after lunch they retraced their steps, but as the afternoon wore on, Alistair began to feel increasingly despondent. He had seen hundreds of trees and rocks, but none had looked like a burning tree or a rock of gold. He walked faster and faster, until he was almost jogging along the path, scanning the surrounds with an increasingly desperate eye.

"Alistair, slow down," Slippers called from some way behind. "We have to stay together."

Reluctantly Alistair slowed his pace, matching it to the lazy meander of the river. And soon, although his eyes were still scanning the rocks and trees, his ears were tuning in to the river, the way it gurgled and burbled over and around stones and branches. After a while he noticed that his feet seemed to be following the rhythm of the river of their own accord. He felt as if he were moving in a trance, hardly aware of moving in and out of the shadows of the plane trees that lined stretches of the river, or the buzz of cicadas, or the slow sinking of the sun, which set the sky ablaze.

A gentle breeze set the reeds rustling and the ends of his scarf fluttering. When he rounded a bend and saw, beneath a tall ridge of rock, a tree whose leaves seemed to have caught flame, his heart skipped a beat. He turned to see if the others had spotted it too. Tibby Rose was right behind him, but Feast and Slippers were still out of sight around the bend.

"Tibby," he breathed, "can you see it?"

Tibby nodded, then pointed. "Over there: look how that rock is glowing where the sun hits it; it looks like—like a rock of gold."

Alistair recited the words slowly.

> *"A burning tree*
> *A rock of gold*
> *A fracture in the mountain's fold,*
> *In the sun's last rays when the shadows grow long*
> *And the rustling reeds play the Winns's north song."*

"Of course," Alistair breathed. "That's why we couldn't see it earlier—the tree doesn't burn and the rock doesn't glow until they're hit by the sun's last rays."

"A fracture in the mountain's fold," Tibby repeated.

"What do you suppose that means?"

The two ginger mice turned to stare at the sheer rock face, then approached and began to trace its sharp creases. Alistair ran his palm along the sheer face until he was stopped by a small fissure. He slipped his hand into the crack, expecting to be impeded by another seam of rock, but instead he was able to extend his whole arm into the space. His pulse racing, he ran his hand further down the crack, which grew wider and wider until, at the base of the rock, he found a hole wide enough to squeeze through. He dropped to his knees and wriggled through into a cavernous space. Here and there the darkness was pierced by light filtering through small holes and cracks in the rock. He walked clockwise around the space, looking for some sign that this place was what he was seeking, though he wasn't sure exactly how he'd be able to tell. But surely it couldn't be a coincidence—that rock shining gold in the sun's last rays, the tree that looked as though it had burst into flame.

He was about a quarter of the way around the cavern when he found it: a light-filled alcove, its roof open to the sky. The walls were whitewashed so that they seemed to glow in the light of the setting sun, and there, painted directly on the wall in vivid colors, was a familiar arrangement of shapes and squiggles with a wide blue stripe running down its center. Holding his breath, Alistair unwound his scarf and held it up beside the painting. They were exactly the same.

With growing excitement, he wrapped his scarf around

his neck once more and resumed his exploration of the cavern. There was something here, he was certain now. Something to do with the secret paths. He had almost finished his circumnavigation, and doubt was creeping in, when he came to an opening carved into the wall, concealed from the mouth of the cavern by a jutting rock. Alistair stepped inside, and then took another step. The rock arched above him, a little higher than his head.

It was a tunnel.

Then, as if from a great distance, he heard Tibby's voice calling his name.

"Alistair? Where are you? Alistair!" She sounded worried.

Realizing he must have been gone for some time, Alistair hurried back to the cavern mouth and crawled through the hole.

Tibby was standing several meters away, glancing around anxiously.

"I'm here," he said.

Turning at the sound of his voice, Tibby said, "I thought you'd disappeared off the face of the earth. Where were you?"

Alistair indicated the crack in the side of the rock face. "In there," he said. "It leads into a huge cavern and, Tibby—I've found it!"

"Found what?"

"A tunnel!"

"A tunnel?" she repeated excitedly. "Where to?"

"I don't know, but it must be one of the secret paths—I

saw a painting that matches my scarf exactly. Hang on . . ." Alistair quickly unwound the scarf from around his neck again and, crouching, laid it out flat on the ground. Tibby kneeled next to him as he found the dash of gold and splash of red knitted into the uppermost part of the scarf, just to the left of the wide blue stripe. Close by, he saw, was a small brown arch.

"Tib, look—do you think that brown arch could be a tunnel?"

Tibby followed his pointing finger. "It makes sense," she said. Peering closer she added, "And there are brown arches running part of the way down this side of the river with more leading off to the side."

"That line running down the left-hand edge must be the coastline of the Cannolian Ocean," Alistair surmised. "So those paths must lead to the coast." He lifted his eyes from their contemplation of the scarf to look at his friend. "Which means . . ."

Tibby's eyes widened as Alistair's meaning sank in. "Which means we can take the tunnels almost all the way to Atticus Island!"

"With no fear of meeting a Sourian patrol!" Alistair cried jubilantly. His parents seemed closer than ever—he couldn't wait to get going. "Let's go find Slippers and Feast."

Feast Thompson and Slippers Pink were rounding the bend. Feast was limping heavily, leaning on the stick.

"Alistair, you're safe," Slippers said with obvious relief. "When we heard Tibby calling we thought something must have happened."

Alistair felt a pang of guilt as he saw the fatigue creasing Feast's face and the anxiety lining Slippers's. He really shouldn't have taken off like that.

But before he could apologize, Tibby was telling them about Alistair's discovery, and he saw their expressions brighten.

A few minutes later, the four of them had crawled through the entrance to the cavern, which was completely dark now that the sun had slipped below the ridge.

"How do you turn on the light?" Feast joked.

"With these," said Slippers. In a niche in the wall, she had found a candlestick and candles.

They lit a candle and Alistair showed the others the alcove and the mouth of the tunnel before returning to the cavern where they'd left their rucksacks.

"We can sleep in here tonight," Slippers decided. "The ground might be a bit cold, since it hasn't been warmed by the sun, but at least we'll be safe."

They improvised a meal of bread and cheese, with some mushrooms from the supply Tibby had picked the day before. As they moved about in the candlelight, their shadows were huge and grotesque against the cavern walls, and Alistair was glad when, as soon as they'd eaten, Slippers Pink blew the candle out to conserve it.

"Well, Alistair, you've done it," Feast Thompson remarked as they lay in the dark. "You and Tibby have found the secret paths, just as Emmeline intended."

Alistair felt a glow of satisfaction at hearing Feast's

words, but he couldn't suppress a tug of impatience. "I just hope they help us to free Mom and Dad," he said, adding, "And that they're useful for FIG." After all, he remembered, it was in order to help FIG that his parents had set off for Gerander and the secret paths in the first place. He still couldn't get over the idea of his gentle mother as a FIG agent. He wondered when she had joined, and if she'd been on many dangerous missions before marrying his father and settling in Stubbins to raise a family. Slippers Pink, who he thought was about the same age as Emmeline, had been on lots of missions, he knew.

"Slippers," he said, "when did you join FIG?"

"When did I join FIG?" she repeated from where she lay on the other side of Tibby, who was on Alistair's right. Her voice echoed slightly off the walls of the cavern. "Let me see, it must be fourteen or fifteen years ago, I suppose. I was at university in Grouch when a friend of mine told me about a secret meeting for Gerandan-born students. All the Gerandan families in Grouch knew each other, although none of us ever spoke about our heritage publicly—you know how Sourians feel about us." Alistair nodded vigorously, having been chased halfway across Souris because of his ginger fur.

There was the sound of shifting, and Alistair guessed that she had rolled over onto her side to face him. "I met Zanzibar at that meeting," she said. "He and his brother and sister had been living in hiding in Gerander since they were children. Their parents had died in prison. Zanzibar grew up determined to free his country. He started FIG, and began to travel around Souris and Shetlock, talking with Gerandan exiles and sympathetic friends of exiles. He was at the secret meeting and, after he'd finished telling us what life was like in Gerander, every person at the meeting joined FIG on the spot. Zanzibar is very inspiring."

"He sure is," Feast Thompson chipped in. "I went along to a meeting with a friend of mine whose father was Gerandan, and I was shocked to hear about the poverty and hunger in Gerander. And the way Gerandans were treated like second-class citizens, unable to travel freely, to express their opinions; any Gerandan who criticized the Sourians was jailed without a trial. Even if you were only suspected of being anti-Sourian you could be taken away for interrogation."

"But Zanzibar didn't speak only of despair," Slippers recalled. "He spoke of hope. He spoke of what we could learn from the experience of Gerander, and how we could use that to build a new and better society."

"Did you see Zanzibar again after that meeting?" Tibby Rose asked.

Slippers laughed. "I'll say I did. I introduced him to my best friend and they got married."

"Zanzibar is married?" Alistair said in surprise. Somehow he had never pictured Gerander's exiled leader as having a family. He always seemed so . . . so solitary when people spoke of him.

"Was married," Slippers said. There was no trace of laughter in her voice now. "His wife—my best friend—died not long after."

"That's so sad," said Tibby. "What about his brother and sister? What happened to them?"

Slippers paused a moment before she replied, "Last I heard, they'd both been captured by the Sourians." Then, before Alistair or Tibby could ask anymore questions, she said abruptly, "We'd better get some sleep. Good night all."

Alistair had hoped to turn the conversation around to his mother, but Slippers Pink had been so definite in her ending of the discussion that he decided to let the subject drop. After all, he would be able to ask Emmeline herself the questions before long. And with that happy thought, he fell asleep.

10

Undercover

Alice couldn't imagine where Solomon Honker was taking them as they filed behind him along the narrow path. Perhaps Alex's guess—that they were going to be traveling by eagle—was correct, though she sincerely hoped not.

A few minutes later they emerged into a small clearing to see a white mouse with tan spots darting nimbly around a tall white basket. A tangle of ropes led to a large swath of sky-blue silk stretched out flat across the ground.

Alex looked transported with joy. "A hot-air balloon! I bet Alistair has never flown in one of these before."

Even Alice, nervous as she was, felt a flutter of excitement.

Solomon Honker approached the tan-spotted mouse and exchanged a few quiet words then returned with her to the small group standing at the edge of the clearing.

"It might not be as fast as an owl, but Claudia says

the conditions are perfect for ballooning." He nodded to the pilot.

"That's right," said the tan-spotted mouse. "Nice and calm. Let's hope it stays that way. If you two are all set"—she raised an inquiring eyebrow at Alice and Alex—"I'll get the inflator fan going."

"Inflator fan?" Alex asked eagerly. "Is that what you use to blow up the balloon?"

"That's right—though we call it an envelope, rather than a balloon," she explained.

Alice watched the balloon (she couldn't quite think of it as an envelope) begin to inflate slowly; Solomon Honker handed her the letter he'd been holding.

"This is a letter from the major commanding your father's old regiment explaining your circumstances and recommending you for service in the palace. If you should happen to meet a Sourian patrol and they ask for your identity papers, show it to them."

"How did you get it?" Alice asked, clutching the letter tightly.

"It's a forgery. A good one, I hope." He smiled drily. "Now listen, Claudia is going to drop you in a field just on the other side of the Winns, about a three-hour walk east of Cornoliana."

Alice, picturing the map which hung on the wall of the classroom, thought she knew where he meant.

"Claudia will return to the field every day at sunset. If you haven't managed to fulfill your objective within two weeks, abort the mission and return to the field.

Understand?"

"Yes, sir."

"Very good. Then I will leave you to say your farewells." He turned toward the path, then stopped. "Oh, and Alice? Don't worry too much about forgetting what you have learned. You have been an excellent pupil, and the information will come to you when you need it. You'll see."

Alice gaped at him. How had he read her fears so accurately?

"And, Alex, I know you're equal to any situation." He allowed a small wry smile to cross his lips. "Good luck, you two."

As he disappeared down the path it occurred to Alice that it was the first time he'd used their real names.

The balloon was semi-inflated by now, and Claudia called, "I'm turning on the burner. You've got two minutes."

Alex was casting longing glances over his shoulder. Alice could tell he was impatient to leave.

"I guess we should be going," she said, as the burner started up with a *whoosh* and the balloon began to rise toward an upright position.

Although Uncle Ebenezer put on a brave face, his mustache was decidedly droopy as he brushed the cheddar crumbs from Alex's whiskers and kissed the top of Alice's head. Beezer looked sad and solemn as she hugged first Alice then Alex.

"We'll see you soon," said Uncle Ebenezer, his voice

thick. Then he hurried up the path without a backward look.

Alice and her brother jogged over to where Claudia was standing by the basket, which was tethered to the ground.

"Jump in," said the tan-spotted mouse.

Alex clambered over the side then reached back to help Alice as she too scrambled in. Claudia pulled out the pegs tethering the basket down then, with one hand on the wicker edge, vaulted neatly in as the basket began to drift slowly upward.

"Okay," she said, "rules of the basket: no sudden movements, let's just try to keep things nice and stable, and if we run into any turbulence slip your arms through those ropes." She indicated some ropes laced through the basket's weave. "Here we go." She adjusted a valve and the flame shot up into the balloon, causing it to rise more swiftly.

Alice stood at the edge of the basket, which came up to chest-height, and waved to her aunt, who was still standing at the edge of the clearing.

A light breeze had sprung up, ruffling Beezer's creamy fur as she stood with her hand shading her eyes against the afternoon sun.

The basket swayed gently as it rose higher and higher, until they were floating past the treetops. The clearing was a small ragged circle of light green grass fringed by the dark green leaves of the trees, and Aunt Beezer was a small waving speck.

"This is brilliant!" Alex cried over the hiss of the

burner. "You can see everything from up here! Look, sis."
He darted from one side of the basket to the other, causing
the basket to rock.

"Not too much moving around," the pilot reminded
him. "We need to keep the basket balanced."

Alice looked where her brother was pointing and saw
the Stetson school and the town below. She had a strange
sensation of weightlessness, floating high above the
ground. She wasn't sure if she liked the feeling or not.

"How long will the trip take?" she asked the pilot.

"Six hours," Claudia estimated. "Depends on the wind."

"How long would an owl take?"

Claudia shrugged. "Maybe three."

Alex looked slightly put out, but Alice had other
concerns than speed.

"You mean we'll arrive in the dark?"

"Yep," Claudia replied.

"But how will you find the field?" Alex wanted to
know.

"I'll find it," said the pilot.

"So you've flown this route before?" Alex persisted.

"Mmm." It was hard to know whether Claudia's reply
was an affirmation or not. She seemed to Alice to be a
mouse of surprisingly few words—though perhaps, Alice
thought, she was just being discreet. She probably didn't
know any of the details of her passengers' mission, nor
was she meant to know.

"How do you go down?" Alex asked as the pilot sent
another spurt of flame into the balloon.

Claudia indicated a rope, which ran right through from the top of the balloon to the basket. "I pull this rope to open the valve up there—what we call the parachute valve." She pointed to a small circular flap. "That lets out some of the hot air, which is causing us to rise."

Alice watched the earth below, following the snaking line of a gleaming river winding through a rocky mountain range. "Are we in Gerander now?"

Claudia glanced down. "Yep."

"Woohoo!" Alex whooped.

Alice stood up to get her first glimpse of the country she'd heard so much about recently—that she was risking her life to save. As she lifted her head above the edge of the basket a cool breeze brushed her fur, and she was sure she could hear the rustle of leaves. "Oh!" she exclaimed as a scent redolent of river and grasses and summer flowers hit her nose.

"Crossing the Winns," said Claudia, lifting her head to inhale the sweet air.

Alice barely had time to take in a broad blue river and fields of gold and green before they were headed out to sea.

"The Cannolian Ocean," Claudia said in answer to Alex's question.

"But doesn't that mean we've left Gerander behind?"

"We'll stay out here, just off the coast, until the last moment," the tan-spotted mouse replied. "Less chance of being spotted by a Sourian patrol."

That made sense, Alice thought, trying to imagine

what they must look like from below. She saw the logic in choosing a sky-blue balloon for a cloudless day. The white basket could look like a cloud or a bird, she supposed. She wondered if Claudia also had a gray balloon—envelope— for cloudy days.

Hours passed, with nothing but the hard, glassy surface of the ocean and the blurred line of the Gerandan coast to look at.

When the chill of the wind started to make her nose twitch, Alice sat on the floor of the basket, her back against its side, her arms around her knees.

Alex, who showed no sign of feeling the cold, continued to lean out of the basket asking questions.

"What's that?"

"A sea eagle."

"Do they attack balloons?"

"Only if we trespass on their territory."

"Will we trespass on their territory?"

"No."

"Oh." Alex sounded vaguely disappointed, as if he'd been looking forward to coming under attack from a giant raptor.

They flew on into the setting sun.

"What's that?" Alex asked.

"Eagle—no, wait." Claudia moved carefully across the basket to where Alex stood and squinted into the fading light. "I'm not sure," she said, more to herself than to Alex.

Alice stood up to see.

Her brother and the pilot were staring at a gray cigar-shaped object moving slowly toward them. It didn't look like a bird—it wasn't soaring or swooping—but what else could it be?

"Maybe it's a cloud," she suggested, but even as she said it she knew that wasn't right either. It seemed more purposeful in its movement, whereas a cloud would just drift.

"It looks like. . . ," Claudia began slowly. "It looks like a dirigible."

"A what?" said Alex.

"A dirigible," Claudia replied, her eyes fixed on the craft moving inexorably toward them. "An airship. Uses hot air, like a balloon, but it's controlled by propellers and rudders."

"Who would be flying a dirigible around here?" Alice asked.

"That's what I'd like to know," Claudia said. "Let's see if it knows we're here."

She adjusted the propane valve to send a jet of flame into the basket, and Alice felt her stomach drop to the floor as they shot upward.

Seconds later, the dirigible too moved to a higher altitude.

"Interesting," Claudia murmured. She tugged at the rope to open the parachute valve, and their ascent slowed. After a few moments, the dirigible did the same. "Very interesting." Alice thought she sounded rather grim.

"Could it be someone from FIG?" Alice asked hopefully.

"Nope. FIG doesn't have any dirigibles."

As the dirigible grew nearer, Alice saw that it was more silver than gray. Silver and . . . what was that printed on its side? It was getting dark and she couldn't quite make it out. She craned her neck.

"I think you'll find it's a purple crown," Claudia told her.

A purple crown on a silver background . . . Purple and silver . . . Alice's chest tightened so that she could barely breathe. "Sourians," she said.

"Sourians," Claudia confirmed.

"What will they do?" Alex, who had relished the thought of an eagle attack, sounded apprehensive now.

"Your guess is as good as mine," Claudia said, her eyes never leaving the approaching airship. "Ram us, maybe? Let's not wait around to find out. Hang on," she instructed. "We're going for a wild ride." She adjusted the valve so that a great spume of flame shot up into the envelope, and the balloon rose suddenly.

The higher they went, the stronger the winds grew, with irregular gusts that battered the balloon and tossed the basket around helplessly. Alice slipped her arms through the ropes on the inside of the basket and tried not to think about her churning insides. Their balloon seemed very fragile now, thrown about at the whim of the wind. What would happen if they fell from this height? she wondered as a particularly strong gust threatened to upset the basket. Surely they were too high; surely the balloon couldn't withstand these winds. They had to descend.

But then she bent her head and saw the dirigible brooding ominously below.

"Hold tight!" Claudia shouted over the roar of the wind. Her face was determined. "Going down!"

And with an almighty tug of the rope they plunged, down, down, until they were beneath the dirigible. Alice's stomach had barely caught up when, just as the dirigible descended to meet them, they shot up again. Alice couldn't suppress a moan as her head began to whirl in concert with her stomach and and she rested her head on her knees.

Alex didn't seem to be at all affected by their dizzying descents and ascents.

"Ha!" he gloated. "That foxed them!"

They'd caught a favorable current at last, and it was sweeping them along at a terrific speed when Alex said in a puzzled voice, "What was that? Something just flew past us. And here comes another one."

Alice lifted her head in time to see a slim projectile hurtle past, narrowly missing the side of the balloon.

"It's a spear!" her brother cried. "They're trying to puncture the balloon!"

Alice kept her head up, transfixed, as a shower of spears flew toward them.

"Incoming!" Alex shouted.

Claudia released a small burst of flame and the balloon seemed to bounce up. Most of the spears passed harmlessly underneath but one hit the basket, the impact jostling them. Alex leaned over the side to pull the quivering piece of wood free from the wicker. "If that's the best you can do . . . ," he muttered at the dirigible trailing in their wake. The flurry of spears finished; either the Sourians had run out or they were finding it too hard to fix on their target now that the last glowing edge of the sun was dipping below the horizon.

"That evens up the playing field," commented Claudia as darkness enfolded them. "Now, let's try to get our own back." She released the parachute valve, and the balloon's progress slowed almost to a halt before beginning to drift down gently.

Alice, now that the buffeting had stopped, felt well enough to stand again.

But her momentary lifting of spirits was dampened as the dirigible hove into view, a dark forbidding mass made visible by the moon rising in the east.

The balloon floated toward land—agonizingly slowly it seemed to Alice—and they were gradually losing altitude. Were they losing power? Looking at the set of Claudia's face, she didn't dare ask. Down they drifted, down . . . down . . . until the smell of salt was strong and Alice could hear the churn and suck of waves below. Then suddenly they stopped. Alice couldn't help but cry out as they seemed to hover in the air, right in the path of the Sourian airship. Couldn't Claudia see the dirigible? It was coming straight for them, looming big and black, closer . . . closer . . . It was almost smothering them. They were going to collide!

"No!" Alice screamed, then *whoosh!* The balloon shot

into the air at the last possible moment while the dirigible, with no time to correct its course, plunged into the ocean.

"Cool!" yelled Alex. "Way to go, Claudia!"

"Yeah," said Alice, when her heart had started beating again.

"That should slow them down for a while," Claudia said. "I don't know how long, though, so we're going to have to make it a quick landing. I won't have time to tie down: when I give the word, you get out fast. Got it?"

"Got it," the two young mice chorused.

"And it could get bumpy," she warned, "so grab hold of those ropes."

Alice obediently hooked her arms through the basket's ropes again as the balloon sailed inland. They tacked to the south—"Best to avoid flying directly over Cornoliana," Claudia murmured, gesturing at a constellation of lights twinkling in the distance—before swinging northeast to descend gradually over a line of treetops toward a large moonlit field.

"Safe travels. I'll see you at sunset."

And then the basket dipped and they were racing toward the ground, the basket hitting at a forty-five-degree angle so that they bunny-hopped along the mown grass before finally coming to rest.

"Go!" ordered Claudia, and Alice and Alex scrambled out.

Claudia released a burst of flame from the valve and the envelope and basket righted themselves. Within seconds the balloon was aloft again, lifting above the trees and catching an easterly current.

They watched in silence until the balloon was no longer in sight. As she gazed into the empty sky it felt to Alice that she and Alex were adrift, and not the balloon: in a strange country with a forged letter, fake identities, and a hastily concocted story. In a bid to dispel the sudden feeling of despair, she stood up and began to brush the grass and twigs from her fur. She didn't know they weren't alone until a prickling between her shoulder blades prompted her to whirl around.

There, spears thrust out, were three Queen's Guards.

"Well, well, well," drawled the tallest, holding the point of his spear at Alice's throat. "What have we here?"

11

The Secret Paths

Alistair's first sensation as they entered the tunnel the next morning, Slippers holding the candlestick aloft, was one of excitement. Here they were, traveling undetected through Gerander—perhaps under the very feet of the Sourian army! But as they moved further and further into the close confines of the tunnel, Alistair couldn't help but feel an invisible weight pressing down on him. Even though he was able to stand without difficulty, and the tunnel was wide enough for them to walk two abreast, the knowledge that they were traveling under who knew how many tons of earth and rock made his chest feel strangely tight, as if the air was thin, though the occasional flickering of the candle told him there must be vents through which drafts were flowing. Here and there the knobs of tree roots protruded from the roof or ran like veins along the wall, usually accompanied by a sharp bend in the tunnel, as if it was skirting an obstacle.

These unexpected bends could be alarming, for if he had fallen too far behind Slippers and the candle, the tunnel would suddenly be plunged into darkness and he would have to feel his way around the corner with one hand brushing along the rough dirt wall.

Although they found niches stocked with candles at regular intervals, Slippers was concerned to conserve them as much as they could. "We'll need light when we're traveling back through the tunnel," she reasoned. "And who knows how many other mice travel these paths and expect to use the candles stored here?"

Other mice traveling the paths? It hadn't occurred to Alistair before, but of course Slippers Pink was right: although the paths weren't known to many, a few families did still retain the knowledge. It was possible they would encounter others in this tunnel. For the first time Alistair wondered why there were secret paths through Gerander, and who had constructed them. He asked Slippers.

"No one knows for sure," she said. "Historians have discovered that before Greater Gerander was united into a single kingdom, the population was split into a number of warring tribes. Perhaps each tribe devised its own way of moving around secretly, and the families who still know of the existence of these paths are descended from those tribes? Or maybe these tunnels are even older," she mused. "Maybe there was an ancient race of mice who lived underground."

Alistair had to admit that the tunnel, cool and dry with a musty earthen smell, did indeed seem timeless.

But he couldn't bear the thought of living permanently underground and was relieved when, not long after this discussion, they saw light seeping into the main tunnel from a narrow branch to the left. That smaller tunnel must lead to the world above ground, he surmised.

The excitement and tension of traveling by secret tunnel wore off quite quickly. There was nothing to look at, just the same unending dirt-packed walls. To pass the time, they told stories: Slippers Pink and Feast Thompson described some of their most hair-raising missions for FIG; Tibby Rose recounted the adventures of Charlotte Tibby; and Alistair recalled the plots of some of his favorite books. They had no way of telling whether it was night or day, so they ate when they were hungry and eventually, when their steps began to drag, they slept. Their pace gradually increased as Feast's ankle mended and, when Alistair and Tibby Rose checked how far they'd gone on the scarf's map, counting off the forks in the path they had passed, they could see that they were making good progress.

They had just stopped by one such fork for lunch on their second day in the tunnel when a shuffling sound in the adjoining tunnel made them pause in their eating. They hurriedly gathered up their things, blew out the candle, and retreated to the far side of the tunnel, where they crouched with their backs against the cool dirt of the wall.

Huddling in the dark, a dark as complete and black as any he had ever known, Alistair tried to stay calm even as his mind threw up frightening scenarios. Had the Sourians inadvertently stumbled across an entrance to the tunnel? Or maybe . . . maybe they had tortured his mother into revealing the secret!

After a few minutes they saw the glow of a flame approaching, and Alistair's heart began to knock alarmingly against his ribs. Then an elderly mouse with curly gray fur, leaning heavily on a knobbly walking stick, appeared. She stopped dead when the pool of candlelight edged toward the four figures crouched against the tunnel wall. The hand holding the walking stick flew to her chest, and the flame of the candle trembled in the other.

"Mercy me," she gasped. "Who's that there in the shadows?"

Slippers Pink moved forward into the glow of the elderly mouse's candle, her almond fur gleaming. "I'm sorry if we've startled you," she said.

"What are you doing in here?" the elderly mouse asked, her voice quavering slightly.

Feast assured her, "We mean no harm."

"We're just travelers," Slippers added. "Alistair, Tibby Rose," she said, beckoning.

The two young mice stepped out of the shadows to join her and Feast. The elderly mouse held her candle higher and peered at them. "What beautiful ginger fur," she remarked, looking from Alistair to Tibby Rose with bright, birdlike eyes. "You're Gerandan, that's for sure. But still, I think you'd better tell me how you came to be in here. I haven't seen anyone in these tunnels for years. Who told you about them?"

"My mother . . . ," Alistair began, then hesitated. His mother hadn't told him about the tunnels, not exactly. Quickly he unwound the scarf from around his neck and held it up. The colors were muted in the light of the candle, but the pattern was obviously visible because the elderly mouse gave a cry of recognition. "My mother gave me this," he said.

The elderly mouse looked at Alistair for a long moment, then Tibby Rose, then back at the scarf. "And did she tell you what it means?"

"She went away the next day, and I haven't seen her since," Alistair explained. "But she sang a song that helped me to find the tunnel."

"Ah, if she knows the song about the tunnels, your mother was from the north," said the elderly mouse. "A special place, the north. The source of the Winns, you know."

"Are you from the north too?" Alistair asked eagerly. Perhaps this elderly mouse knew his mother.

"Oh, no," said the elderly mouse. "I'm from east of the Winns; our paths are quite different from these tunnels. I'm from another branch of the Winns family, you could say." She laughed softly to herself. "But my grandfather was from the north, and he told me of the tunnels. Not many know the old paths these days. They can only be passed down within families, you see, and so many families have fled—or worse." Her voice had dropped to an ominous whisper. "I dread the day the paths are discovered by the Sourians. To me, that will be the day when Gerander is truly lost."

"We were hoping that perhaps the paths could be used to free Gerander," Alistair said tentatively.

"Use the paths to free Gerander?" the elderly mouse repeated, tilting her head inquisitively.

"Perhaps we should introduce ourselves properly," Slippers Pink interjected. "I'm Slippers Pink, and this is Feast Thompson, Alistair, and Tibby Rose." She pointed to each of them in turn. "We're members of FIG."

"FIG? But that's Zanzibar's resistance group, is it not?" Before anyone could answer her, the elderly mouse slapped her own wrist and said, "You must excuse me, I've completely forgotten my manners. I'm Althea."

"Yes," Slippers said with a smile. "We are led by Zanzibar."

"Poor Zanzibar," said Althea, the light in her eyes dimming. "In prison these many years."

"No he's not," Tibby Rose interrupted. "He's free!"

"Free?" Althea stamped her walking stick once on the ground and thrust her face close to Tibby's. "Did you say 'free,' Miss Tibby Rose?"

"It's true," Alistair chimed in. "Isn't it, Slippers?"

"It is," Slippers Pink confirmed. "He's in hiding, but he's free."

"Well, mercy me. Why hadn't I heard? I may be old, but I'm not so forgetful that I wouldn't remember a thing like that."

"I suspect the Sourians haven't exactly been advertising the fact that Zanzibar escaped from them," Feast said wryly. "And that's why FIG wants to use the secret paths: so that information like this can be spread among Gerandans."

"I see, I see." Althea was nodding rapidly. "That's a very good idea. Yes, a very good idea. Why, if everyone knew about Zanzibar being free, it would give them great hope and courage. So is that why you are here? To spread this news?"

"Not exactly," said Slippers. "We've only recently arrived in Gerander from Shetlock. Our first goal was to find the secret paths, and now that we have done that—"

"We're going to Atticus Island," Alistair interrupted. "To rescue my parents."

"Your parents are on Atticus Island?" said the elderly mouse. "Oh dear." Alistair could hear the weight of sorrow in the words. "Oh dear."

"And we must be getting close to the tunnel which will take us to that stretch of coast, wouldn't you say, Tibby Rose?" Feast asked. Alistair could tell he was trying to inject a note of optimism into his voice to counter the dark foreboding in Althea's. "We'll be with Emmeline and Rebus soon."

"What's that? Emmeline?" Althea said.

"That's my mother's name," said Alistair. "Do you—?"

But Althea was already shaking her head. "No, no. I don't know your mother. I did know of a mouse called Emmeline once, but surely it couldn't be. . . ." She fixed her birdlike eyes on Alistair for a few seconds, then said, "No, I'm sorry, Alistair. Atticus Island . . ." She pressed her lips together. "You'll be needing help to get to the island, and I have a cousin living very close by, as it happens. William Mackerel. He's a fisherman, living in Cobb, which is the nearest town to that despicable place." She tapped her walking stick on the earthen floor thoughtfully, then said, "I'll walk with you as far as the tunnel leading to Cobb."

"We'd be much obliged," said Slippers Pink.

"You two young ones walk up here with me," said Althea, directing her gaze at Alistair and Tibby Rose. "You can carry my candlestick, Miss Tibby Rose, and I'll lean on your shoulder if I may, Master Alistair."

"So the secret paths you use in the east aren't tunnels?" Alistair asked as they set off at a surprisingly fast stride, leaving Slippers Pink and Feast Thompson to follow at a more sedate pace.

"No," said Althea. "They're not." She tipped her head consideringly. "Or perhaps they are. But not in the way of these tunnels."

"Have you taught your family about the secret paths that you know?"

"Alas, no. I'm still waiting for the right one. I'll know when he or she comes along. You always do. But sometimes you have to wait a generation or two. Your mother was lucky to recognize you so early."

"I've never understood why my mother gave the scarf to me and not my brother or sister," Alistair confessed.

"It's like I said," Althea replied. "You just know who the right one is. I was taught by my aunt, and she was taught by her great-grandfather. Who knows who you'll teach? Maybe you'll have to wait for generations too."

Alistair had to laugh at the thought of himself as a great-grandfather.

"But the times are changing," Althea continued. "You've told your friends about the tunnels, after all."

Alistair nodded guiltily, even though he knew he never could have found the tunnels, let alone reached them, without the help of Tibby Rose, Slippers Pink, and Feast Thompson. Or Oswald, he added to himself, feeling another stab of guilt.

"And perhaps that's as it should be," the elderly mouse mused. "For if the secret of the paths can help to free Gerander from tyranny, what greater purpose could they serve?" She stumped along in silence for a few minutes, then said, "But I'm an old mouse, and it's too late for me to change my ways. The old traditions still live strong in me. I could only ever share the secret within my family. What they choose to do with it"—she lifted her shoulders—"is up to them."

Only by his disappointment did Alistair realize that he had been hoping they would learn more of the secret paths from Althea.

"We're getting close now," Althea said. "I can smell the sea. Do you smell it?"

Alistair lifted his nose and sniffed. The dusty, earthy smell of the tunnel was slowly but surely giving way to the salty tang of sea air. "Yes," he said.

"I never understood why William Mackerel preferred

to live here by the sea," Althea said. "Every day the pounding of waves against the shore. Me, I like the whisper of the trees that grow alongside the Winns." She gave a peculiar flutelike sigh. "As much a whistle as a whisper, I suppose. Not everyone can hear it, but to me it's the most beautiful music."

She released her grip on Alistair's shoulder and danced a few steps, gliding and weaving with her feet never leaving the ground, so that an intricate pattern was traced into the earth behind her.

"Wow, where did you learn to dance like that?" Tibby asked. "It leaves such a pretty pattern on the ground."

"I've been doing it since I was a girl," said Althea. "Come on, I'll show you." She handed Alistair her walking stick and took Tibby Rose by the arm. "Now glide out and round with the left foot, straight through with the right . . . that's the way." Alistair, chuckling to himself, followed their braided steps as the old mouse and the younger one danced through the tunnel.

"Don't just laugh away back there, Master Alistair," Althea called over her shoulder. "Make yourself useful and give us some accompaniment. Like this." And she began to breathe and sigh her strange whistle. At first all Alistair could produce was a hissing sound, and it was Tibby's turn to laugh, but with Althea's encouragement—"Inhale between your teeth, that's right, now exhale . . . ah, you've got it"—he was whistling and sighing along behind them in no time.

When Tibby had mastered the complicated steps,

Althea patted the younger mouse's arm then released it. "You dance very nicely, Miss Tibby Rose," she said approvingly. "But that's enough for an old mouse like me. Besides, we're almost at Cobb, so if Master Alistair would be so good as to give me my stick and his shoulder . . ."

Alistair gave Althea her walking stick and she put her hand on his shoulder as before. She seemed to be leaning on him more heavily now, as if the dancing had worn her out, and the trio slowed their pace.

"Your turning is just up ahead," the old mouse said as Slippers and Feast came up behind them. "It's been many years since William Mackerel and I last spoke, and I'm afraid I can't recall where in the village he lives. But if you should find him, mention I sent you." She shrugged. "He might help you or he might not. There's no telling with William Mackerel. The only thing he really cares for is pigeons. One pigeon, that is—and dead now, I'm sorry to say." Her voice had sunk almost to a whisper. "I'll take my leave of you now. My family worry if I'm away too long."

And she must have traveled quite some distance, Alistair realized, if she lived to the east of the Winns. She would face a long journey home.

"Will you be all right?" he asked. "Have you very far to travel?"

"Don't you worry," she said dreamily. "I'll have the murmur of the Winns below, guiding my feet toward home. And you—you have your scarf to guide you."

12

Cornoliana

Alice swallowed, and felt the tip of the tall guard's spear prick her throat.

"Name?"

"Rita," Alice answered, a bit breathlessly. Had the Queen's Guards seen the balloon? Had they failed in their mission already? She clasped her hands together to hide their trembling.

"What about you?" said a shorter, stouter guard, poking his spear at Alex's belly.

"Do you mind?" Alex replied, swiping away the spear. "Don't go poking me like I'm some common Gerandan."

At first Alice was impressed by Alex's unruffled demeanor, but the guard clearly wasn't; indeed, he seemed to take offense at Alex's insolent tone.

"I asked you a question," snarled the guard, aiming the point of his spear at Alex's heart now.

"R-Raz," quavered Alice, "tell him your name." Oh,

why was her brother antagonizing the guards?

"Well I don't need to tell him now, do I, sis?" said Alex. "You just did." He turned back to the guard and lifted one shoulder in a shrug. "So now you know."

The guard, bristling at having his question repeatedly ignored, stamped his foot. "But you were meant to tell me," he whined.

"Hold on there, Groodley." The third guard, who appeared to be the leader of the trio, stepped forward. "Stand down, Longnose."

The tall guard dropped his spear, and Alice instinctively rubbed her throat.

"So, Raz and Rita, I'm Captain Scorpio," said the third guard. "How about we dispense with the spears, and you dispense with the attitude and show us your papers?"

Papers! Of course! Alice thrust the letter she was holding at Captain Scorpio. "Our papers burned in a fire," she said. "But we've got this."

The captain scanned the letter, nodding as he did so.

"What does it say, Captain?" Groodley had been trying but failing to read over Scorpio's shoulder. "Shall we take them prisoner?" he asked hopefully.

"We most certainly shall not, Groodley," the captain responded, folding the letter and handing it back to Alice. "These young orphans are two of our own. Their dad is a hero—killed by rebel Gerandans while serving in the Crankens. Now they're on their way to Cornoliana to work in the palace."

"You're going to work in the palace?" Longnose

shuddered. "Better you than me."

"Is General Ashwover very fierce?" asked Alice.

"Oh no, the general's harmless enough—it's Lester you've got to watch out for."

"Who's Lester?" said Alex.

"He's the general's eyes and ears and right-hand mouse," Captain Scorpio explained. "The general runs Gerander, but it's Lester who runs the palace. And a more unpleasant mouse I've never come across," he reflected.

"A friend of mine, Jackson Johnson, was a sentry at the palace," said Groodley. "Lester once came into the mess hall and demanded to know why Jackson Johnson had spaghetti in his whiskers. When Jackson Johnson said he didn't, Lester tipped a plate of spaghetti over his head and told Jackson Johnson never to contradict him."

"Poor Jackson Johnson," said Longnose, shaking his head in sympathy, but it seemed to Alice that the smirking Groodley found his friend's misfortune rather entertaining.

"So these two are free to go then, Captain?" asked Groodley. He sounded disappointed.

"I don't think so," Captain Scorpio said, and Alice's breath caught in her throat. Were they prisoners after all?

"The gates of Cornoliana are closed at sunset, and I don't like the idea of you two wandering around in the dark," Scorpio continued, turning to the two young mice. "Our camp isn't far from the city walls. You can stay with us tonight, and we'll take you to the east gate in the morning. How does that sound?"

"That sounds . . . very kind, thank you." The one thing Alice hadn't really expected from Sourians—and Queen's Guards in particular—was to be treated with kindness.

"Are you hungry?" Captain Scorpio asked as he led the way through a line of cypress trees to the road. "Groodley, Longnose, who has some field rations to spare for our young friends here?"

"Not me," said Groodley quickly.

"I do," said Longnose. He shrugged his pack from his back and stooped to retrieve an orange and half a sandwich.

Alice took the orange and Alex the sandwich, and they set off down the road into the dying rays of the sun.

"Are we far from your camp?" Alice asked as the darkness closed in around them.

"A couple of hours' walk. Why, are you scared of the dark, Rita?" The captain's voice was teasing.

"N-no," said Alice, though it was creepy in the twilight, with the bushes by the side of the road looming in unexpected shapes.

"We don't usually have call to venture into these parts ourselves," the captain remarked. "It's mostly just farmland around here—but we were sent to investigate possible FIG activity."

Alice gulped. "FIG?" she said, trying to sound both innocent and curious.

"Were you looking for fruit?" Alex asked through a mouthful of sandwich.

Scorpio laughed but his voice was serious when he said,

"No, not the fruit—the Gerandan rebels." He sighed. "Most Gerandans are grateful for our presence; they understand that their country is too poor and backward to survive without Sourian strength and organization. But there are always a few bad apples, I suppose. Anyway, it seems it was just a false alarm."

Most Gerandans were grateful for the occupation? That couldn't be true—and yet the kind captain sounded as if he really believed it.

As they walked on through the darkness, Alice continued to mull this over, along with the surprising information that the Queen's Guards had been on the lookout for FIG activity. What kind of activity? Was it possible that there was another FIG operation underway in the same region? Yet both Tobias and FIG had mentioned the difficulty of transporting FIG operatives into Gerander secretly, so it was unlikely that there would be other FIG members so close by. But if there wasn't another FIG operation going on, that meant the Sourians had been expecting her and Alex! The captain didn't seem to suspect them, though. . . . Alice sighed. She wondered what her brother had made of it all. It was really very confusing.

Her confusion, she had to admit, was made worse by the fact that she was feeling bone tired. It was hard to believe that only that morning she had woken in Stetson, with no idea that she'd be in Gerander by nightfall.

Her brother, as usual, didn't seem to know the meaning of the word tired. He was chatting happily with

Groodley, whose attitude toward Raz from Tornley had completely changed once Alex started peppering him with questions about Gerandan food.

"Dirt," Groodley was sniffing now. "It all tastes like dirt. The basic ingredients are all right, mind you— it's just that the Gerandans have no talent for cooking whatsoever. If I were you, I'd try to make sure you get all your food from the soldiers' mess when you're at the palace. The army brings their own cooks, you know."

At last Captain Scorpio pointed to a dull orange glow emanating from a hilltop and said, "There's our camp," and they trudged up the short steep slope to where three rows of tents stood.

Flaming torches posted every few meters lit their way as they walked between two rows of large, square white tents, their shadows flickering on the canvas. Mice were lounging around the tent flaps chatting. Some were playing board games and others were polishing their boots. They all saluted Captain Scorpio respectfully as he passed, and he greeted many of the guards with a little joke or comment.

"Watch out for Boggles here," he said, stopping near a group playing tiddlywinks and placing a hand on the shoulder of a plump gray mouse. "He wins so often I'd swear he has springs on his thumbs."

"Is that a letter from home, Shirley?" he asked a slender mouse who was reading a letter with a crease of anxiety furrowing her brow. "I hope your husband's broken tail is healing well."

They went straight to the mess tent for a bowl of tomato soup. "Gerandan tomatoes," Groodley said, "but Sourian soup, you see?" He smacked his lips. "That's what makes it good."

Finally, when Alice feared she was about to drop on her feet, Captain Scorpio said, "There's a couple of spare cots in the sick bay—Longnose, why don't you show them the way?"

And at long last she was in bed. Curling onto her side, she asked her brother, "Alex, remember what Captain Scorpio was saying about how they were investigating possible FIG activity? They were expecting activity right where we landed!"

"It's just a coincidence," Alex said, then yawned loudly. "He obviously didn't suspect us or he would have arrested us. Besides, who could have told them? We didn't even know we'd be landing in that field today until right before we took off, so it's impossible that the Sourians could have known."

"But what about the dirigible?" Alice asked. "Isn't it strange that it just happened to be flying around in the same patch of sky that we were?"

"Another coincidence." Alex's voice was growing fainter. "Stop worrying, sis. Everything will be . . ." There was a long pause.

"Alex?" said Alice impatiently. "Everything will be what?"

But her brother was asleep.

As she stepped out of the tent the next morning, Alice could see why the soldiers had chosen this site to make their camp. Their position on the hilltop gave them a good view of the surrounding countryside. The hill seemed to be marooned in a sea of golden wheat, the feathery tips of the grain gleaming in the sun. Lines of tall, dark green cypress trees separated the fields from the road. Beyond the wheat fields were patches of gray-green interspersed with bursts of yellow and the occasional red dot of a farmhouse roof.

"Cornoliana's on the other side of the plain."

Alice turned, startled, to see Captain Scorpio.

"Once you've had some breakfast, Groodley and Longnose will accompany you to the city gate."

"Thank you, Captain Scorpio," said Alice.

"I've got two kids of my own back in Souris," the captain replied. "Seeing the two of you alone in the world with no one to look out for you . . . It reminds me how lucky I am that my family is safe and well." Once again Alice was struck by the kindness of the Sourian soldier— until he added, "And it makes me all the more determined to ensure that the Gerandans are kept in their place so no more good men like your father have to die in defense of our country."

The way he said that Gerandans should be "kept in their place," it was as if he didn't understand that this was their own country! Was it possible for someone to be good and bad at the same time? Alice wondered.

They had a quick breakfast of fruit and yogurt, then

the four mice set off across the golden plain. It was only a half-hour walk, and Groodley passed the time telling them more horror stories about the dreaded Lester. He told the stories with a certain relish, and it seemed to Alice that he hadn't really forgiven them for being innocent Sourian orphans rather than evil FIG spies.

To stop herself becoming too frightened by his stories, Alice focused instead on her surroundings. As they left the fields of wheat behind, she saw that the patches of gray-green she'd noticed from the guards' camp were olive groves, and the bursts of yellow were sunflowers, their heads tilted toward the sun. As they drew closer to the high castellated stone wall encircling Gerander's capital, they passed through a series of market gardens. On either side of the road were neat squares of earth with rows of lettuce, and beans strung along wire and vines of plump red tomatoes.

Before long they were at the city's east gate.

Longnose saluted the red-coated sentries and said, "Captain Scorpio sends his compliments and asks that you escort these two young mice to the palace gates."

"They're going to see Lester," explained Groodley.

The two sentries saluted, and one replied, "Why would anyone want to see Festering Lester?"

Groodley chortled. "Festering Lester—good one."

"Good luck," said Longnose to Alex and Alice.

"You'll need it!" added Groodley.

They turned and strode away.

"Well, come on then," said the guard who'd referred

to Festering Lester. "Better not keep Lester the Pester waiting." She set off at a brisk pace, calling over her shoulder, "I'll be back soon, Pearce. Try to keep the rampaging hordes from the gates until then." She sighed. "Guarding that gate is the world's most boring job," she said as she led Alex and Alice down a narrow street, "in the world's most boring city."

"It's so old!" Alice exclaimed as they passed rustic stone buildings painted in faded shades of cream and ocher and topped with red-tiled roofs.

"Just goes to show how backward the Gerandans are," sneered the guard on her left. "In Souris, if a building gets old we knock it down and build a new one."

But Alice hadn't meant it as an insult. She was enchanted by the tall, rickety buildings that seemed to lean in toward one another as if for support. Even the cobblestones were worn smooth, as if mice had been walking these streets for centuries. It occurred to her that her ancestors might have walked on these very stones.

They wound through a maze of cramped alleyways. At street level there were tiny shops: outside one, woven baskets were tacked to the wall and lined up along the window ledge; another had a collection of terra-cotta pots in all shapes and sizes arranged on either side of the doorway; a third had leather belts and bags strung in the window. A glimpse into a dark workshop revealed a mouse blowing glass through a long tube. And from the worn pillowcases and ragged towels draped on clotheslines high above the streets, it was obvious that the upper levels of these buildings were living quarters.

They came out into a wider street and Alice started to sense the grandeur of the city. The buildings here were larger and sturdier, with arcades at street level and porticos above the doors. Many had some kind of ornamentation carved in stone above the high arched windows. Then they rounded the corner into an enormous plaza and were confronted with the most beautiful building Alice had ever seen.

"Is this the palace?" she gasped. A pair of bronze doors divided into panels and adorned with various scenes stood almost as high as their old apartment block in Smiggins, with a smaller pair of wooden doors on either side. Above each door was a rose window of stained glass. The building was richly decorated in strips of pink, white, and green marble, which outlined a series of tall arched windows—with more stained glass—and square panels inlaid with intricate terra-cotta patterns. At the very top were a dozen or so niches, in which marble statues were just visible. Set back from the facade Alice could see an enormous red-tiled dome roof.

"The palace? Nah, that's just the cathedral." The guard looked at it critically. "It's all right, I suppose. But the cathedral in Grouch is much bigger." And with a sniff she dismissed the breathtaking building.

They hurried across the large square, past the cathedral, and along another elegant avenue. With all this beauty Cornoliana should have been a happy, vibrant place, but the mood on the streets was somber. Mice went about their business with their heads bowed and shrank from them as they passed. Alice saw a child cry out on seeing them, only to be swiftly hushed by his parents, as if they were afraid to draw attention to themselves. She couldn't help but notice how thin they were, these sad-looking mice. There was no way any of them could be said to look grateful. The only mice who appeared at ease, lingering in the cafés and gazing in shop windows, wore red coats. They seemed strangely unaware of the Gerandans, who moved through the streets of their own capital city like shadows.

At the end of the avenue they crossed a bridge over a shallow, fast-flowing river into another enormous square. An imposing building stretched along the full length of its far side.

"Right," said the guard. "Cross the square and you're at the palace gates. Give my love to Fester." She sniggered unkindly then turned on her heel and marched away, the heels of her boots clattering loudly on the cobblestones.

"Ready?" said Alex, when the guard had gone. He sounded unusually nervous.

Alice swallowed. This was where their undercover operation really began. She tightened her grip on the letter in her hand. "Ready." And she began to walk across the square.

13

Billy Mac

The tunnel ended in a hole they had to crawl through. It was raining when Alistair clambered out onto a long, deserted beach resounding to the roar and thud of crashing waves. He blinked in the light, which hurt his eyes, despite the dull gray of early evening. The sand was sodden and clung to his feet. It must have been raining for some time. Another crack in a mountain's fold, Alistair thought, as he turned to look back at the sheer cliff rearing above them.

"Cobb should be over the headland to the south," Slippers said. "And there's bound to be a lot of Queen's Guards so close to Atticus Island, so let's take it nice and easy."

A path led over the headland and they followed it in a stop-start fashion, Feast going on ahead to survey the terrain, beckoning them forward when he had ascertained the coast was clear. Although they didn't have far to travel, it seemed to take a long time and involved much standing in puddles and hiding in wet bushes.

The houses of Cobb were huddled together beneath a big brooding sky, their backs to the gorse-studded hills encasing the town. Some of the buildings were whitewashed, others a faded brown stone the color of butterscotch. They all had steep red-tiled roofs, narrow chimneys sitting atop them like exclamation points, and small many-paned windows. In most houses a light was shining against the gloom, and they could see straight into parlors and kitchens.

They walked up and down the main street, which was wider than the rest and ended abruptly at a neat walled harbor. On the harbor's edge was a tavern, and from here came the only noise in the silent town. The flurry of red shapes within suggested that this was why they hadn't yet encountered a Sourian patrol: all the Queen's Guards were in the tavern. Alistair couldn't blame them for wanting to get out of the driving rain.

They hastily retraced their steps up the main street, noting the number of small alleyways leading off it.

"I don't know how we're going to find William Mackerel," Slippers fretted. "We can't exactly go knocking on every door in town asking for him—the Queen's Guards would hear about it in no time." She glanced back down the street toward the tavern. "Did Althea say anything about her cousin that might help us to identify him?"

"She said he was crazy about pigeons," Alistair offered.

"Unless there's a flock of pigeons circling his house I can't see how that's going to help," said Slippers Pink. "But it's something I suppose."

And so they slipped up and down the narrow streets, keeping their heads beneath the level of the windowsills and their bodies pressed against the damp stone walls.

It was Tibby Rose who spotted the door knocker in the shape of a pigeon, and soon they were all peering through the window at a lone mouse mending a net by the fire.

"What do you think, Feast?" Slippers asked.

"One way to find out," said Feast. "Let's chance it."

Slippers lifted the pigeon-shaped knocker and rapped three times on the door.

Alistair watched through the window as the mouse by the fire looked up in surprise, appeared to hesitate, then put down his needle and twine.

The door was opened by a mouse as tall as Feast Thompson, though thinner and considerably older. He had wiry copper fur and a dour expression.

"What d'ye want?" he asked gruffly.

"We're looking for William Mackerel," Slippers Pink said.

"Why d'ye want him for?" said the copper mouse.

"Are you William Mackerel?" Slippers countered.

"Mebbe I be, mebbe not. Depends who're doing the askin'."

Slippers hesitated, and Alistair could tell she was reluctant to give the fisherman their names.

The coppery mouse snorted and began to shut the door.

"Your cousin from the east sent us," Slippers said quickly.

"My cousin?" the fisherman repeated, and though his expression was as dour as ever, the door stayed open. "Which cousin?"

"Althea."

"Cousin Althea sent you, did she?" He sighed. "Aye, I be William Mackerel, though folk calls us Billy Mac. Ye'd better come in." Billy Mac glanced up and down the street, then ushered them inside.

Alistair, his fur soaked through to the bone and his sodden scarf weighing heavily around his neck, looked longingly at the blazing fire, but Billy Mac didn't invite them to sit by the hearth.

"Ye'll have to stand here by the door," he told them. "If anyone sees you through the window theys be asking questions. If I draws the curtain theys be asking questions too. There be a lot o' curious folk in Cobb."

Over the fire a pot was bubbling merrily and the air was rich with the aroma of fish soup. Feast Thompson sniffed the air appreciatively, but Billy Mac didn't offer them a bowl.

"Delicious-smelling fish soup," Feast ventured.

"Fish soup?" growled Billy Mac. "Dunno what yer talking about."

"The soup in that pot." Feast pointed.

"In that pot? No fish in that pot. I gives all me catch to the Queen's Guards. That must be mushrooms you can smell. No law against gathering mushrooms as far as I know." He glared at Feast Thompson fiercely, as if daring the other mouse to contradict him. "Now what be your business with Billy Mac?"

"We don't wish to intrude," Slippers began.

Billy Mac grunted as if to suggest they already had.

"We're looking for a way to get to Atticus Island."

"Atticus Island?" Billy Mac laughed scornfully. "Ye come here and disturb me supper—of perfectly legal mushroom soup—to ask me how to get to Atticus Island? I can tell ye this: the surest way to Atticus Island is to be asking questions like how to get to Atticus Island. I should think ye'd best be off before we all end up there." He raised his hands in a shooing motion.

"Please, Billy Mac," Alistair said. "My parents are prisoners there and—"

Billy Mac shut his eyes and shook his head. "Why me?" he grumbled to himself. "Just a poor fisherman trying to mend me net."

Tibby Rose, Alistair noticed, was paying little attention to the conversation, but was studying the little parlor with bright, inquisitive eyes. It looked as much like a workshop as a parlor. The net Billy Mac had been mending was slung over a towel rack by the fire, and a thick needle was stuck into a ball of twine that rested on a stool alongside. Pots of paint were stacked unsteadily in one corner, and coils of rope were scattered among mooring buoys and crab pots. Amid all this clutter were a big comfy armchair and a dainty occasional table on which stood a collection of pigeons: ceramic pigeons and a porcelain plate with a pigeon painted on it, even salt and pepper shakers in the shapes of pigeons.

"You collect pigeons?" Alistair asked when he noticed the copper mouse glaring in his direction.

"And what be wrong with that? I had a pigeon for a friend once, and a better friend I never had. If I want a few keepsakes to remember him by what business be it of yours?"

"None at all," said Slippers Pink. "One of my best friends is an owl." A look of anxiety flashed across her face, which she quickly masked, and Alistair knew she was remembering Oswald and the eagles. But Billy Mac was looking at her with a more kindly expression.

"An owl innit half the bird a pigeon is, but mebbe yours is an exception," he allowed. "What's its name, yer friend?"

"Oswald," said Slippers.

"Me pigeon friend was Bert. A beautiful speckled feller, he was. Until. . ." Billy Mac's coppery face creased and his voice broke. "Until them Sourians got their hands on him." He turned to gaze out the window at the dark street. "They thought he was carrying messages, you see. But Bert—he was never inter politics. I'm not saying he didn't hate the Sourians, mind." The expression on Billy Mac's face was dark. "But Bert just wanted to live a quiet life. We had that in common."

Billy Mac shifted his gaze back to his unexpected visitors. "But now Althea has sent yer to me, and I suppose I have to help yer. She was very good to me when Bert died, was Cousin Althea."

"You could start by telling us what you know of Atticus Island," Slippers suggested.

"Dunno if you can call it an island really," said Billy Mac, rubbing at the coppery fur on his chin. "At high tide most of it disappears. As for the prison, she's nobbut one tower on a cliff."

"Could we sail across there and land in secret, do you think?"

Billy Mac's mouth turned down at the corners in reply. "Only one safe place to land a boat, and that's on the far side of the island. But with the Sourians coming and going . . ." He let the sentence trail off, then added, "And there be lots o' comings an' goings o' late."

"But surely you locals know of some way to get to the island that the Sourians don't know about," Slippers said persuasively.

"I may've heard tell of a way," Billy Mac said cautiously. "Folks say there's an underwater tunnel. Least there's a song they sings hereabouts." He cleared his throat then began to sing self-consciously in a rough, quavery voice:

> *"It's one way in and no way out,*
> *When the tide turns roundabout.*
> *Enter where the third rock cleaves,*
> *But once you're in you'll never leaves."*

"*Never leaves?*" echoed Slippers, clearly horrified. "This underwater tunnel, it is safe, isn't it?"

"Dunno. Never swum it, have I?"

"Why not?"

Billy Mac looked at Slippers as if she was daft. "Why not? More like why would I. There's nowt I want on Atticus Island. But it could be that bit's just to scare the little 'uns. Other Bill who lives up the street reckons how he swum it as a boy. Reckons the never leaves bit is just to say that you can't leave by the same tunnel ye swims in by."

"So how do you leave?" asked Feast Thompson.

Billy gave a grim smile. "There be no song 'bout that."

"But Other Bill got off the island, didn't he?"

"Aye," Billy Mac conceded. "But could be the place weren't overrun by Queen's Guards in those days. He's older'n the cliffs themselves is Other Bill."

"We can worry about getting off the island after we've got on," Slippers decided. "But it's very important we get there. Do you know this place, where the third rock cleaves?"

"Reckon I know it well enough."

"Would you take us there?"

"If you be wanting to swim the tunnel, it'll be three days afore the tide runs right for it."

"We have to wait three days?" Alistair protested.

"Three days," the fisherman repeated. "And if ye think you're gunna stand here in me entrance hall for three days, ye've got rocks in yer head. Ye'll have to find someplace else."

"Do you know somewhere we can stay?"

Billy Mac barked a laugh. "I s'pose there be no point directin' you to the inn since they're hardly likely to give a room to four mice with no names, eh?"

Slippers smiled briefly but said nothing.

"There be a cave," Billy Mac said at last. "You could bide there a time, I reckon."

Slippers's smile grew warmer. "Thank you, Billy Mac," she said. "Now if you could just tell us where the cave is we'll leave you in peace."

Billy Mac sighed. "There'll be no peace for Billy Mac if you go blundering through town telling everyone ye know me, will there?"

"We're not going to—"

Billy Mac raised a hand against Slippers Pink's protestation.

"I'll just have to show ye meself." He stumped around the small parlor-cum-workroom, pulling on galoshes and rummaging through a pile of canvas until he found a fisherman's cap.

"Excuse me, Billy Mac," said Tibby Rose. "Would you be able to spare some nylon twine?" She pointed to the reel sitting on the stool.

"Spare some twine?" Billy Mac hooted in disbelief. "A poor fisherman like me can scarcely spare the time o' day and you want me to spare some twine?" Then, at Tibby's chastened expression, he muttered, "I might have another ball o' the stuff around here." He fished around in a crab pot full of odds and ends, finally dislodging the twine Tibby had asked for. Tibby crammed it into her rucksack.

"Now let's get ye shifted to that cave. Me mushroom soup won't wait forever."

"Does it ever stop raining?" Slippers wanted to know as he opened the front door a crack and peered out.

Billy Mac looked at the sky in surprise. "Rain? This innit rain. This be a fine summer's eve. Just a wee bit overcast is all."

And gesturing to them to follow, he stepped out onto the rain-slick street.

14

The Palace

lice had thought the cathedral was big, but the palace dwarfed it. She counted ten sets of double doors across the front, with a second story that had at least twenty pairs of long windows. A third story was set across the middle portion of the building like a crown. It wasn't as richly decorated as the cathedral—it was imposing rather than ornate—but when the sun came out from behind a cloud the drab stone gradually began to glow gold, the many windows glittering like stars, and the severe facade softened.

Two Queen's Guards stood sentry on either side of a pair of elaborate wrought-iron gates tipped with gold.

"Here goes." Alex took the letter of introduction from Alice's hand and stepped forward, holding out the piece of paper, and addressed the sentries confidently. "Hello. My name is Raz and this is my sister, Rita, and we've come from Souris to work in the palace."

The shorter of the sentries took the letter, scanned it quickly, then handed it to her taller companion. "They'll be needing to see Lester."

The taller sentry made a face, then said, "Are you sure it's my turn?"

"Yep," said the first emphatically. "You'd better get that spot off your coat." She pointed to a speck on the tall sentry's red coat, which he hastily brushed away.

"All right," he said with a sigh. "Let's get on with it."

He turned and marched ahead of Alice and Alex across an expanse of gravel to the palace steps, passing between statues of an imperious-looking mouse in royal robes. Alice noted that while the bases of the statues looked stained and weathered, the statues themselves were gleaming white, as if new statues had been put on old pedestals.

"Who's Lester?" Alex asked the sentry's red-coated back innocently.

"He's General Ashwover's right-hand mouse," the sentry explained. "He looks after the running of the palace. And disciplining the troops." He nervously brushed the spot on his coat where the speck had been.

They stepped into a cavernous entrance hall. Purple and silver banners were draped from fluted marble columns, the silver sparkling in the light of dozens of enormous crystal chandeliers. The floor was a dazzling mosaic of tiny tiles in jewel-like colors, and the walls were painted with giant frescoes showing mice draped in togas plucking grapes from vines and dancing in flower-strewn gardens.

Immediately before them a wide marble staircase swept up, branching away to the left and right, but rather than climb the staircase they turned left down a corridor near the foot of the steps. After the grandeur of the entrance hall, this corridor seemed rather shabby and narrow, Alice thought as they walked past a dozen nondescript doors— all shut—before turning right, then right again. Then they climbed a set of stairs, and weaved through several more corridors.

"It's like a maze," Alex observed. "How do you keep from getting lost?"

"You need to have a good sense of direction around here," said the sentry, tapping his temple with his forefinger. "Plus, I've got one of them photographic memories."

They descended some stairs, and came to a halt in front of an inconspicuous wooden door. The sentry tapped on it then, at the occupant's command, opened the door.

A tiny mouse with neatly combed gray fur and enormous pearl earrings looked up from her desk with an impatient expression.

"Who are you?" asked the sentry in obvious astonishment.

"I am the Undersecretary Assisting the Head of Floral Arrangements in the Department for Banquets," she replied loftily. "Who are you?"

"Er, nobody," said the sentry. "Wrong office." He backed out of the room and closed the door behind him.

He stood scratching his head for a moment, muttering,

"Left then right then right then stairs then—hang on, did I go up when I should have gone down? That must be it."

He set off again, striding along corridors and around corners, up a grand stone staircase and down a shabby wooden one, finally arriving at a door that looked rather like the last one. The sentry knocked, waited, then pushed Alice and Alex ahead of him into the room. "Sir," he began, then stopped. A dozen mice were sitting around a long table, watching a coffee-colored mouse with an enormous nose who was scrawling something on a whiteboard.

The coffee-colored mouse turned at the interruption and glared down his enormous nose. "This meeting is classified top-secret," he barked. "Who are you? Do you have security clearance?"

The sentry seemed to wilt under his gaze. "I'm . . . I'm . . . sorry," he gasped, then fled the room and took off down the corridor so fast Alice and Alex had to run to keep up.

They cantered up two flights of stairs and zigzagged wildly along corridors—some of them, Alice was sure, they had already been down more than once.

The sentry was breathing raggedly and Alice and Alex were panting when a sharp voice rang out behind them.

"Wooster! Why have you abandoned your post?"

All three mice turned to see a mouse in a white jacket and black boots. His smooth black fur had a sheen like an oil slick.

"Lester!" the sentry cried, almost weeping with relief. "I mean, good morning, sir." He bent his head deferentially.

"Well?" demanded Lester. "What are you doing here?"

"I was coming to see you, sir. These two just showed up at the gate with a letter saying they are to work here."

"Showed up at the gate, eh?" Lester turned his beady black eyes on Alice and Alex. "Where is this letter?"

The sentry handed it over. Alice watched with her heart pounding as Lester read the letter once, then a second time. Why wasn't he saying anything? Could he tell it was a fake?

"Very well," he said finally. "Wooster, you may—" He stopped. "Wooster," he said slowly, "did you polish your boots this morning?"

"Y-yes, sir," stammered the sentry.

"Then why, I wonder, does your left boot have a heel print on it?"

Wooster gazed down at his boot. "But, sir," he said, "there's no—"

Lester lifted one big black boot then brought it down hard on the sentry's left toe.

Wooster's eyes went very wide and he opened his mouth as if to scream, but no sound came out.

"I'm . . . sorry. . . sir," he gasped at last. "It . . . won't . . . happen . . . again."

"See that it doesn't," Lester snapped. "Dismissed."

Wooster gave a brisk nod, then staggered off down the corridor.

Lester opened the nearest door and ushered the two young mice inside.

"So," he said, as he sat behind his desk, gesturing to

Alice and Alex to sit in the two low wooden chairs facing him. "Raz and Rita from Tornley."

Alice had to crane her neck to see him over the top of the desk. "Yes, sir."

Lester looked down at the letter he was still holding. "Father a Sourian soldier killed in the Crankens, I see."

Alice and Alex nodded.

"Mom—Mom said he was a hero," Alice added. "That he died fighting . . . filthy Gerandans." She had faltered on the last words, and hoped that it sounded like she was grief-stricken rather than reluctant.

"Good man," said Lester approvingly. "And your mother . . . ?"

"Died of an illness, sir," Alice whispered.

"Indeed. Well, unlike the filthy Gerandans your father fought, we Sourians look after our own. You will be given important jobs here in the palace. You will be well fed and have comfortable beds to sleep in, just as your father would have wished."

"Thank you, sir." Alex sounded both brave and grateful, Alice noted, as befitted an orphan boy who had been given a golden opportunity.

Lester rose and moved soundlessly to the door despite his big black boots. "Come," he said, beckoning. "I'll take you to the office of Fiercely Jones."

The route from Lester's office to the office of Fiercely Jones seemed remarkably direct. One right turn, one flight of stairs, through a door leading onto a terrace, across a springy green lawn to what looked like a good-sized potting shed concealed from the terrace by a screen of flowering bushes.

"Jones," called Lester impatiently. "Where are you?"

There was a sound of someone moving about inside the shed, then a gruff voice said, "What is it?" The door opened to reveal a gardener, his long tawny nose just visible beneath the brim of a battered brown hat. "Oh, it's you," he said. "Sir." He touched a hand to his hat.

"Jones," said Lester, "meet Raz and Rita. They're orphans of a Sourian hero and they've come all the way from Souris to help with your special project. They're to be treated as palace staff. Settle them in, and put them to work. Raz, Rita, this is the palace's head gardener, Fiercely Jones."

Lester turned on his heel and strode away, leaving Alice and Alex alone with Fiercely Jones.

The gardener regarded them dourly for several seconds, then sniffed. "About time they saw fit to give me helpers," he said. "I've been told the gardens need to be completely replanted with only purple flowers. That means hyacinths, lilacs . . . I wonder if it's too late to plant wisteria? Violets, lavender . . . I think cornflowers can pass for bluish purple, don't you? Asters, clematis, crocuses, hydrangeas . . ."

"Is he really going to list every purple flower under the sun?" Alex muttered under his breath as the gardener went on.

"Petunias, verbenas, pansies, peonies . . ."

"Why would anyone want a garden that only had purple

flowers?" Alice wondered aloud.

"Geraniums and zinnias. Got that?"

"Yes, sir," Alex responded quickly. "Purple zinnias. Lovely, sir."

"Good," said Fiercely Jones, though he gave Alex a shrewd look. "Follow me."

The gardener stumped off across the lawn, through an immaculately maintained formal garden, across a small park dotted with topiary, skirting a hedge maze and under a pergola groaning beneath a climbing rose and into a rose garden ablaze with flowers of scarlet and yellow and flaming orange, punctuated with the gentle glow of soft pink and peach and apricot.

"You can start by digging up that bed there," Fiercely Jones ordered. "I want all those beautiful, rare roses, which were planted by my grandfather and which I've tended since I was a lad, gone by dinner time."

"What about lunch?" Alex protested. "I can't work on an empty stomach."

Fiercely Jones looked at Alex expressionlessly. "Gerandans do," he said, then stumped away toward his potting shed.

"I don't see what's so important about this job," Alex complained as they began to dig.

"Me neither," said Alice. "Ouch!" A drop of blood appeared where a thorn had pricked her finger. "But maybe there's something important about purple flowers."

"Well, if there is, we're hardly likely to learn about

it out here," said Alex. "How are we meant to discover palace secrets from out in the garden?"

"That is a problem," Alice admitted. "We'll just have to be on the lookout for opportunities."

They worked for several hours in the garden bed, learning nothing more than the many ways in which thorns could prick, scratch, stab, and puncture, before Fiercely Jones returned and escorted them to a courtyard at the rear of the palace, directed them to wash their hands under a pump, and showed them into the kitchen through the back door.

Inside, the gardener removed his hat and gestured to the mouse standing by the stove. "This is Cook. She prepares the food for the palace staff and servants, and she'll be giving you your meals."

Cook was a stout mouse with long fur the color of milky tea, partially covered by a voluminous white apron.

"Who are these two then?" She was looking at Alice and Alex, but her question was directed at Fiercely Jones.

"Raz and Rita," he said. "They're the kids of one of the Queen's Guards. Were the kids, I should say. Orphans now."

Cook, far from looking sympathetic, glared at Alice and Alex resentfully. "So now I'm expected to feed Sourian brats out of our meager share? Why can't they eat in the mess with the guards?"

Fiercely Jones looked around nervously. "Now, now, Cook. Mind your tongue, eh? Lester said they're palace staff, same as us."

"Hmph," Cook responded, turning her glare on Fiercely Jones, but she didn't say anything more.

Fiercely turned to Alice and Alex. "Right, I'll see you two in the morning. At the garden shed by five."

"Five in the morning?" Alex squawked.

"That's what I said." Fiercely Jones gave Alex an even stare, then pulled on his battered hat and left by the back door.

"We start work at five in the morning?" Alex repeated, with a wounded expression.

"I suppose you young Sourians aren't used to hard work." Cook set two bowls down at one end of the kitchen table and put two ladlefuls of soup into each. "I'd advise you to get used to it. We've no room for slackers around here."

Alice picked up her spoon and dipped it into the bowl and Alex, looking subdued, did the same—only to drop the spoon immediately. "This—this isn't soup," he said in disgust. "This is nothing but hot water."

"That's what servants eat around here," Cook returned smartly. "And many in Gerander would think us lucky. Of course, if you were a Queen's Guard like your dad you'd get three hearty meals a day—delicious apple pies and spicy carrot soup and fish fried in butter and cheesecake with raspberries. . . ."

Alice found it hard to continue sipping at the watery soup while this recitation was going on.

"But that's not for the likes of us. Gerandans, and Sourian servants, get this soup. And if you don't like it, all the better," hissed Cook, bringing her face down close to Alice and Alex. "My grandchildren will be dining on your leftovers."

Alice dropped her spoon with a gasp.

"What is it, girlie?" asked Cook. "Surprised?"

Alice was about to express her outrage at the miserable treatment of Gerandans by the Sourian occupiers when she remembered the role she had to play. "I certainly am surprised," she said. "Everyone in Souris warned us about how awful Gerandan cooking is, but I never believed it could be as bad as this." She turned up her nose and pushed her bowl away. "I'd rather starve."

"That can be arranged," Cook muttered darkly under her breath.

"Yeah," said Alex, catching on. "We might be servants here, but we're not just any old servants; we're the children of a Sourian hero of the Queen's Guards. I'm sure our father's old colleagues wouldn't be pleased to hear how we're being treated by the Gerandan servants."

Alice winced inwardly to hear how his voice dripped with contempt when he said the word "Gerandan," but she had to admit his performance was brilliant. She thought she saw a flash of fear in Cook's eyes as she turned back to the soup pot.

"All right, all right, there's no need to be telling tales, boyo. I think I've found a bit of fish at the bottom of this pot after all."

She tipped the watery soup from their bowls back into the pot simmering on the stove, gave it a stir, then refilled the bowls. This time, their portions were thick with chunks of potato and pieces of fish. It still wasn't quite enough to assuage Alice's hunger, but she suspected it was as good as a servant—even a Sourian one—was likely to get.

She tucked into her soup as Cook went back to her pots and pans, clattering them with unnecessary force it seemed to Alice. For a while the only sounds in the kitchen were clattering and slurping, so that Alice was startled to hear a smooth voice close behind her say, "Settling in all right, then?"

It was Lester.

Cook paused in her work, her back stiffening.

"Yes, sir, thank you, sir," Alice murmured, and Cook's shoulders relaxed.

"Cook, the Deputy Head of Banqueting will be calling on you in the morning. We will be holding some very large banquets in the near future, and that will mean some changes to staffing levels."

"Changes to staffing levels? I should think so. I've only got one kitchen hand," Cook complained, "which won't do at all if you're talking large banquets. It's hard enough to—"

Lester held up a hand to silence her. "More kitchen hands will be arriving from Souris shortly, along with a highly accomplished Sourian chef."

Cook seemed to whiten under her milky fur. "A Sourian chef? There's no need for that," she objected.

"I'll be the judge of what's needed in the palace." Lester's voice was hard.

Cook swallowed. "Of course, sir."

Lester slipped out the door as silently as he had arrived, only to ooze back in almost immediately.

"Your father, Jaz . . . was he a tall mouse with small ears?"

Alice realized with a start that he was addressing her and Alex.

"Our father's name was Jez," she corrected. Was Lester's mistake deliberate? she wondered. Was the question about his ears a trap? She tried desperately to recall what Jez of Tornley had looked like but found she couldn't. Her mouth felt suddenly dry. There had been a photo in the file, she remembered. Why hadn't she paid more attention?

"Big ears," said Alex calmly. "Our father had big ears."

"Is that so?" said Lester. "I must have been thinking of someone else."

Alex continued eating steadily as Lester slipped out the door. The clink of her spoon against the bowl alerted Alice to the fact that her hand was trembling. Fortunately, Cook didn't appear to notice. She was bent over the stove, her shoulders shaking.

"A Sourian chef?" she was saying to herself. "They can't mean to—to let me go. Cooks have always run the palace kitchen, even after the Sourians took over. My mother cooked for King Martain; it near broke her heart when the old king was forced out. And I always thought that a Cook would run the kitchen for Zanzibar one day." She suddenly clapped a hand over her mouth as if aware of what she was saying. As she turned to see if she had been overheard, Alice dropped her head to stare into her soup bowl.

Alex, still slurping, gave no sign of having heard Cook's treacherous words.

"Cook, where does that door go?" he asked when he noticed Cook's gaze directed their way. He was pointing not toward the door that Lester had used, but to one on the other side of the hearth.

Cook turned to look where he was pointing.

"Oh that." She sniffed dismissively. "Servants' staircase. In the old days, when King Martain lived in the palace, servants moved around via their own passageways so as not to disturb the royal family and their guests. Out of bounds now. The Sourians want us out in the open where they can see us."

"Isn't it better this way?" Alice asked. "Wouldn't you rather use the same stairs and passageways as everyone else?"

Cook lifted one broad shoulder. "Perhaps," she said. "But these days I find that I don't care about disturbing the guests; it's the 'guests' who disturb me." She gave them a meaningful look, then said, "Right, I'll show you where you're to sleep, then I'm off home to my family. The little ones will be waiting for their supper."

She ushered them out the back door into the cobbled courtyard and pointed to a wooden staircase climbing the outer wall of the palace. "You'll find a room up there."

Alice, who was looking forward to sinking into a comfortable bed, led the way up the stairs. One flight.

Two. Three. The staircase grew more and more narrow, the steps more rickety. By the time she glimpsed a doorway at the top of the sixth flight of stairs, Alice's hopes of a comfortable bed had faded.

When she pushed open the creaking door a couple of minutes later, her heart sank.

"It's a good thing the attic is warm," she remarked as they stood in the dingy room under the eaves regarding two pallets of straw. "I'd hate to rely on this." She held up a blanket so worn that it was transparent in parts.

"Warm is an understatement," said Alex. "It's stifling in here. I wonder if this window opens." It was impossible to see through the grimy panes, but with a few tugs Alex managed to get it open, and they both breathed welcome drafts of fresh air.

The view was mostly of palace rooftops, but they could see the lights of the city across the river. Somewhere out there, Alice thought, were mice just like them. And with this comforting thought, she lowered herself onto one of the pallets and fell into an uneasy sleep, aware every time she rolled over of the straw digging into her side.

Sometime in the night she woke abruptly to a growling sound. After a few anxious moments, she identified the sound as her stomach. She turned to see if her brother was awake—but his blanket was tossed back and the pallet was empty.

"Alex?" she whispered into the dark room. "Alex, are you there?"

There was no reply.

Rising, she went to the open window, thinking he might have climbed out onto the roof to escape the heat, but there was no stirring in the shadows. Where could he have gone? For a moment she considered going to look for him, but the thought of wandering alone through the dark, perhaps happening across the oily Lester. . . . She shivered and sank back onto her pallet. She couldn't.

She lay wide awake in the dark, fretting over the whereabouts of her brother, for what seemed like hours. When at last Alice heard the door squeal on its hinges and then the rustle of straw of the pallet next to her, she reached over and punched at the sound.

"Ow!" said Alex. "That was my arm."

"Where were you?" Alice demanded.

"Exploring," said Alex. He turned to face her, his eyes shining in the dark. "This place is enormous, sis."

"I know that," said Alice huffily, still cross. "I read about it in the files. Two hundred and forty-three rooms, seventy-three chimneys, one hundred and eighteen bathtubs, thirty-nine staircases, blah blah blah."

"And that's just the stuff they want you to see," said Alex.

"What do you mean?"

"I mean that those are only the rooms that the royal family lived in. Then there's all the places the royal family never set foot in. Sis, there are dungeons here, and heaps of other attic rooms, and you can even climb out onto the roof and walk all over it. There's all these underground cellars and miles of hidden staircases and passages for the servants."

"Alex," Alice groaned, "I can't believe you went in there. You heard what Cook said. Imagine if you'd been caught."

Alex seemed unconcerned. "But I wasn't. Anyway, stop your griping; I brought you a present."

Something hit Alice's shoulder and bounced onto the thin blanket. It was a piece of cheese.

"Where did you get this?"

"I was hungry, so I paid a visit to the kitchen."

Never had a piece of cheese tasted so delicious, Alice thought as she lay on the hard straw pallet nibbling the piece of cheddar. "Still," she said, "you shouldn't steal food. If anyone catches you we could be sent away before we've had a chance to find anything out."

"I don't know what we're going to find out from the gardener besides the names of every purple flower under the sun," Alex said. "Anyway," he grumbled, "if I don't steal food we'll starve on what that horrible Cook feeds us."

"True," Alice said, thinking of the watery soup Cook had first dished up. "Though once we reminded her we were Sourian, the food improved a—oh no!" She sat up.

"What?" said Alex. "Here, I found some strawberries too."

"Cook's not the horrible one—we are!" She absent-mindedly took a strawberry from her brother's outstretched palm.

"Huh?"

"Remember what Cook said? Her grandchildren dine on our leftovers."

"So?"

"So the more we eat, the less food there is for her grandchildren to eat. That's why she gave us watery soup at first: she was trying to save some fish and potatoes for her family. Alex, from now on you have to steal all our food in the middle of the night."

"Um, okay." Alex seemed surprised by his sister's sudden change of heart.

"Cook's grandchildren will starve unless we leave a lot of leftovers."

"Oh. I get it." Alex sounded somber.

"Just steal little bits of lots of things so it's not too obvious," Alice advised as she lay down to sleep once more.

"Alice?" said her brother into the dark.

"Mmm?" Alice murmured sleepily.

"I don't think I'm going to enjoy being Sourian."

Alice closed her eyes. "Me either," she said.

15

Atticus Island

For the next three days, Alistair, Tibby Rose, Slippers Pink, and Feast Thompson waited for Billy Mac's return. Their situation was far from comfortable. The cave, in a small cove to the south of Cobb, was dark and damp and barely large enough for the four of them to squeeze into. When it wasn't raining—which was rare— Alistair sat on the rocks near the cave and stared across the choppy gray water at Atticus Island. Though, as Billy Mac had said, it was hardly an island; it looked like nothing more than a chain of dark, jagged rocks. He thought of the years his parents had spent in this desolate place, years in which they must have long ago ceased to hope for a reprieve, and he longed to embark on the rescue immediately. The waves that crashed relentlessly on the shore only increased his restlessness.

The others seemed to adjust better to the period of waiting. Feast worked out a timetable of shifts, so that they each took a turn keeping watch for movement on the path at the far end of the beach. When they weren't on watch, Feast and Slippers slept or studied the sketched map of Atticus Island that Tobias had given Slippers, or played cards with a tattered deck they kept in the front pocket of their rucksack. Tibby Rose, who was used to amusing herself after her solitary upbringing, used the nylon twine from Billy Mac to fashion a net, knotting strands of the twine at regular intervals lengthways and crossways, then tying rocks to one end for what she called the lead line, which sank. She spent hours of each day wading through the shallows, dragging the net. By evening she had usually caught enough tiny fish to add flavor and substance to the soup they made by boiling water they fetched from a freshwater spring at the base of the cliff, seasoning it with wild herbs.

Finally, just before dawn on the fourth day, Slippers, who was on watch, hurried into the cave.

"There's a boat coming," she said.

"Is it Billy Mac?" Alistair asked, hope rising in his chest.

Slippers shrugged. "Can't tell. Let's stay out of sight till we know for sure."

They huddled in the cave as a pale blue boat, bobbing in the swell, neared their hiding place. It wasn't till it drew alongside the rocks that they were able to recognize the coppery figure of Billy Mac on the deck.

"Right," he said, as they gathered on the rocks, "which of you is doing this daft thing?"

Slippers and Feast exchanged a look. "It had better be

me," she said. "You've got to watch your ankle, Feast."

Feast nodded.

"And me," said Alistair, adding, "Tibby can't swim."

Slippers shook her head. "I don't think so, Alistair," she said. "It's too risky."

"If anyone should be taking the risk it's me," Alistair argued. "They're my parents."

Slippers looked pained, as if she wanted to forbid him, but Alistair just stared at her resolutely.

Finally she lifted her shoulders in surrender. "Short of tying you up, I don't think I can stop you," she said. "But, Alistair, I am in charge of this rescue, okay? I give the orders." She looked at him steadily until Alistair nodded his agreement.

Slippers sat on a rock and pulled off her long black boots. If Billy Mac was surprised to see that the almond mouse had gingery pink feet he didn't let on; he just extended a coppery arm to help her onto the boat. Alistair clambered after her.

He stood for a moment, accustoming himself to the roll of the deck, then turned to look at Tibby Rose, who was watching him calmly, though the twitching of her tail betrayed her nervousness. "Good luck," she said.

"Thanks," said Alistair. And then the boat was moving away, and he turned to face the forbidding silhouette of Atticus Island.

The journey was a quick one—the outgoing tide was running in their favor—and soon the chain of rocks Alistair had been staring at for days loomed ominously above them. But there was no sign of the infamous prison, no tower was suddenly revealed as they approached the dark, jagged teeth protruding above the waves.

As they neared the third rock from the left, Billy Mac slowed the boat and pointed.

"It be down there," he said. "About a meter under."

Alistair looked, but he couldn't see anything beneath the churning water.

"In that case," said Slippers Pink, "I guess this is our stop. Thank you, Billy Mac. Coming, Alistair?" And she leaped nimbly onto the railing of the deck, balanced precariously for a few seconds, then dived cleanly into the sea.

Alistair's own entry into the water was more of a belly flop, and he flailed in the heavy swell for a moment, gasping and winded, before settling into a rhythm and treading water.

Slippers resurfaced, her almond fur sleek and wet against her head, and said, "There does seem to be a tunnel. Take a look."

Ducking his head under the water, Alistair kicked down until he saw a fissure in the rock. It was smaller than he'd expected, about as wide and high as his outstretched arms.

As he kicked toward the surface, he was starting to comprehend just how dangerous their swim was going to be. Once they entered that tunnel, there'd be no turning back. And how did they know it really was a tunnel and not just a dead end? Just from a stupid song and a story of Other Bill's? Was he really going to risk his life, and Slippers

Pink's, on such flimsy evidence? Then he thought of his parents, of four long years in a prison cell. He looked at Slippers Pink, at the trepidation on her face. Was she having second thoughts? But Slippers just said, "Billy Mac's moved off pretty smartly." Turning, Alistair saw the little fishing boat had already departed, leaving them stranded by the rock, a long way from shore. "So either way we've got a swim ahead of us," Slippers continued. "Shall we give this tunnel a try?"

Alistair was by now so apprehensive he couldn't even speak, just nodded once.

"Take a deep breath," Slippers advised, "and hold it for as long as you can before letting it out very slowly. Try to make that breath last. And stay close." She looked both determined and resigned as she inhaled slowly and deeply, then slid beneath the surface.

Alistair breathed in, feeling his lungs expand, then dived down.

The first thing Alistair noticed as he followed Slippers Pink into the tunnel was the silence. The roar of the waves, which had been a constant soundtrack the last few days, abruptly ceased. The second thing he noticed was that visibility was limited in the murky light; he could only just make out the indistinct form of Slippers Pink swimming ahead of him.

He moved his arms and legs in a steady rhythm, and when he felt his lungs start to burn he let out a trickle of air, trying to ignore how his heart was beginning to knock in his chest. The tunnel was longer than he'd expected, and he started to grow anxious. How much farther could it be? As he became aware of the air pushing out of his lungs he simultaneously became aware of the heaviness of his limbs in the water, which felt thick now, as if it was resisting his effort to move through it. The walls of the tunnel seemed to be closing in, to be physically squeezing the air out of him, and he thought the murky light was dimming. He tried to keep panic at bay, tried to keep swimming steadily, tried to hold on to the last of the oxygen in his lungs, fixed his eyes on Slippers Pink. . . . But where was she? For through the gloom Alistair saw that the tunnel forked—and he had no idea which way Slippers Pink had gone! But there was no time to think, he had to keep moving, he was out of air, desperate to breathe, and he thought he saw a glow in the left-hand fork, perhaps it was the surface, air, he needed air. There was nothing steady about his movements now; Alistair was frantic, hands clawing at the water. Why wasn't the tunnel ending? What if he had taken the wrong fork and the tunnel didn't end? Several times he jerked his head up convulsively, as if to surface, only to hit the roof of the tunnel and be reminded that there was no way out but forward. If there was a way out. The salt water was stinging his eyes, his chest was aching with pressure, heart pounding, pulse racing, head feeling light, eyes filled with light. . . .

As his head broke the surface, Alistair drew a huge breath, and was almost overwhelmed by dizziness from the rush of oxygen into his bursting lungs. For a few seconds he thought of nothing but his next breath, gulping at the air gratefully as if each inhalation might be his last. His limbs were trembling, though whether from exertion or relief he couldn't tell. The panic he had felt in the tunnel still felt very fresh—but he was alive!

Treading water as his breathing steadied, he looked around. He was in the center of a small pool, one of a series of pools strung together like pearls across an expanse of dark, slippery rock. Blocking his view of the shore was an uneven jumble of rocky peaks and crumbling cliffs, silhouetted against the sky like a ragged row of teeth. He'd made it! He was on the far side of Atticus Island! He looked around for Slippers. At first he couldn't see her, and his heart began to beat quickly again. What if she had taken the wrong tunnel? Then he spotted her several meters away, standing with her hands on her hips in shallow water in the shadow of an overhanging rock. Her almond fur was all slick from the water, but her brow was furrowed with anxiety as she gazed intently into the rock pool in front of her.

"Slippers," he called.

She looked up, and a huge smile spread across her face. Alistair couldn't help smiling back.

"Did you take the left fork?" she asked, hurrying over, and when Alistair nodded she said, "I took the right fork. That explains why you've come up in a different place to me."

"I didn't know which way you'd gone," he told her, saying nothing of the terror he had experienced.

But she must have understood something of what he had gone through, because her face clouded over. "I've cursed myself a thousand times in the last couple of minutes," she confessed. "When I got to the fork I could see a faint glow from the right-hand tunnel and presumed that must be the one to take—and it wasn't till I'd entered it that I realized you mightn't have seen which way I'd gone, because I'd be blocking the light. But there was no room to turn back, I had to go on, not knowing if you were still behind me or if. . . ." She broke off, and Alistair realized that she had been no less terrified than he. Imagine if she had reached his parents only to have to tell them that their son had . . . Alistair shook his head to dispel the image of himself drowning in the tunnel.

"Well, we made it," he said. "Just don't tell me that was the easy bit!"

Slippers Pink bit her lip and glanced up at the rocky peaks. "I guess we'll find out," she said.

As he gazed along the chain of rocks, Alistair could discern the outline of a tower on one of the cliffs.

"There," he said.

Slippers peered in the direction he was pointing. "Ah yes," she said.

"What a horrible place to put prisoners," Alistair burst out. "There's no food, no source of fresh water. It would be almost impossible for a boat to land except in perfect weather conditions. What if they run out of supplies?"

"The prisoners don't eat," Slippers surmised grimly.

Alistair couldn't help wondering how his parents

would be changed by their years in this terrible place.

They picked their way carefully across rocks coated in slippery seaweed, trying to stay low, but Alistair knew it was impossible that they could approach the tower undetected; there was nowhere to hide, and his ginger fur was bound to make him conspicuous. Still, though Alistair watched nervously for the telltale flash of red that signified the presence of the Queen's Guards, he saw nothing, just the sparsely vegetated cliffs, the black slivers of rock, the deep blue sea and white foam of crashing waves. Gulls wheeled overhead—perhaps they were the lookouts? But they seemed immersed in their own business, and didn't show any apparent interest in the mice who warily approached a path cut into the cliff.

"This looks like the only way up," Slippers observed as they stepped onto the narrow trail. "Which means it's likely to be the only way down, too."

The path was so steep and winding that it was impossible to see more than a few meters ahead. Anyone waiting above them would have a clear advantage: one push and they would be plunged off the edge onto the rocks below. It was more than exertion from the climb that was making Alistair's breathing speed up as the path wound higher and higher.

About a quarter of the way up, Slippers called in a low voice, "There's another path joining this one. It looks like it goes back down to the rocks. You wait here, I'm going to see where it leads." She disappeared down the second path, only to reappear a few minutes later. "The good news is, there's a boat tied up down there," she said. "Which gives us a way out of here."

"What's the bad news?" said Alistair.

"There's a boat tied up down there," she said. "Which means that even though we can't see them, there are definitely guards around here somewhere."

But they'd seen no guards by the time they reached the top of the path, no guards yelled at them to halt as they ran across the small patch of grass between the path and the tower, and there were no guards blocking the prison's entrance.

Alistair was panting slightly as he began to climb the stairs behind Slippers Pink, but he barely noticed. His senses were on full alert, expecting to hear a cry of alarm at any moment as their presence was discovered. He tugged the ends of his scarf nervously, but all was silent as they passed the first-floor landing, and when they reached the second-floor landing too. Slippers held out a hand to stop him, then peeked cautiously around the edge of the doorway.

"Quiet as the grave," she said when she drew her head back. Her whisper sounded loud in the stone chamber. "No sign of the Queen's Guards—or anyone else for that matter. This is strange," she murmured uneasily. She reached behind her absently to smooth the fur on the back of her neck, then stepped through the doorway, beckoning to Alistair to follow.

They were standing at the end of a long corridor. One side was lined with heavy wooden doors, each with a small barred window at about head height. The other side was a wall of rough-hewn stone with tiny openings every few paces to let light in. Even so, there was barely enough light to see by as they started down the corridor.

"Emmeline and Rebus should be in the seventh cell along," Slippers said.

Alistair's pulse was racing now, and he wished that Slippers Pink would move faster. They were almost there! He was about to see his parents for the first time in four years!

"Even if they were being kept apart from other prisoners, you'd expect to at least see some of those other prisoners," Slippers Pink muttered, almost to herself. She stopped at the door of the third cell, which was ajar. There was no one inside.

"Come on," said Alistair impatiently. "They're just up here."

He moved briskly up the corridor ahead of Slippers Pink. "Four . . . five . . ."

"Alistair," Slippers called sharply, "wait for me."

"Six . . . seven!"

The door to the seventh cell was closed, but when Alistair pushed at in frustration, it swung open. He darted inside, his whiskers trembling in anticipation.

The cell was empty. A square of light from a small barred window set high in the opposite wall fell on the bare stone floor, dimly illuminating the bare stone walls. A single metal cot was pushed against one wall. There was no sign of his parents, no sign of anyone. At first Alistair simply stared in disbelief. His disappointment was like a great weight lodged in his chest, stopping him from breathing. He swallowed hard, feeling a lump rising in his throat. "Slippers," he said in a small voice. He took a couple of steps backward. "Slip—"

There was a clang of metal and he spun around just as the cell door slammed shut.

16

Trouble in the Tulips

Five a.m. found Alice and Alex at Fiercely Jones's shed, bleary-eyed.

"Sleep well, did you? Straw pallets cozy enough for you, were they? Heh heh heh." The gardener's mirthless chuckle suggested that he was not displeased at the notion of their discomfort. "I've got a job that will wake you right up, don't you worry."

He led them 'round to the back of the shed, where they were greeted by the foulest stench ever to assault Alice's nose. Whatever it was, there was a pile of it that looked almost equal to the shed itself in size.

"What—what is it?" she choked out, after she regained her breath.

"Fertilizer," said Fiercely Jones.

"Fertilizer?"

"Manure. And you're going to shovel it." He pointed to two shovels. "Shift it." He pointed to a wheelbarrow.

"Then spread it." He flicked a thumb over his shoulder.

"Spread it where?" Alex gasped, holding his nose.

"On the two hundred and thirty-eight garden beds we'll be replanting."

"Two hundred and thirty-eight garden beds?" Alex wheezed in disbelief.

"You can start on the tulips."

A week passed, the days blurring into one another as each morning Alex and Alice rose just before dawn, spent a long day shoveling, shifting, and spreading manure, washed themselves under the cold-water pump in the courtyard, then presented themselves in the kitchen for a meager supper. Then, still hungry, they climbed the stairs to their sweltering attic room and fell onto the hard straw pallets. Alice usually slipped into a light doze until she heard the rustle of straw that meant her brother was about to go off on one of his raiding expeditions to the kitchen—often via some other part of the palace in search of information for FIG. Alice was too frightened to go exploring herself, though she did wonder whether it might in fact be less terrifying than lying awake, imagining scenarios in which Alex was discovered roaming by Lester, and imprisoned, or tortured . . . or worse. By the time he returned she was always a nervous wreck, too wound up to eat much, too tense to sleep.

On their eighth evening as servants of the palace, Alex returned to the attic with two hard-boiled eggs—he'd heard someone approaching the kitchen and had had to leave before gathering anymore food. He also had some disturbing news.

At first Alice had trouble understanding the news, since her brother had stuffed the whole egg into his mouth in one go.

"There's someone in the dungeon?" she repeated, not sure she'd heard right.

Her brother nodded vigorously. "He looks pretty young, too," he said, spraying flecks of yolk on Alice's fur.

"Alex, yuck," she complained, brushing away the specks of yellow. "Who is he? Why is he there? Where did he come from?"

"Don't know, don't know, and don't know," said Alex. "I didn't have a chance to ask. There was a guard down there with him—I had to scarper before he saw me. But I'd say he's Gerandan, since he's got orangey fur, and he can't have been there long, because I checked out the dungeon the night before last and he wasn't there then."

Alice nibbled at her egg thoughtfully. "This could be important," she said. "You should go back again tomorrow night and see if you can find out anything more."

She finished her egg and lay back on her pallet, exhausted and still hungry. She was sure she'd never be able to sleep with the hunger pangs gnawing at her insides, but exhaustion won and she drifted off into a light doze. She dreamed she was crossing the border hidden inside a pile of manure. The manure was heaped on top of her and as fast as she tried to dig herself out it kept coming, filling her nose and mouth so that she couldn't breathe. She woke gasping for breath, and saw that the moon had barely shifted in the sky. She'd probably only been asleep for a few minutes. She gazed out the small window and thought about the prisoner in the dungeon. Had he been caught stealing food, perhaps? Or said something bad about Souris and a Queen's Guard had overheard? Or maybe he was a spy, like them. . . . Alice didn't get back to sleep that night.

By the next day, her senses were dulled from lack of food and sleep, so that it was something of a relief to be working alone with Alex in the garden at some distance from the palace, with no need to act the part of Rita or remember their cover story. But her relief was replaced with apprehension when, that afternoon, a trio of mice strode across the grass. Alice recognized Fiercely Jones, of course, and the odious Lester, but the third was a mouse she'd never met before. His fur sprang from his body in short gray bristles, and he was wearing a dark blue coat with gold buttons. His boots were the tallest and shiniest Alice had ever seen.

"Where are you up to with these flowerbeds, Jones?" the gray mouse demanded in a high voice. "We don't have much time, you know."

"Coming along, General, coming along," said the gardener. "Least I've got some help at last."

"Stand to attention when you see the general," Lester barked at Alice and Alex.

So this was General Ashwover! Alice and Alex

obediently stopped their shoveling.

"General, these are the two newest additions to our household. Their father was killed in the line of duty in the Crankens, and their mother fell ill and died. They're from Tornley."

"Tornley, eh?" said the general.

"Yes," said Lester. "Interesting place, Tornley. I'm very fond of the Parmesan they make there." He looked at the two young mice blandly.

Alex affected a look of surprise. "Really?" he said. "That's odd. We're famous for our mozzarella."

The general turned to his lieutenant. "Quite right. I don't know what you're on about, Lester. They make mozzarella in Tornley, not Parmesan."

"My mistake," murmured Lester.

"It's the way that the mozzarella is aged that makes it so special, isn't that right, young man? How is it aged, exactly?"

"Er, yes sir, General," said Alex. "It's aged in icy crevasses."

"Icy crevasses? Well, that is unusual." Fortunately, before he could inquire further, the general's nose began to twitch. "Let's move on, shall we, Lester? The smell around here is a bit, er, ripe."

"The tulips in the eastern part of the grounds should just about be blooming, General," Fiercely Jones offered, and the trio moved away.

Alice and Alex picked up their shovels and resumed work.

"The general isn't nearly as scary as I'd imagined," Alex mused after a few minutes. "I wonder how come he's so—" But before he could finish his thought they heard a distant bellow and looked up to see a dozen or more Queen's Guards rush past.

"What's going on?" Alex asked one of them.

"Something afoot in the flowerbeds," he gasped.

"In the flowerbeds?" Alice and Alex looked at each other, mystified.

"Let's go see," said Alex, and still clutching their shovels they hurried after the Queen's Guards.

When they reached the edge of the crowd, they pushed through the sea of red coats till they had a view of the offending flowerbed. There, clearly spelled out in purple tulips, was the word "FIG."

"Oh!" Alice exclaimed.

"Disgraceful, isn't it?" said a guard to her right.

The general was roaring his outrage at Fiercely Jones. The gardener, whose hat had fallen off, stood ashen-faced before him.

"WHAT is the meaning of this?" roared the general.

"I don't know," whispered the terrified gardener.

"WHO is responsible?" roared the general.

"I don't know," the gardener whispered helplessly.

Suddenly Alice's arm was seized in a tight grip.

"Hey!" she said, pulling away, but the grip tightened.

"Let's ask Raz and Rita," said a smooth voice by her ear. Lester moved forward, dragging Alice by the arm and pushing Alex along in front of him.

General Ashwover turned to the gardener's helpers, fur bristling. "What do you two know about this then, eh?"

As Alice gaped at the general, Alex said, "I'll tell you what I know: it's an abomination." He spat on the ground beside him. He turned to address the red-coated crowd. "If my father were here . . ." He waved his shovel threateningly. "The culprit must be caught!"

As the crowd of Queen's Guards shouted their approval, Lester released his grip on Alice's arm and moved to Alex's side. "And caught he will be!"

The crowd shouted again, though somewhat less enthusiastically now seeing as it was Lester doing the talking.

"This matter will be fully investigated," Lester promised, though to Alice's ears it sounded like a threat. "And you mark my words"—his gaze traveled around the gathered crowd—"the perpetrator, or perpetrators, will be punished." The final words were spoken in a menacing hiss. Had Alice imagined it, or had his gaze lingered on her and Alex?

As the crowd dispersed, and she and Alex walked back to the garden bed where they'd been spreading manure, dozens of questions clamored in Alice's mind. Who would plant the word FIG in the flowerbeds, and why? Was there really a FIG supporter here at the palace? Maybe there was even another undercover FIG agent here? But then would another undercover agent really put them all at risk by alerting the Sourians to their presence? That didn't seem very smart. No, more likely, someone was trying to frame her and Alex. . . . Someone like Lester; he was always trying to trap them, it seemed to Alice, with his supposedly innocent mistakes about the Parmesan of Tornley or their father's small ears. But why would he frame them unless he knew the truth? And if he knew the truth, why bother to frame them, why not just throw them in the dungeon?

When they reached the garden bed, Alex threw down his shovel. "This is ridiculous," he growled. He started to stalk away across the grass.

"Alex—I mean, Raz, where are you going?" Alice hurried after her brother. "Raz, wait!"

"I'm going to the kitchen," Alex ground out when she'd caught up. "I'm going to tell Cook I can't keep working like this on one pathetic meal a day—and then I'm going to tell Lester exactly what I think of him and how he treats the orphans of a Sourian hero."

"No!" said Alice. "You can't go see Lester. It's too dangerous. It's just the hunger that's making you act like this. Al—Raz, stop!"

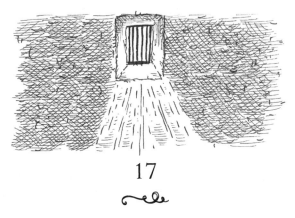

17

Keaters

"Slippers Pink?"

Alistair rushed to the door, grabbed at the bars of the opening and pulled, but the door was shut fast.

"What . . . ?" Pressing his face to the bars, he could just make out a figure hurrying down the corridor. "Slippers? What's going on?" Anxiety made his voice come out high and squeaky. "Slippers!"

But there was no reply. The corridor was silent and deserted. Slippers Pink was gone.

Alistair sank to the ground and put his head in his hands, his thoughts whirling. Where were his parents? Tobias's source had been sure they were here, had given them specific details about which cell Emmeline and Rebus were in. Was it possible the source had lied, that Alistair had walked into a trap? Maybe—and the thought so filled him with despair that he let out a small choked sob—maybe his parents had been dead all along? But if this was a trap, didn't that mean Slippers was part of it? She had been right behind him—she must have been the one to lock him in the cell. Perhaps she had been trying to lose him in the underwater tunnel, had been disappointed when he surfaced in the pool! Yet why would she do such a thing? The only thing of value he had was his scarf, and the song, and Slippers already knew the song, and she would have had plenty of opportunities to take the scarf if she'd wanted it. And besides, he had seen the look of joy and relief on her face when he had emerged from the underwater tunnel. There was no way that was faked. He trusted her. After everything they had been through together, how could he not?

Alistair raised his head and leaned it back against the door to stare at the shadowy ceiling, trying to think more calmly. If it wasn't Slippers who had slammed the cell door shut, then who? Maybe that hadn't been Slippers hurrying down the corridor. But who else had known he would be here? There was no one else around. And where was Slippers now?

He continued to sit, dazed, staring at the ceiling, for a few more minutes, until the cold of the stone floor began to seep into his fur. Tightening his scarf, which felt a bit stiff and scratchy after its dousing in salt water, he stood up and began to pace, moving between the door and the small patch of light from the high window, rubbing at his arms to warm himself.

He didn't know how much time had passed—it could have been anywhere from five minutes to an hour—when he heard a snuffling from a dark corner of the cell where the light from the window couldn't reach.

His heart leaped. Could it be . . . ?

In three steps he was there, kneeling down by a huddled figure, reaching forward to touch rough fur. "It's me," he said. "Alistair."

But the huddled figure gave a squeak of alarm and sprang up, and Alistair saw that it was neither his mother nor his father, but a small, shabby black mouse who was rubbing his eyes and glaring at Alistair with a mixture of suspicion and fear.

"Wh-who are you?" demanded the black mouse. "Where are Rebus and Emmeline?"

Alistair's plummeting spirits rose again. "They're my parents! I came here to rescue them. Do you know where they are?"

"If I knew where they were, I wouldn't have asked you."

"Oh," said Alistair, "of course. Sorry. But I was expecting to find them here."

"Me too," said the black mouse. He sounded more puzzled than suspicious now. "They were here when I fell asleep." He smothered a yawn and looked around the cell with a slightly bewildered air, as if Emmeline and Rebus might be hiding in the shadows. "That must have been some deep sleep though. I still feel a little groggy. Maybe the guards put something in my breakfast."

"Breakfast?" said Alistair. "It's late afternoon now."

The black mouse yawned again and stretched. "Like I said, some sleep. And you're Emmeline and Rebus's son, you say? Odd coincidence, you turning up right when they've disappeared." His sleepy expression had turned shrewd and watchful.

"I know it must seem that way, but . . ." Alistair shrugged helplessly. "I . . . I really thought they were going to be here. I haven't seen them in four years." Something in his voice must have convinced the black mouse that Alistair was who he said he was, because when the prisoner spoke again it was in a softer voice.

"So which one of the three are you then, eh? You're obviously not Alice. Not big enough to be Alex. And then there's that ginger fur, which none of the others have got, right? You must be Alistair."

Alistair just stared. "How did you . . . ?"

"Oh, I've heard all about you from your parents. After all"—the black mouse held his arms out wide to indicate the empty cell—"there's nothing to do in here but talk."

It pleased Alistair to think of his parents talking about him and his brother and sister to this stranger. It wasn't that he thought their parents would have forgotten them exactly, but it did make them feel closer somehow. Nothing could make up for the disappointment of bursting into the cell to rescue his parents only to find them gone, but at least he was now in the company of someone who had been speaking to them that very morning.

"How are they?" he asked.

The black mouse paused as if searching for the right words. "We're none of us who we were after a stay on Atticus Island. Emmeline is fearful thin, and Rebus's fur is a bit patchy." He rubbed his shabby black fur ruefully. "But they're in as good spirits as can be expected. They were lucky to have each other." He smiled somewhat sadly. "If only I had my wife with me . . . Not that I would wish her in this evil place," he added hastily. "Only, it does a body a power of good to have company. I was in solitary before they put me in here with Rebus and Emmeline." A shadow of despair passed across his face, then he brightened. "But now you're here. And, forgive me if I'm wrong, but didn't you say something about a rescue?"

Seeing the hope on the black mouse's face, Alistair suddenly felt embarrassed. "I'm sorry, er . . ."

"Keaters," the black mouse supplied.

"I'm sorry, Keaters, but the thing is, well I was coming here to rescue my parents, only someone slammed the door shut behind me."

"Wait," said Keaters. "How did you get into the cell in the first place?"

"Through the door," said Alistair, and now he felt both embarrassed and foolish. He remembered Slippers's unease, how she'd called to him to wait, how she'd rubbed at the back of her neck. What was it Feast Thompson had said? It's like she's got a sixth sense for danger.

"The door was open?" asked Keaters in disbelief.

Alistair nodded miserably. "And I just walked straight in, and now look where it's got me." He sighed. "I should have listened to Slippers."

The black mouse suddenly looked alert. "Did you say Slippers? As in Slippers Pink? She's here on the island?"

"That's right," said Alistair. "I came here with Slippers. Do you know her?"

"Do I know her?" Keaters repeated. He laughed—a rusty-sounding laugh, as if it had been a long time since he had last done it. "Slippers and I go way back." He chuckled, perhaps remembering something from the past. "Way back. We joined FIG together. And she's here now you say? Well, that's splendid. If anyone can get us out of here it's Slippers Pink."

"You're right," said Alistair. "But I don't know if she's still here or not," he admitted. "I called and called after the door slammed shut, and she didn't answer. She was right behind me. I don't know what could have happened to her. Do you think the guards caught her?"

Keaters looked grave. "I'd say so. They've probably put her in a cell on another floor."

"It was the strangest thing though," said Alistair. "I didn't see or hear any guards, then suddenly—*bang!*—the door closes."

The black mouse shook his head. "That's not the strangest thing," he said. "The strangest thing is that they left the door open in the first place, with me inside." He slapped a palm to his forehead. "I could have walked right out of here, but instead I went and slept through the whole thing." He strode over to the door, grasped the bars of the opening and shook them, clearly hoping that the door wasn't really locked. When he was unable to shift it, he paced the floor, much as Alistair had done earlier. Alistair could understand Keaters's frustration at finding out that he could have walked free.

Abruptly, the black mouse slumped onto the cot, and Alistair sat too.

"So where do you think they've taken them?" he asked Keaters eventually.

The black mouse, who had been staring moodily at the door, started. "Emmeline and Rebus?" He shook his head. "There's only one place a prisoner ever goes from here: the Cranken Alps."

Alistair gulped. If his parents were already in bad health, how would they survive the mountains' appalling conditions? He remembered the cold bleak valley he and Tibby had crossed. Then, standing once more as the cold, hard metal slats of the cot grew too uncomfortable, he gave a hollow laugh. How would he survive himself? Like Keaters had just said, the next stop after Atticus Island was the Cranken Alps. It looked like he might be reunited with his parents after all. Though how long it might be before that happened was anyone's guess.

He turned to look at Keaters, to find the black mouse regarding him with a curious expression.

"How did you get all the way to Atticus Island from Shetlock without being caught by the Sourians?" Keaters asked.

"I, er . . ." Alistair hesitated, not sure how much he should tell the other mouse. "Oswald helped," he said finally.

"Ah yes." Keaters nodded knowingly. "The owl. But even owls can't travel long distances undetected. You must have used the secret ways, hmm?" The black mouse winked.

Relieved, Alistair nodded, and his hands stole up to clutch the ends of the scarf, which contained the map of the secret paths. He tugged the ends nervously.

Keaters's bright eyes followed the movement, then met Alistair's gaze with an understanding smile. He opened his mouth as if to say something, but before he could speak they heard a screech of metal, as if somewhere else in the building a door was swinging open.

The two mice exchanged looks.

"Do you think it's the guards?" Alistair whispered hoarsely.

The black mouse, with an expression of panic on his face, gave a curt nod. "They must be doing their rounds. I just hope . . ." The black mouse swallowed. "I hope they won't beat me again."

"Beat you?" Alistair's mouth was so dry he could barely choke the words out.

Keaters inclined his head. "It's their idea of fun," he whispered, a tremor in his voice.

Alistair glanced wildly around the cell, looking for a place to hide. "There must be a way out of here," he said, trying to suppress the whimper rising in his throat.

"I'm sure if there was, Emmeline and Rebus would have found it," Keaters said, but he rose from the cot and moved to stand beside Alistair. His gaze roamed the cell, moving from the solid door to the high window, into the shadowy corners then back to the window and door. Suddenly he narrowed his eyes and rubbed his chin thoughtfully. "Is it just me, or do the bars up there"—he pointed to the small window in the wall—"look different from the bars down here?" He pointed now to the bars set in the door's opening.

Alistair squinted. "I'm not sure," he said. "I don't think—"

"There is a difference," said Keaters firmly. "I'm sure of it." He pointed to the window again. "Those bars are rustier than the bars in the door. And do you know what that means? It means they're weaker. . . ."

Alistair, who was beginning to see what Keaters was driving at, felt a small flower of hope bloom inside him. "But how would we get up there?" he asked.

The black mouse turned to face him, his eyes shining. "Determination," he said.

Alistair would have preferred a ladder, but if determination was all they had, he was more than willing to give his share. After all, what did they have to lose?

The two mice contemplated the wall, looking for possible handholds, but there were none.

"Typical Sourians," muttered Keaters darkly. "Everything has to be neat and square. There's not a single bump or crevice in the whole wall."

"But aren't you Sourian?" asked Alistair.

"What?" Keaters looked at him in surprise.

"You said you joined FIG with Slippers Pink," Alistair pointed out. "She told me that she joined when she was at university in Grouch."

"That's right," said Keaters. "I suppose I am Sourian— by birth. The fact is, I've been working for FIG for so long that I really feel more Gerandan."

"I've been Gerandan my whole life without even knowing it," said Alistair.

"Sometimes," Keaters said solemnly, "I think the world would be a better place if we didn't think in terms of Gerandan or Sourian or Shetlocker. What's the difference between any of us, really? We're all mice."

"That sounds like something my Uncle Ebenezer would say," Alistair said wistfully, thinking of his stout, cheerful uncle. How upset he would be to learn that instead of rescuing his parents, Alistair had wound up being the third member of the family to be captured.

"Ebenezer?" said Keaters delightedly. "Rebus's brother? Rebus used to tell us the most hilarious stories about their escapades when they were lads. It sounds like Rebus got Ebenezer out of all kinds of scrapes."

"No," Alistair corrected him. "It was the other way—" Then he stopped. Ebenezer's stories had always sounded rather far-fetched. Who knew how much he had exaggerated? "Anyway," he kicked at the wall with his foot, "I don't think we're going to be able to scale this."

Keaters turned his attention back to the wall. "I don't suppose so."

Alistair could tell that he was losing confidence.

"Maybe if I gave you a boost?" he suggested.

Keaters shook his head. "Too high," he said briefly. The black mouse's whiskers were drooping now.

Alistair cast desperately about the cell. If only there was something of use, but there was nothing. Nothing except the cot. The cot . . . with metal slats . . .

"Keaters," said Alistair excitedly, "what if we lifted the cot so it was leaning against the wall? The slats would be like a ladder." It seemed to him like the kind of clever idea that Tibby Rose might have come up with.

Keaters turned from the cot to the window then back again, measuring with his eyes. "It might work," he said. He sounded cautious, but Alistair could see hope flaring in his eyes once more. "Let's try it."

They stood one at each end of the cot, then on the count of three heaved together. It was much heavier than Alistair had imagined, and they were only able to inch it over in slow stages. They were both breathing heavily by the time they had got it into position. Alistair was disappointed to see that it didn't reach the high window.

"It won't work," he said gloomily.

"Let's not give up so easily," said his cellmate. "Come on!" And with Alistair close behind, the small black mouse nimbly climbed the slats to perch on top of the cot.

"Looks rather different from up here, doesn't it?" remarked Keaters. "That window's a way off still, but perhaps not impossible. Now how about that boost you offered me?"

Bracing himself against the cool stone wall for support, Alistair cupped his hands together. Keaters stepped onto the makeshift stair, and stretched.

"Almost . . . ," the black mouse gasped. "But not . . . quite . . ."

Alistair lowered his hands so that Keaters could step

back onto the top of the cot.

"I was so close," said Keaters, holding his hands about shoulder-width apart. "There has to be a way." He closed his eyes for a moment, then opened them. "Alistair, what if I stood on your shoulders?"

"Sure," said Alistair. "If you think it would work."

He squatted so that the older mouse could step onto his shoulders, then slowly began to rise. His leg muscles screamed with pain as he moved to a standing position, his hands scraping against the stone of the wall as he scrabbled for balance, his shoulders feeling like they were about to buckle.

"I don't know how long . . . ," he began breathlessly, but was interrupted by Keaters's crow of triumph.

"I've got it! I can reach the bars!"

The weight on Alistair's shoulders suddenly eased, and he looked up to see his cellmate hauling himself up onto a narrow window ledge.

"Hooray!" Alistair cried.

He watched anxiously as Keaters began to test the bars, rattling one after the other. But one after the other they held firm. Alistair was barely breathing now. They'd come so close. He'd really thought . . .

"This one's moving!" Keaters called. He was grasping the second last bar. Alistair held his breath as Keaters grunted and gave an almighty push. "Almost . . . almost . . . yes!" The bar broke clean through, and the black mouse hastily bent both ends out to create a gap. His head disappeared as he thrust it out, then reappeared again a few seconds later.

"It's a long way down," he reported. "But I reckon we could jump. What does it matter if we get a few bruises? We'd be free!" He thrust his head through the gap once more and inhaled loudly. "Free air," he murmured. "Lovely." Looking down at Alistair again he said, "Right, let's get you up here." He kneeled down and extended his hand.

Alistair stood on tiptoes and reached up, but he was nowhere near Keaters's proffered hand.

"Stretch," Keaters urged.

"I am stretching," Alistair said in frustration. "I can't reach. What are we going to do?"

"I suppose I could jump down and then try to get back into the tower to let you out," Keaters suggested.

"But what if you can't get back in?" Alistair asked. "Please don't leave me here alone."

"No, you're right, it's too risky," Keaters agreed. "Besides, we're in this together. 'All for one and one for all,' right?"

"Right," said Alistair, smiling weakly as he recognized the quote from *The Three Musketeers*, one of his favorite books, which he had lent to Tibby Rose. He thought of his friend, waiting on the beach with Feast Thompson for Alistair and Slippers Pink to return. Of course, they were expecting them to return with Emmeline and Rebus. Now it looked as though he wouldn't be returning at all. He only hoped Slippers had managed to escape somehow. His gloomy thoughts were cut short by a cry from Keaters.

"I've got it!" said the black mouse. "Throw me your scarf, and I'll use it to pull you up."

Yes! He was saved after all! Alistair hastily began to unknot his scarf, but as he held the precious map in his hands, feeling the unaccustomed sensation of cool air on his neck, he hesitated.

"Quick," Keaters urged. "Throw it to me. The guards will be coming 'round with dinner soon."

Still, Alistair hesitated. He wanted to throw the scarf, wanted to escape this miserable cell, but something was holding him back. Keep it safe, and never lose it, his mother had said when she gave him the scarf. Keep it safe. . . . Now that he knew how valuable the scarf was, not just because it was a memento from his mother but because of the secret knowledge it contained, it was more important than ever to keep it safe. And how well did he know Keaters really? Tobias's source had said that Emmeline and Rebus shared this cell, but there had been no mention of Keaters. Now Keaters was here and his parents were not. Then again, Keaters knew all about Alistair and his brother and sister, knew about Rebus and Ebenezer's boyhood adventures. How could he have known if not from Emmeline and Rebus? And he even knew Slippers Pink—they had joined FIG together.

"Throw it," Keaters repeated impatiently.

Alistair stood clutching his scarf, racked with indecision.

Suddenly he heard a key scraping in the lock of the cell door.

"It's the guards!" Keaters yelped. "If they catch us like this we've had it. It's now or never, Alistair. Throw me the scarf or I'm going without you."

Trembling with fear, Alistair quickly balled up the scarf and prepared to throw it, just as the cell door burst open.

18

Settling Old Scores

When Alice and Alex reached the kitchen, Cook was banging pots and pans around on the stove with even more force than usual.

Alex seemed nonplussed by the scowl on Cook's face, and Alice took advantage of his silence to ask, "Is something wrong, Cook?"

"I'll tell you what's wrong," snapped Cook. She gave the onions sizzling in butter in a large frying pan a brisk stir then cracked an egg into a bowl and snatched up a whisk. "General Fancy-pants wants a six-course dinner for some visiting mucky-mucks. 'And mind you make it a special dinner, Cook,'" she said, imitating the general's high voice. "'My guests have very discerning palates.'" Cook dropped the whisk, picked up a small knife, and with a flick of her wrist expertly minced a clove of garlic. "Meanwhile, it's four o'clock already, the general will have a fit if his tea tray isn't in his office when he returns, those potatoes won't peel themselves"—she inclined her head toward a teetering mound of potatoes on the large kitchen table—"and them fish won't bone themselves"— she waved her elbow in the direction of a bucket of fish on the draining board—"and my useless kitchen hand is in bed with the measles. That's what's wrong, girlie."

"We'll deliver the tea tray for you, then come back and peel the potatoes," Alex offered. His bad mood seemed to have vanished.

"You will?" Cook looked as surprised as Alice felt. "Well . . . all right then." She swept the garlic into the pan with the onions and gestured to a large silver tray on which was placed a plate with an assortment of cookies and cupcakes, three porcelain teacups on small saucers, three silver spoons, a silver sugar bowl, and a small jug of milk. "You can take that one, boyo, and girlie, you take the teapot. And mind you hurry back."

Alex carefully picked up the tea tray and Alice the silver teapot etched with a flower motif, and they headed for the stairs.

"What did you do that for?" Alice demanded as the kitchen door swung shut behind them. "I don't want to go anywhere near General Ashwover's office."

"Yes, you do," Alex contradicted her. "Think about it, sis: from what Cook said, the general isn't in his office at the moment—which gives us a great opportunity to snoop around. Maybe we'll find out something important that we can report back to FIG. All we've learned so far is how to shovel manure."

"I suppose you're right," Alice conceded. "But let's be quick about it. We don't want to end up in the dungeon." She felt a chill as she thought of that lonely young mouse Alex had described.

They kept their mouths shut and their heads down as they reached the main hall. Sentries armed with spears were posted at every door and on each side of the giant staircase.

"What are you doing here?" asked one of the red-coated guards suspiciously. "I thought you worked outside with Fiercely." He looked pointedly at Alex's muddy feet.

"Cook said we were to deliver the general's tea tray to his office," Alex told him. "Kitchen hand is sick."

The guard sniffed at the tea tray appreciatively. "Wish she'd send a tea tray to me." At a hiss from the sentry on the other side of the stairs he straightened and said brusquely, "Second floor."

Up the wide crimson-carpeted staircase they scampered to the second floor. There they encountered two more sentries, each guarding a long corridor.

"Tea tray for General Ashwover," Alex said.

The guard to their right indicated over his shoulder with the point of his spear. "Last door on the left," he said.

The corridor was lined with portraits of mice in heroic poses: one stood on the prow of a ship in a stormy sea; another had his foot on the head of a slain dragon. But as they got closer to the end of the corridor, the portraits were all of Queen Eugenia: standing, sitting, singing, speechifying and, in one, stamping her royal foot.

"Guess who's the president of the Queen Eugenia fan club," said Alex.

He tapped lightly on the last door to the left and, when there was no response, led the way into the general's office.

The room was dominated by a large mahogany desk, which faced the door. Light flooded in from the two windows behind the desk, framed with brocade curtains. A door was discreetly set into the wall to the left of the desk, while to the right was the largest portrait of the Queen they had seen yet, in which, standing beside her in a blue jacket bristling with medals and lavishly trimmed in gold braid, was General Ashwover himself.

"Shut the door behind you, sis," Alex instructed.

"Okay, but we have to be quick," Alice urged again. "The guards know we're in here."

Alex had deposited his tray on the desk and was already rummaging through the drawers.

"This one's just full of paperclips and rubber bands," he said. He slid it shut and pulled open a lower drawer.

Alice carefully placed the teapot beside the tray and started flicking through the pile of papers on the general's desk. "Ah, this is more like it," she said. "Alex, look at this—it's an order requesting a thousand more troops be sent from Souris to Gerander." But before she could speculate on the significance of the order, she heard voices in the corridor.

"Alex, someone's coming," she whispered.

"Quick," said Alex. "Under the desk."

They had barely slipped out of sight when the door opened. Peeping out from their hiding place, Alice saw the furry gray legs of the general stride into the room.

"Oh good," he said, "the tea tray is already here. And I see Cook has made my favorite cupcakes with passionfruit frosting."

He moved toward the tray, revealing the legs of his two visitors. One pair of legs was silvery gray, the other coal black.

Alice started so violently she banged her head on the underside of the desk.

She heard a soft "Ouch" and knew that her brother must have banged his head too. Her heart racing, she turned to look at her brother. She could just make out his eyes gleaming in the shadows. "It couldn't be," he breathed, just as a voice said sweetly, "But, General, dear, will a thousand more troops be enough to subdue the Gerandan rebels once and for all?"

Alice and her brother knew that sweet voice all too well: it was Sophia, and those coal-black legs no doubt belonged to Horace.

This was confirmed when a familiar gloomy voice asked querulously, "Why don't those rebels just go home and let us get on with it?"

"This is their home, Horace," Sophia reminded him. "At least it was. But soon," she added, with obvious satisfaction, "it will be our home—and dear Queen Eugenia's. But surely we will need more than a thousand troops, General?"

Alice's mouth dropped open. Her home? And Queen Eugenia's home? What on earth did she mean?

"No, no, you misunderstand, Sophia," the general was saying as he rounded the desk and dropped into his chair. "One thousand troops is merely an advance party. We will have at least five thousand to accompany Her Majesty when she journeys from Grouch to Cornoliana. By the time she declares Cornoliana the new capital, and herself the Queen of Greater Gerander, we will also have several thousand more troops amassed at the border of Gerander and Shetlock, and the entire Sourian navy ranged off the Shetlock coast. Then we will give President Shabbles of Shetlock a choice: Shetlock can reunite with the kingdom of Greater Gerander voluntarily—or we will take his country by force." There was a scraping sound as the general pulled the tea tray across the desk to sit in front of him.

"It sounds like an excellent plan, dear General," Sophia said approvingly.

"Thank you," said the general modestly, his voice muffled by a cupcake. "Her Majesty was gracious enough to say that she, too, thought it a fine plan. I was thinking of suggesting that we rename the capital Eugeniana in her honor."

"Lovely," said Sophia absently. Her legs had moved closer to the desk on which the tea tray stood. "Those cupcakes do look delicious," she said.

"Mmmph," the general agreed, but he made no move to offer them around.

Sophia sighed and sank down into one of the chairs pulled up to the desk. Her feet were so close that Alice had to shuffle backward so that Sophia didn't feel Alice's breath on her toes.

"And how are matters progressing with Songbird? I hope our contribution has encouraged him to sing more sweetly."

"Lephter!" the general called, and a shower of crumbs sprayed onto his lap and the floor around his feet.

"Sir?" Lester oiled into the room so fast he must have been outside eavesdropping, Alice thought. She was reminded suddenly of Tobias's secretary, who also seemed to be perpetually lurking outside his superior's office.

"Update us on Songbird's latest communiqué, will you?"

"Certainly, sir," Lester replied. "He became quite cooperative once he found out we had a hostage."

"I'm glad to hear it. And well done to you for that idea, Sophia and Horace," the general said, generous with his praise if not his cupcakes.

"Songbird has now given us a lot of valuable information, but I'm afraid he is being rather obstinate on the matter of Zanzibar. He is still refusing to reveal Zanzibar's location. Though it seems he's willing to betray almost anyone else. See here, he's given us a full list."

There was a rustle of paper then Sophia said, "Ah, this makes it all nice and clear."

"Sophia, what is it?" asked Horace. "Tell me."

"It's a list, Horace, dear," said the silvery mouse. "It is a complete list of the heirs to the House of Cornolius, and their last known whereabouts—though a few seem to be merely 'in transit.' And there's no mention of Zanzibar's hiding place, of course."

"How long is the list?" queried Horace. "I thought there was just one other heir besides Queen Eugenia: Zanzibar."

"Zanzibar is the primary threat, of course," Sophia agreed. "But there are other heirs. Zanzibar has a brother, a sister—and don't forget the next generation."

"You mean they all have to be killed?" Horace asked. He sounded rather weary, Alice thought.

"That's right," Sophia said. "It would be best if Queen Eugenia's was the only claim to the throne of Greater Gerander. Simpler."

"Exactly," said Lester. "And thanks to Songbird, we can just work our way through the list. Look, I believe you have some old scores to settle with these two."

"Indeed we do," Sophia replied. "And I see the ginger brat is high on the list."

"Ginger brat?" echoed the general. "Which one's that?"

"This one," Sophia said, and Alice guessed she was pointing to someone on the list. "Queen Eugenia is particularly interested in him. If you see a ginger brat with a scarf, let me know."

A ginger brat with a scarf? That had to be Alistair! How many ginger mice in scarves could the Sourians possibly know?

"What's this question mark below his name?" Sophia asked. "Is Songbird holding out on us?"

Lester bent over the list. "Ah, that—no, that relates to

a rumor. Something Keaters thought he heard years ago. We're still seeking confirmation. But the good news is, the brat with the scarf may be within reach. Songbird has given us some very helpful information—the brat is on his way to Atticus Island, apparently."

Atticus Island? Did that mean Alistair was on a mission to rescue their parents? Alice felt hope flare within her, only to be abruptly dampened as she realized that he was unlikely to succeed if the Sourians knew all about his mission.

"Though Songbird has left out a few details which we'd rather like to know. Like, how can he be so sure that the brat would make it all the way to Atticus Island without us capturing him? The rebels must have devised some way of moving around the country while evading our patrols. But Keaters has been preparing a little trap. He'll worm the brat's secrets out of him. I'm expecting word any time."

Someone called Keaters was going to trap Alistair?! Alice began to tremble. They had to do something. . . . Stop Keaters—stop Songbird. But how? She had no idea who they were. They had to get back to Stetson, to warn FIG. Oh, if only the Sourians would hurry up and leave the room so she could get out from under this desk!

"Keaters?" Sophia snorted. "Are you sure he's the right mouse for the job? He always makes things so needlessly complicated. All those elaborate tricks and schemes, 'worming' secrets out of our enemies. What's wrong with simply kidnapping the brat and forcing him to reveal his secrets?"

"We tried that, Sophia, remember?" Lester said. "You were supposed to kidnap him. Instead you ended up bogged down in a wild-goose chase."

"We—" Sophia began, but Lester interrupted her.

"The trick is not to let the brat know he's been captured. How does that old saying go? Ah yes: you catch more flies with honey than with vinegar."

"Now hold on just a minute," said Sophia. She sounded offended. "I don't need lessons from anyone in how to persuade our enemies to cooperate."

Alice, who had herself been fooled by Sophia's sweet manner, had to agree. But General Ashwover wasn't interested in the rivalry between the spies.

"So Keaters is taking care of the brat, eh? Excellent, excellent," the general was saying. "Though really, Her Majesty won't be satisfied until she has Zanzibar." He slumped back in his chair again.

Sophia's silvery voice chimed in, "You know, General, I think it's just a matter of applying a bit more pressure. Songbird has been trying to bargain with you. It's time to show our friend in FIG exactly who's in control here. We do have our hostage, after all."

The general chuckled, a high, unpleasant sound. "Hee hee hee. You're quite right. I think Songbird will find the whiskers are on the other cheek now. Lester, tell Songbird . . ." He idly picked up another cupcake and chewed thoughtfully. "Tell Songbird the information about the ginger brat with the scarf is good, but not good enough. Queen Eugenia wants Zanzibar too, or . . . how should I put it? Ah yes, I have it. Unless Zanzibar's hiding place is revealed to us, Songbird's own chick will be . . ." The general let out a series of high giggles. "Songbird's own chick will be pushed out of the nest."

"Very good, General," Sophia said appreciatively as Lester bustled officiously from the room. "I'm sure that will achieve results." She stood up and stretched. "Such a long and dangerous journey we've been on," she remarked. "Wouldn't you like a spot of tea and a cupcake, Horace dear? I would. Excuse me, General." Alice heard the rattle of cups and saucers as Sophia pulled the tea tray across the desk away from the general. After a pause, the silvery voice rang out again. "General, does Cook usually write on the cupcakes?"

"Write on the cupcakes? Don't be absurd."

"But look," Sophia persisted. "This cake has a *G* on it."

"A what?" The general's knees shifted as he leaned across the desk. "Well I suppose it does look a bit like a *G*," he conceded gruffly. "Perhaps it stands for 'General,' since they're my cupcakes. But look at this one." The chair creaked as he leaned farther forward. "There's no *G* on that. And what about this one? No *G* on that."

"No, General," Sophia agreed. "You've picked up an I, and . . ." She studied the general's second cupcake. "An *F*."

"*G, I, F*? Bah!" There was a soft thud as the general threw his cupcakes back onto the tray. "What's got into Cook? What on earth would possess her to spell out GIF on my cupcakes?"

Sophia added her cupcake to the two the general had

discarded. "Not GIF, General," she said. "Look."

The general said aloud, "*F, I, G*...Why that spells FIG!" He pushed back his chair. "Lester!" he roared.

Almost at once the oily black mouse appeared in the doorway.

"Yes, General?" he said smoothly.

"Get Cook in here at once!" General Ashwover ordered.

"Right away, General," the secretary promised.

"Why must I be plagued by these petty acts of sabotage?" the general blustered. He slumped so low in his chair that Alistair and Alex had to squeeze to the outermost edges of the desk. Even so, their whiskers were almost tickling the general's kneecaps.

"Did you see the flowerbeds?" he demanded. "I ordered them replanted in readiness for Her Majesty's arrival, and when the flowers bloomed they spelled FIG. Can you imagine if Queen Eugenia had seen that?" The general's high voice sank to a hoarse whisper. "Her Majesty would not be pleased."

"No," Sophia agreed. She sounded distracted. "She wouldn't. General, these cupcakes are remarkably good. I'd like to meet this Cook of yours and ask her a few questions."

"That's why I've sent for her," the general said irritably. "This business of sabotaging cupcakes is inexcusable. I—"

There was a rap on the door, and when the general barked, "Come in," Lester entered, followed by a frightened-looking Cook clutching a wooden spoon.

"Here's Cook, sir, as you requested," purred Lester.

"Thank you, my man," said the general. "Now, Cook, what is the meaning of these cupcakes?"

"I-I'm sorry, General, sir," said Cook. "I don't know what you—"

"You used fresh butter, didn't you, Cook?" asked Sophia.

"I did, ma'am," said Cook, turning to the silvery gray mouse in confusion. "And eggs freshly laid, and—"

"But what about the writing, Cook?" Ashwover bellowed. "Why did you write 'FIG' on my cupcakes?"

"FIG on your . . . ?" Cook raised a hand to her chest. "But, General, I did no such thing."

The general moved forward in his chair. "Then how do you explain this?"

Cook bustled over and squinted at the cupcakes. The shock in her voice sounded genuine as she said, "I can't explain it. But I can tell you this, General: I have a six-course dinner to prepare for your guests here. . . ."

Sophia gave a happy murmur.

". . . and I have no time for such nonsense as writing on cupcakes."

"Then who did?" the general wanted to know. "Could it have been your kitchen hand, perhaps?"

"Not likely," said Cook definitely. "He's got measles. I had to get those two young mice of Fiercely's to give me a hand this afternoon. Though I don't know where they've got to," she added crossly. "They promised to come back and peel my potatoes, and they never did, and potatoes don't peel themselves you know, General."

"No," said Ashwover. "I don't suppose they do."

"Two young mice of Fiercely's?" Sophia butted in. "Who are they?"

"Fiercely Jones is the gardener, ma'am," Cook explained. "And he's took on a couple of new helpers of late—young orphans from Souris."

"You don't say," murmured Sophia, stroking her long whiskers.

Alice froze.

"What do these helpers of Fiercely Jones look like, Cook?" Sophia asked.

"Well let me think," said Cook, wrinkling her nose thoughtfully. "The girlie is a chocolatey brown with a white patch." As Alice peeked out apprehensively from under the desk, Cook rubbed her hip in the approximate place of Alice's white patch. "And the boyo is white with a brown patch." Cook tapped her shoulder. "Here."

"Thank you, Cook, you may go," Sophia said. The door closed behind her, and there was a few minutes' silence, during which Sophia made the appreciative noises of someone whose mouth was full of cupcake.

Finally the general heaved a sigh. "Well, Cook didn't do much to shed light on the situation."

"Oh, I don't know about that, General," Sophia disagreed. "It sounds to me like our young friends are close at hand, doesn't it, Horace? They carried the cupcakes here from the kitchen, but they didn't return to the kitchen as promised. Where are they now, I wonder. . . ."

Suddenly Sophia pushed her chair back and dropped to the floor.

Alice screamed as Sophia's face come into view, staring right at her.

"Aha!" cried Sophia. "These are no young orphans from Souris, General. They're spies!"

As Sophia's hand shot out to grab her, Alice wriggled backward, colliding with the knee of the general, who reared back in surprise. She was trapped!

She felt a hand seize her wrist. "No!" she cried, but then she heard Alex say urgently, "This way, sis!" He dragged her under the general's chair and, to the sound of startled gasps from those assembled in the room, they shot out from under the desk and bolted for the door set into the wall.

"Alex," Alice cried as they plunged into darkness. "Where are we?" She stumbled and almost lost her footing as the ground dropped away abruptly. They were on a set of stairs, she realized.

"Servants' stairs," said Alex, releasing her wrist. "Stay close."

Alice put one hand on the rough stone wall to guide her as she scampered down the winding stairs behind her brother. Above, she could hear Sophia's voice, sharper than usual.

"Where do the stairs lead, General?" Sophia demanded, her voice loud against the bare stone.

"I don't know," came back Ashwover's voice. "They're the old servants' stairs."

"Then they must lead to the servants' areas. Someone alert the guards." Sophia's voice was growing fainter the further Alice descended, but she clearly heard the silvery voice say, "I'm going after them."

"I'll wait here!" the general called after Sophia, as the stairwell above Alice echoed with the pounding of footsteps.

19

The Traitor

"A listair!" a voice cried. "What are you doing?"

Alistair started. It was Slippers Pink!

"Slippers! Keaters, it's okay—it's Slippers Pink." But when he glanced up at the window, the black mouse had vanished. "Keaters?"

"Alistair?" Slippers Pink was staring up at him in astonishment. "What are you doing up there?"

"Er, we were escaping," Alistair said. He looked at the balled-up scarf in his hand, then at the empty windowsill. "Me and Keaters. But he must have jumped. We thought you were the guards, you see."

"Keaters," Slippers sniffed. "I should have known." She rubbed the back of her neck reflectively. "Put your scarf back on, Alistair, and come down from there. We need to get moving."

Alistair hastily knotted his scarf around his neck and clambered down the metal slats.

"You've had a close call there, my boy," Slippers said when Alistair was standing on the floor in front of her. Her voice was grim, but she laid an affectionate hand on his shoulder.

"What do you mean?" Alistair asked.

"Keaters," Slippers growled. Then she held up a hand and peered around the edge of the doorway. "All clear. Right, follow me and I'll explain as we go."

They set off down the corridor, back the way they had come hours earlier, past cell after empty cell.

"Just as you entered the cell looking for Emmeline and Rebus, I saw a shadow move in the next cell along. I ducked into the nearest cell myself and waited, and sure enough I heard a cell door bang, and you call out, then I saw a mouse rush away down the corridor. I thought it was odd that he wasn't wearing a guard's uniform, so I followed him." She shook her head wearily. "I ended up chasing him all over the island. We had quite a tussle at the end. I wasn't able to make him talk." She rubbed her knuckles ruefully. "Probably because I had to knock him out so he didn't push me over a cliff. At least I got the key to the cell though."

As they reached the bottom of the stairs Alistair hastened toward the door, eager to leave the cold stone tower far behind him. But Slippers Pink grabbed his arm. "Wait," she said in a low voice. "We need a plan to get off this island. Since there is not another soul here, I'd presume Keaters and his accomplice arrived by the boat we saw."

"There's no one else?" said Alistair. "No one at all?"

"No guards, no prisoners," Slippers Pink confirmed. "Strange, huh?"

"Very," Alistair agreed. "So our plan is to take their boat?" He was relieved to hear that they wouldn't be returning via the underwater tunnel; he didn't think he could face it again.

"Before they do," said Slippers Pink. "And we don't have much time. Knowing Keaters, he won't bother looking for his accomplice; he'll only be interested in saving his own sorry skin. He's had a head start, and he'll be watching for us, which will make it all the harder."

"So what should we do?" asked Alistair.

"Look and listen," Slippers Pink explained.

They sat just inside the door to the tower, from where they had a good view of the reef below. The only sound was the waves crashing onto rocks.

Alistair was dying to ask Slippers about Keaters, but every time he opened his mouth to whisper the question she raised her slender hand and shook her head.

Many minutes passed, and then manymore, until Alistair was starting to feel sure that Keaters must have already left the island. Then Slippers Pink touched him lightly on the arm and pointed.

"There," she breathed.

Out of the shadows of the tower limped a small black mouse. He must have injured himself jumping from the second story of the tower, Alistair surmised.

"He was probably waiting for us to leave so he could

follow us," Slippers said. "I imagine he's still trying to catch you. Now he'll be thinking that we somehow slipped by him."

As the black mouse slid and stumbled down the cliff path, Slippers said, "Let's go after him—but quietly. The element of surprise is the only weapon we have."

They had just about caught up with Keaters when he stopped suddenly. Slippers ducked behind a rock, pulling Alistair down into a crouch beside her.

"What's he doing?" she asked. "Oh, I see." The black mouse had hidden the oars in a clump of gorse and was pulling them out.

"I'll take that," said Slippers Pink, stepping out from behind the rock and seizing one of the oars.

"You!" said Keaters.

"That's right," said Slippers pleasantly. "It's been a while, hasn't it, Keaters?"

"Not long enough," snarled the black mouse, raising the second oar above his head threateningly. "But here's a thought—maybe this mission doesn't have to be such a dead loss after all. How about you hand over the ginger brat or I'll bring this oar down on your head? Are you there, Alistair? Come on out like a good boy or I'll give your friend Slippers a nasty headache."

"Don't listen to him, Alistair," Slippers said quickly. "Stay where you are."

But Alistair had a better idea. Concealed by the rock, he slid off the path and clambered down, taking care not to disturb any loose rocks, until he was standing in the water lapping at the base of the cliff several meters below. From here, he began to wade unseen toward the boat.

"Still hesitating, Alistair?" said Keaters. "I have to tell you, I'm not all that keen on the pauses and hesitations. I prefer a decisive character, myself. I'll make it easy on you, okay? If you haven't come out by the time I count to three, Slippers will be having a nice long sleep. Like I did when the guards slipped something into my breakfast—oh wait, that's right. There were no guards. I made it all up." He laughed cruelly. "Just like I sawed through the bars of the cell so I could escape and leave you stranded there to die once you'd told me your secrets. So what are your secrets, hmm, Alistair? It's something to do with that scarf, isn't it? That scarf would be mine now if only Slippers Pink hadn't turned up. Still the same old spoilsport, aren't you, Slippers? Shall I just give her a little tap on the head, Alistair, or would you like to come save her?"

"Stay where you are, Alistair," Slippers repeated. "I've got an oar too and I've been looking forward to getting my own back on this miserable traitor for a long time. Just you try it, Keaters," she dared him.

Alistair reached the boat and tried to climb onto the path below the black mouse, but the wet rocks were slippery and he fell to his hands and knees, scrambling desperately to get to his feet.

"One . . . ," Keaters began. "Two . . . Decision time, Alistair."

With a desperate lunge, Alistair grabbed the black

mouse by the tail and yanked.

"Thr—ooph!" Keaters's feet shot out from under him and he landed heavily on his stomach. As he lay there, winded, Slippers Pink skipped neatly over his prone body, collecting the second oar on the way.

"Neatly done, Alistair," she complimented him. She climbed awkwardly into the boat. "Push us off, will you?" She maneuvered the oars into position as Alistair quickly untied the boat and gave it a shove until it was bobbing in deeper water. As he hauled himself into the boat Slippers began to row—though not very well, Alistair noted, as she pulled too hard on the left oar and sent them circling back toward the cliff.

"Perhaps I could do that," he offered.

"Ah yes," said Slippers Pink, handing him the oars. "I'd forgotten. You have quite a lot of rowing experience, don't you?"

"Too much," said Alistair.

As he pulled hard on the oars, pleased to see he hadn't lost the knack, he observed, "It looks like Keaters is getting up."

Slippers, who had her back to the shore, turned to watch. The shabby black mouse was shaking his fist at them. It looked like he was yelling something, but Alistair couldn't make out what.

"Good riddance," Slippers said. "Now somehow we need to get around to the other side of this cliff and back to the beach where Feast and Tibby are."

The next half-hour was a tense one, as Alistair put all

his strength into rowing against the current that tried to wash them back onto the rocks, while Slippers Pink watched for hazards and screamed directions over the sound of crashing surf.

"Head farther to your left," she called. "I think I see a channel."

Too breathless to turn around and see for himself, Alistair did as he was told.

"Now a hard right, but look sharp—the passage is pretty narrow."

Alistair's shoulders ached, but he continued to row hard through the pain. Within minutes the boat was scraping between two rocks and then, thankfully, they were in calm water, with the current pushing them forward. Alistair pulled up the oars and let the boat drift while he tried to catch his breath.

"Nice going," said Slippers Pink approvingly. "There's no way I could have handled that myself."

Alistair glowed at the compliment, glad to feel that he was contributing something useful after he'd been so foolish as to walk into Keaters's trap. He finally asked the question that had been on the tip of his tongue ever since Slippers had burst into the cell.

"How do you know Keaters? He said the two of you go way back."

"Keaters!" said Slippers Pink, and her voice was filled with contempt. "That double-crossing, two-faced toad. Ha! We go way back all right. I suppose he told you that we joined FIG together?" She looked at Alistair, who nodded. "Well, it's true, we did. But what I'll bet he didn't tell you was that he joined in order to spy on us. Oh, he was very clever about it. It was years before we worked out how it was that Queen Eugenia seemed able to anticipate our every move. By the time we worked out we had a traitor in our midst, it was too late." Slippers Pink fell silent. Her voice was heavy when at last she continued, "One of the people he betrayed was my dearest friend in the world. Another was Zanzibar."

"He . . . he's the one who betrayed Zanzibar?" Alistair's blood ran cold at the thought. "What did he want with me? He was going to leave me to die!"

Slippers didn't say anything, but shook her head.

"So the whole thing was a setup," said Alistair bitterly. "Him being in the cell where my parents were supposed to be, deciding we should try to escape. I was the one who thought of using the cot, but that was probably part of his plan too. And I walked straight into it." Alistair felt disgusted with himself. "It was all too easy when I think about it. Why though? Why go to all that trouble over me?"

Still Slippers was silent.

"Maybe," said Alistair slowly, recalling how insistent Keaters had been that Alistair throw him the scarf, "it wasn't me he wanted; it was my scarf. He knew it was important somehow." He clutched the ends protectively. He'd been so close to giving it up, too. If Slippers hadn't burst in . . . "So he didn't really share a cell with my parents then?"

"I doubt it," said Slippers.

"But he seemed to know so much about me."

"Mm," agreed Slippers Pink, her lips a tight line. "I'd love to know where he's getting his information."

As they drifted out of the channel, Alistair took up the oars again. If the channel came out where he thought, the beach was behind him and the cave near the rocks to his left.

Settling into a steady stroke, he considered what Slippers Pink had said. How had Keaters and his accomplice known that Alistair would be on Atticus Island? He ran through the possibilities. Althea? No, not possible. Billy Mac, then? Now that he thought about it, the fisherman hadn't been all that friendly, but he'd still agreed to take Alistair and Slippers Pink to the island. Maybe he was part of the trap too? It occurred to him that if this was the case, Tibby Rose and Feast Thompson might be in real trouble. He almost groaned aloud at the thought that after all the day's disappointments, it might yet grow a lot worse. He was about to mention his fears to Slippers Pink when suddenly she sat up straight and pointed.

"I think I see them."

Alistair craned his head around. Yes, there were two shadows, one large and one small, sitting at the far side of the cove. He corrected his course, then resumed rowing with increased vigor. It was possible that at least one thing might go right today.

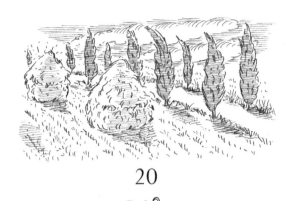

20

The Rendezvous

They burst through a door and found themselves in the kitchen. Alice looked around wildly for any sign of Queen's Guards, but all she saw was Cook, standing at the kitchen table. She had a faraway look in her eyes, as if she was still trying to comprehend the scene she had witnessed in General Ashwover's office. When she registered the presence of the two panting mice in her kitchen, she looked startled but not surprised.

"Who are you really?" she demanded. "You're not Sourian servants at all, are you?"

"No," managed Alice, still puffing. "We're Gerandans . . . undercover . . . and Sophia is right behind us."

"Get in here." Cook opened the oven door.

Alice was about to protest when she heard footsteps on the servants' stairs. She and Alex clambered in and Cook pushed the oven door shut. The oven was warm from recent use but not, Alice was relieved to find, hot. As she and Alex jostled for space it seemed that there were too many arms and legs and tails and ears to belong to only two mice, but at last they managed to curl up into two small neat balls. Even so it was a tight squeeze, and Alex's whiskers were poking into Alice's right ear in a most uncomfortable way.

"Oh, ma'am, thank goodness," came the distant sound of Cook's voice. "Those two horrible children were here. I went after them with my rolling pin but they got away."

Sophia's silvery voice sounded distorted from inside the oven. "Thank you, Cook, I—" She paused. "It certainly smells delicious in here," she remarked. "What's that over there on the dresser?"

"That's my blue cheese crumble," Cook replied.

Alice could feel her legs starting to cramp, but still Sophia continued to linger.

"And there . . . is that a chocolate cake?"

"A triple chocolate cheesecake."

"And in the oven?" Sophia asked. "I can just make out something through the glass. Two things, in fact . . ."

"The oven, ma'am?" Cook cleared her throat. "In the oven are two big ripe pumpkins."

"Pumpkins?" Sophia sounded surprised.

"That's right, ma'am. I'm making slow-roasted pumpkin confit, which I'll serve with goat's cheese. It's a Gerandan delicacy."

"A delicacy, you say? I adore delicacies. May I take a peek?"

"I'm sorry, ma'am," said Cook firmly, "but you know how it is with confits. They're very temperamental. If I open that door it'll dry those pumpkins right out and they'll be ruined. Then the general will be upset, on account of he wants this dinner to be absolutely perfect for you. And if the general is upset, that Lester will make a slow-roasted confit of my head."

"I quite understand," Sophia assured her. "I'll leave you in peace. I have the utmost respect for the careful preparation of meals. Now, about those little brats . . ."

"They went that way!" said Cook. "You'd better hurry."

"Oh, there's no need to rush," said Sophia casually, sauntering toward the door. "I'll get them in the end. They know that as well as I do."

In the close dark space of the oven, Alice couldn't repress a shiver.

Seconds later, Cook opened the oven door and Alice and Alex climbed out. As they were shaking their limbs to try to restore blood flow, they heard someone clump up the back steps. Alice squeaked in terror as the back door opened.

Fiercely Jones pushed his hat back on his head and regarded Alice and Alex balefully.

"The Queen's Guards have turned my potting shed upside down looking for you." He advanced on them threateningly. "I'll keep a watch on 'em, Cook, and make sure they don't escape. You run for the guards."

Cook moved to stand between the gardener and his erstwhile helpers. "Fiercely, wait—you don't understand.

Raz and Rita aren't Sourian at all; they're Gerandan."

The gardener stopped short. "What?"

"The Queen's Guards are after them because they're spies. We can't turn them in."

Fiercely Jones squinted at Alex and Alice down his long nose.

"Is this true?" he asked them.

The two young mice nodded vigorously.

"We're not really called Raz and Rita. We were sent by—" Alice stopped. Should she reveal who they were and what their mission was?

"Sent by who?" Fiercely was clearly suspicious.

Alice and her brother exchanged glances.

"FIG," said Alice.

"FIG?" said Cook. "But that's Zanzibar's resistance group."

"Zanzibar is still in hiding, of course, since he escaped from prison," Alice explained, "but—"

"Wait," the gardener interrupted. "Do you mean to say that Zanzibar is free?"

"That's right. He escaped from the Cranken prison and—"

"He's free!" Cook hugged herself gleefully.

Alice glanced around nervously, mindful of Lester's uncanny way of appearing soundlessly. "I think we'd better get out of here," she said.

"Of course," said Cook immediately. "Fiercely, we have to help them."

"Wait here," said the gardener. "I'll be back in a jiffy."

Then he pulled his hat down over his eyes once more and slunk out.

"You really shouldn't have written FIG in the icing though," Cook scolded. "You wouldn't have been caught if not for that. And you almost got me into terrible trouble."

"But it wasn't us," Alice protested.

"It wasn't you?" said Cook, astonished. "But who else could it possibly have been? You don't mean to tell me there are other Gerandan spies in the palace?"

"No . . . At least, I don't think so." Tobias had said that FIG was having trouble infiltrating the palace, hadn't he? She wasn't sure of anything anymore.

All three paced the kitchen anxiously, until finally they heard a squeal and a clunk outside the kitchen door. Cook opened the door a crack and peered out, then gestured to Alice and Alex. It was Fiercely Jones, pushing a wheelbarrow full of manure. The sound they had heard was the wheelbarrow's squeaky wheel.

"What are you doing moving manure around now?" asked Cook. "You were meant to be finding a way out of here for Raz and Rita."

"This is their way out of here," returned the gardener.

"Pushing a wheelbarrow of manure?" asked Cook.

"In the manure," said Fiercely Jones.

Alice groaned.

"Isn't there another way?" Alex asked.

"None that I can think of," said the gardener. "Get in, and be quick about it."

Hidden in the manure it was just how Alice had

dreamed it. Her nose and ears were soon clogged with the foul-smelling substance. All she could do was keep her eyes shut tight and try to breathe as shallowly as possible so as not to inhale manure into her lungs.

Then they began to move. Slowly, it seemed to Alice, so slowly. Was the gardener taking them on a tour of the palace grounds? Why was it taking so long? Finally the wheelbarrow began to rattle and bump, as if they were crossing gravel.

"Aren't you going the wrong way with that, Jones?" Alice could just make out Wooster's voice through the manure in her ears.

"No, sir," said the gardener, his tone aggrieved. "As if it's not enough that I have two hundred and thirty-eight flowerbeds to attend to in the palace grounds, now Mr. Lester's wanting purple flowers growing around the city walls. Meanwhile, those two useless helpers he gave me have skived off somewhere, and I have to shift all this manure myself."

"It's no wonder those helpers were useless—they weren't really servants at all. They were Gerandan spies!"

"You don't say," said Fiercely Jones in an uninterested voice.

"And I'm the one who escorted them into the palace," said Wooster. He sounded quite proud of himself.

"But don't you worry," said his partner confidently. "There's no way they'll slip by us."

"That's a comfort, ma'am," said the gardener. And then they were on the move again, bumping over cobblestones before passing smoothly over the planks of the bridge on the far side of the square.

"Fiercely, was it you who spelled out FIG in the flowerbed?" Alex asked as they trundled along.

"It was not," came the gardener's definite reply. "Why would I want to be drawing attention to myself like that?"

"Then who—"

"Quiet," Fiercely Jones growled. "I can't walk down the street talking to a heap of manure. People will think I've gone crackers."

From then on they were wheeled in silence, the only words exchanged being those between the gardener and the guards standing sentry at the city gate.

Inside the manure, it was growing decidedly hot, and Alice was just starting to remember hearing stories about how things could actually be cooked in manure when the wheelbarrow trundled to a stop.

"All right, you can get out here," came the voice of Fiercely Jones, and then the wheelbarrow was tipped up, depositing Alice, Alex, and a heap of manure by a simple stone bridge which crossed a shallow stream. "We came out the south gate, and if you follow this here stream to the east you'll get to the Winns."

"Thank you!" Alice called, as the gruff old gardener turned the wheelbarrow around and headed back in the direction they'd come.

Fiercely Jones didn't respond, merely raised a hand without looking back.

"Last one in's a rotten egg," said Alex, looking

longingly at the clear stream. Then, wrinkling his nose as he regarded his manure-covered fur, he added, "Of course, we already smell worse than rotten eggs."

The two reeking mice slid down the bank toward the water, and were about to dive in when Alice put up a hand to stop her brother. She'd heard a shout in the distance.

"Quick," she said. "Hide under the bridge."

The voice grew closer, still shouting, and Alice could make out the distinctive rhythm of boots marching in time.

"It's a Sourian patrol," she breathed.

"Left, left, left, right, left . . ."

Then the boots were on the bridge, clip-clopping on the wooden boards, and she heard someone mutter in an undertone, "What's that disgusting smell?"

She held her breath until she heard a voice reply, "It must be the river. Eeeuw! I've heard a lot of bad things about Gerander, but I never expected the rivers to stink."

"No surprise really," said the mouse who had first commented.

"I suppose," said the second.

And then they were gone.

When the clatter of heels had faded, Alice and Alex walked into the river and hastily washed the manure off their fur. Then they crossed the bridge and set off down the road, which followed the course of the stream, walking briskly, but not so briskly that they were in danger of catching up with the patrol.

Finally, Alice was able to share some of the thoughts

and fears that had been occupying her mind since they had overheard Sophia and the others in General Ashwover's office.

"Alex," she said, "did you hear what Sophia was saying about the ginger brat with the scarf? That must be Alistair!"

"I don't know," said Alex. "Maybe they were talking about another ginger mouse with a scarf. Why would Alistair be an heir of Cornolius and not us?" He had clearly been doing some thinking too. "And I should think I'd know if I was an heir of Cornolius."

"Maybe we are," Alice said slowly. "Remember how Lester talked to Sophia about settling old scores? And then, when she saw us under the desk, she didn't seem all that surprised. It's as if we were already on her mind. And Lester—remember all those questions he asked about our father and about Tornley? It's like he suspected we weren't who we said we were and he was trying to trap us. But why should he suspect us?"

"Which leads us to the most important question," Alex said. "Who's the traitor? Who's Songbird?"

They walked on and on, the stream burbling away beside them, speculating as to Songbird's identity, but not getting anywhere.

"The only thing we know for sure," said Alice finally, the realization yawning before her like a dark abyss, "is that Songbird knows a lot about FIG's operations."

"We know one other thing," Alex reminded her. "We know that the Sourians have a hostage. It must be that mouse I saw in the dungeon."

Alice put a hand to her mouth. "You're right!" She stopped. "Maybe we should have tried to rescue him?"

Alex grabbed her arm to hurry her along. "Keep walking, sis. We've lost our chance." His voice was somber. "There's no way we can get back into the palace now. And you've forgotten something: we need to get back to Stetson as quick as we can. We have to let FIG know that someone called Keaters has set a trap for Alistair and that Zanzibar is in danger—before it's too late."

They picked up their pace as the road swept around to the left, then ended at an intersection with a larger road.

"I know this road," Alice said when she had glanced left and right. "It's the one we walked along the night we first arrived in Gerander. That hill in the distance there, away to the left, that's where Captain Scorpio's camp is. If we turn right, it'll take us almost all the way to the field where Claudia let us off." She looked over her shoulder to where the sun was creeping toward the horizon. "I just hope we make it there by sunset."

"Let's pick up the pace then," said her brother, and they began to run, passing golden fields, some newly shorn and dotted with haystacks and others screened from the road with cypress trees.

"I think the field where we're meeting Claudia is just up ahead," Alice panted. "The silhouette of those cypresses looks familiar."

They were almost to it when, in the distance, they saw a block of red coming toward them.

"It's another patrol," said Alex with a weary groan. As they darted off the road and into the nearest field he urged, "Into that haystack, sis." And they dived in.

The hay poked at Alice's arms and legs, making her itch, and she wriggled in discomfort.

"Keep still," Alex hissed. He was peering at the road, and Alice shifted forward till she too had a clear view.

The patrol was getting closer, and Alice's heart almost stopped when she realized that the guards were actually searching the haystacks. Had they been seen? She watched in horror as a guard suddenly plunged his spear into a neighboring haystack. "Alex, look!"

"Uh-oh! This way," said Alex, and the two of them backed out of the haystack—right into a pair of Queen's Guards.

"Ha!" the first guard crowed. "I told the sergeant I saw a couple of mice running for the haystacks."

"Didn't think we were smart enough to look on both sides of them, eh?" said the other.

"Papers," the first one demanded, holding out a hand.

"We, er, we don't have any," said Alex.

"Don't have any papers?" The guard smiled, showing a row of pointed teeth. "Then you are in a sticky situation, aren't you?" He called over his shoulder, "Sergeant! Over here, sir."

The rest of the patrol rounded the haystack, and now Alice and Alex were surrounded by six red-coated guards, each holding a spear in a threatening pose.

"They were backing out of this haystack, and they don't

have any papers," said the sharp-toothed guard. "They're in a lot of trouble, aren't they, Sergeant?"

"I'll say they are," said the sergeant. "Who are you, and what are you up to?"

"We're . . . we're. . . ." Alex stopped.

As the guards drew closer, looking ever more menacing, Alice did the only thing that occurred to her: she burst into tears.

The guards looked taken aback.

"Stop that," the sergeant ordered, but Alice didn't.

"It's all my fault," she sobbed. "We're orphans, you see, and we were sent from Souris to work in the palace. . . ."

Through her tear-filled eyes she saw that most of the guards had lowered their spears.

"But L-l-lester . . . ," she hiccoughed.

"Yes?" said the sergeant, leaning forward. "Lester?"

"Lester was so mean that we . . . that we . . . ran away," Alice finished with a wail.

The sergeant straightened. "Ha," she said. "Don't talk to me about Lester. I was posted to the palace for a year, and I found myself hoping that a Gerandan spy would sneak in and assassinate him."

"Please don't send us back there," Alex begged, putting an arm around Alice's shoulder as she continued to whimper. "We just want to go home to our grandparents in Tornley."

The sergeant tilted her head to one side to study them for a moment, then nodded. "Okay. As far as I'm concerned, we never saw you."

"But we'll have to put it in the report, Sergeant," said the mouse with the sharp teeth.

"Put what in the report, Ringbark?" asked the sergeant.

"About the two mice that we found hiding in the haystack," said Ringbark.

"What two mice?" said the sergeant, tipping a wink at Alice and Alex, who crept silently backward until they were hidden in the haystack once more. The other guards were trying to stifle their laughter.

"Those two mice!" shouted Ringbark in frustration, turning to point at the spot where Alice and Alex had stood.

As Alice and Alex pushed their way through the other side of the haystack and took off down the road, they could hear the roars of laughter of the patrol.

When at last they pelted between the trees at the edge of the field where they would rendezvous with Claudia in the balloon, Alice turned toward the west and caught the glint of the sun above the trees.

"We've made it!" said Alice, and Alex punched the air with his fist. "Yes! Stetson here we come!"

Then there was a movement in front of them, and another kind of glint. With a sickening sense of dread, Alice recognized the silvery gray mouse who stepped out from behind a slender trunk, recognized the silvery glint of metal from the knife in her hand. Sophia.

Alice looked around wildly, thinking to turn back, only to see a coal-black figure with a mournful expression step out of the shadows behind them. It was Horace.

"I wouldn't bother running," Sophia said. "I think you'll find Queen's Guards treat FIG spies with rather less sympathy than Sourian orphans. My bag, please, Horace dear."

Horace hurried over, carrying Sophia's large bag. Still holding the knife, and with her gaze fixed firmly on her two captives, Sophia fished in her bag and produced a coil of rope.

"Tie them up, will you, dear?" she said to Horace.

"You won't get away with—" Alex began, as Horace wound the rope around his wrists, but Sophia interrupted him.

"Please spare me the clichés," she said with a yawn. "I'm really not interested in anything you have to say." She peered into the depths of her bag and produced two lace handkerchiefs with the letter *S* embroidered in one corner.

She shoved one into Alice's mouth, the other into Alex's.

"You know, Horace dear, what I really don't like about these two—and there are many, many things," she added, looking at her captives with distaste, "is the amount of extra work they cause us. Now I suppose we'll have to go all the way back to the palace with them. What a bore. Unless . . ." Her expression brightened and she asked, "Horace, I don't suppose you remembered to pack my magic carpet, did you?"

"Your magic . . . ?" Horace cast an anxious glance at the bag. "I'm sorry, Sophia, I . . ." Horace stopped. "That was a joke, wasn't it?" he said gloomily. "I wish you wouldn't do that."

Sophia laughed delightedly. "There, there, Horace. I'm only teasing. You couldn't possibly believe that I own a magic carpet!"

Alice knew how Horace felt. She didn't believe in magic carpets herself, yet she wouldn't have been at all surprised to find out that Sophia had one.

"It would be handy to fly, though," the silvery mouse said thoughtfully. "I don't suppose you two know where we could find a hot-air balloon?"

It was as if the silvery mouse was a mind reader, Alice thought in dismay. Or . . . as if she knew about their rendezvous. But how could she? And then Alice remembered: Songbird. The traitorous Songbird who was revealing all FIG's secrets to the Sourians must have told Sophia and Horace about the hot-air balloon, which would land in the field at sunset.

Almost as soon as she'd had the thought a big blue shape appeared over the trees. Oh no! Go back, Claudia. Alice put all her energy into the thought, willing the pilot to turn around lest she be caught too.

Sophia looked up. "Now I wonder who this could be?"

Alice watched mutely as the unsuspecting pilot worked the rope to let hot air out of the valve and the balloon began to descend. Down, down, down . . . and she saw that the pilot didn't have the tan-spotted fur of Claudia. No, this pilot was white. And with a sudden jolt she recognized him: the pilot was Solomon Honker! They were saved!

She turned to look at her brother, widening her eyes and raising her eyebrows to indicate her relief. If anyone could take on Sophia and Horace it was Solomon Honker.

The balloon bumped along the ground and came to a stop a few meters away. Solomon Honker switched off the burner and climbed out of the basket as the balloon slowly began to deflate.

As he walked toward them, Alice thought he looked different somehow. He wasn't wearing a bow tie, for one thing, and he didn't have either the cantankerous expression of their teacher or the friendly demeanor he'd had when they saw him in the cafeteria. If anything, he seemed more like the serious mouse who had bid them farewell in Stetson. But when he spoke, his manner was decidedly jaunty, and his words stunned Alice with the force of an electric shock.

"Anyone need a lift to Grouch?"

21

Back to the Source

"Alistair! Oh, I'm so happy you're okay."

Alistair climbed out of the boat and waded through the shallows onto the shore where Tibby Rose was waiting impatiently.

"You were gone so long and I thought—" She didn't finish her sentence, but threw her arms around him. "I just couldn't bear it if anything had happened to you." Then she took a step backward. "But, Alistair, where are your parents?"

Alistair felt as if the sand he was standing on was about to cave in. Since the moment he had discovered Keaters in the corner of the cell, his focus had been on escape— escape from the cell, escape from Atticus Island. He hadn't thought ahead to this moment, when he would be standing on a beach, having returned from Atticus Island . . . without his parents. He opened his mouth to speak—then found he couldn't. The words wouldn't come.

"Alistair?" Tibby's voice was quieter now, her eyes filled with concern.

"They . . . they . . . they weren't there," he croaked finally, his words barely carrying over the pounding of the surf. Suddenly he was aware of a chill breeze ruffling his salt-encrusted fur, and he began to tremble with the cold. "Th-th-they . . . they weren't there, Tibby." And now his voice was cracking.

He felt a warm, solid hand on his shoulder and looked up into the sympathetic gaze of Feast Thompson. "They weren't there, Feast. They weren't there!" He was trembling violently now, his body so racked with shivers he could barely stand. The crashing waves, the wind, the sand beneath his feet all seemed to recede.

As if from a great distance he heard Slippers Pink say, "Feast, quick, catch him. I think he's going into shock."

He wanted to assure them that he was okay, but he felt so far away from his legs, his voice, that he didn't know how. And then a black fog engulfed his brain and he was falling.

When he opened his eyes he was lying beside a crackling fire, staring at the shadows of flames as they flickered on a wall of rock. He lay quietly for a few moments, taking in the scene. Tibby was sitting next to him, a book in her hands, his scarf stretched across her knees. The colors glowed in the firelight, and Alistair knew she must have washed it. On the other side of the fire, Slippers Pink and

Feast Thompson were talking in low voices.

"Good book?" Alistair rasped.

Tibby glanced down and saw his open eyes and smiled.

"Great book," she said, slamming it shut.

He sat up, swaying for a moment as a wave of dizziness washed over him.

"Where are we?"

The hum of conversation from Slippers and Feast had stopped, and his voice sounded uncommonly loud, echoing in the stone chamber.

"Hey there, stranger," said Slippers softly. "How are you feeling?"

"I'm okay," said Alistair, though it wasn't exactly true. He felt numb, like all the emotion had been wrung out of him leaving him dry and empty.

"We're back in the tunnel," Feast told him.

"Feast carried you all the way," Tibby chimed in. "While you two were on Atticus Island, we did a bit of exploring, and we found a path through the scrub that meant we could get back to the tunnel without having to go through the town."

"After you fainted, we decided we'd better make a hasty exit from the beach in case Keaters and his friend had a rendezvous planned with the Queen's Guards," Slippers explained.

Alistair nodded. It made sense. Keaters was working for the Sourians, after all.

"So what do we do now?" asked Tibby.

"We have to go to the Cranken Alps," Alistair broke in.

"To the prison there. That's where my parents are now," Keaters said."

"Alistair," Slippers said in a reasonable tone, "we can't go to the Crankens. It's too dangerous."

"But we have to rescue them," Alistair protested. "That's our mission."

"Our mission was to find the secret paths and rescue Emmeline and Rebus from Atticus Island," Slippers corrected him. "We've found the secret paths and we've been to Atticus Island."

"But my parents . . ." Alistair could hear how his voice was rising, and struggled to control it. "Tibby and I have crossed the Crankens before," he said. "We can do it again."

"But you were lucky, Alistair," Slippers pointed out. "You only had to traverse a couple of valleys. The prison is deep in the mountains, and none of us is equipped for that."

"Nor are we equipped to take on a whole garrison of Queen's Guards," Feast added.

"Besides," Slippers continued, "we don't even know if Emmeline and Rebus are there."

"Keaters said they were," Alistair argued.

"Keaters is not exactly renowned for his honesty," Feast observed drily.

"But if they're not there," Alistair began, then stopped. If his parents weren't in prison in the Crankens, where were they? He had been told they were alive and in prison on Atticus Island. If they weren't really in prison on Atticus Island, did that mean . . . ? He swallowed as his mind followed the sentence through to its logical conclusion. Did that mean they weren't really alive?

Shoulders slumped, he stared into the fire as Slippers said, "We walked into an elaborately constructed trap. The question is, how did Keaters know we were coming?"

"There's that leak Tobias was talking about." Feast sighed heavily. "If even Timmy the Winns can be caught . . ."

Alistair slumped further at the reminder of Timmy the Winns.

"We have to face the fact that no FIG operation will be safe until that leak is plugged," Slippers said. She stood up. "We have to go back to Stetson and tell Tobias what happened," she decided. "Until we know who the traitor is, it's just too risky to continue."

"And if the traitor is in Stetson?" Feast asked.

Slippers shuddered. "That's just too dreadful to contemplate."

Alistair shuddered too. Alex, Alice, and his aunt and uncle—possibly all the family he had left—were in Stetson. He got to his feet. "Let's hurry," he said.

If the others were surprised by his change of heart, no one said anything. Tibby handed Alistair his scarf, their rucksacks were hastily repacked and the fire quenched, all in silence.

When they had shouldered their packs, Feast took a candle from the niche in the wall, lit it, and led the way down the dark passage, followed by Tibby, then Alistair with Slippers Pink bringing up the rear.

As they retraced their steps, a journey that he had been expecting to make with his parents, Alistair realized that despite the crushing disappointment of returning without them he was lucky to be returning at all. Because of him, he and Slippers nearly hadn't made it back.

He slowed his pace a little so that he and Slippers Pink lagged a bit behind the others. "Slippers," he said quietly over his shoulder to the shadowy figure behind him, "when we were back on the island—I'm sorry that I didn't listen when you told me to wait."

"It's okay, Alistair," she said kindly. "I understand. You thought you were going to see your parents. You were thinking with your heart and not your head. That's the hardest part about the kind of struggle we're engaged in—learning when to think with your heart and when with your head. Sometimes I wonder if Tobias did the right thing sending you on this mission."

Alistair hung his head miserably. He didn't blame Slippers for thinking that after he'd messed up so badly.

But she continued, "Not because I think you've done anything wrong—just because it is so very difficult to think with your head and not your heart when loved ones are involved." Then she said in a voice so soft Alistair thought she must be talking to herself, "Believe me, I know."

They walked on in silence until they reached the fork in the tunnel where Althea had left them. Tibby pointed to the patterns she and the older mouse had traced in the dirt floor with their feet.

"I hope Althea made it home all right. It sounded like she had a long way to go."

As did they. Without anticipation to spur him on, the underground miles seemed endless to Alistair. For most of the time Tibby walked beside him, and though they didn't speak much, her presence was comforting. His despair weighed on him like a heavy burden, one that never lifted and threatened occasionally to overwhelm him.

"It's like my parents have died all over again," he confided to Tibby, his voice tight from the constriction in his chest.

She said nothing, just put a small, warm hand on his shoulder until he was breathing easily again.

For two days they walked underground, and the shadowy, subterranean path fitted Alistair's dark, heavy mood. Eventually, small landmarks they had noted in their first hours in the tunnel, days before, told them they must be getting close to the cavern near the source: a sharp rock protruding knee-high in the center of the path; a patch of feathery tree roots growing through the roof of the tunnel to brush the tops of their heads. Slippers raised the question which had been at the back of Alistair's mind, though he had feared to voice it.

"I wonder if Oswald will be there?"

For of course if Oswald didn't appear at the rendezvous point, they had no certain way of getting back to Stetson—and none of them knew if Oswald had even survived the eagles' attack.

"Let's cross that bridge when we come to it," Feast suggested.

At long last they reached the cavern where the tunnel began and squeezed through the entrance one by one into the warm still air of early evening.

Blinking in the unaccustomed light, Alistair's heavy heart immediately felt lighter as he breathed in the scent of the Winns, so sweet compared to the dank mustiness underground. The tops of the trees on the opposite bank were rimmed with gold from the setting sun and the sky above was a clear cloudless blue. The broad river reflected the sky so that the sense of air and spaciousness seemed endless after the closeness of the tunnel.

Gazing at the scene, Alistair had the strangest feeling that time had stood still while they'd been gone; that all of it—the tunnel, Althea and Billy Mac, the frightening swim, and the terrible events of Atticus Island—had been a bad dream. He turned to look at the ridge behind him, the last sliver of sun just skimming its top, and even as he watched he saw a gold sheen wash across the rock face, saw the bush appear to ignite in flame.

As they retraced their steps north, toward the river's source, everything looked much as they'd left it—the reeds still swayed, the cicadas hummed undisturbed, the old stone house slumbered on—until, finally, they reached the source of the Winns. Alistair rubbed the fur on his arms as he felt the chill emanating from the pool.

The sun had disappeared behind the ridge and the sky was a deep violet, the pines etched in black against it.

"Oswald?" Slippers Pink called softly. There was a rattle of leaves in the treetops as if in reply, but there was no answering hoot, no rush of wind as a large brown bird swooped from a branch.

Slippers let out a heavy breath which sounded close to despair, but Feast said, "At least wait till the moon has risen before we give up on him, Slips. You know Oswald likes the companionship of the moon when he travels. Alistair, Tibby Rose, why don't you fetch some firewood?"

The two ginger mice headed into the trees at the northern edge of the clearing and began to collect kindling.

"What do you think we'll do if Oswald doesn't come?" Tibby asked in an undertone.

Alistair snapped a long stick in half and placed it in his friend's outstretched arms. "I don't know, Tib. I don't even know if there is another way." A twig became caught in the ends of his scarf; as he was untangling it he had a thought. "Unless—" He was about to suggest that there might be a secret path they could use. Hadn't Althea said that she lived to the east of the Winns? Perhaps there were paths on the other side of the river, maybe even one that led to the border with Shetlock? But his thoughts were interrupted by a murmuring, and as Tibby said, "Unless what?" he put a hand on her shoulder and a finger to his lips to silence her. "Listen," he breathed in her ear, and felt her stiffen in alarm.

That murmuring—was it coming from the trickle of water that slipped down the hillside to the south of the clearing to become the river? No, it was coming from the other direction, from above them. As the murmur grew more distinct, Alistair felt a jab of fear between his shoulder blades. It was voices he could hear, and that could only mean one thing.

On trembling legs he and Tibby Rose picked their way between the trees and undergrowth back to the clearing, careful not to step on any dry twigs, barely daring to exhale lest the rustle of leaves alert the Sourians to their presence.

Together they tiptoed back into the clearing to alert Slippers Pink and Feast Thompson.

With a few quick gestures, Feast signaled that they should take their rucksacks and hide in the bushes on the far side of the pool. By the time the voices reached the clearing, there was no trace of the FIG members.

Through the leaves of the bush he was crouched behind, Alistair could make out the silhouettes of four mice.

"Is this the place?" said a deep voice.

"I think so," came a gravelly reply. "The sarge reckoned he saw an owl coming and going."

"But how does he know it's their owl?" a third voice squeaked.

"Well, if it's an owl, it has to be theirs, doesn't it?" said Gravelly Voice.

"All owls look alike to me," yawned a fourth voice.

"So what do we do now?" Deep Voice asked. "I don't see any owl."

"We wait," said Gravelly.

And wait they did, while the four Queen's Guards moaned about having been chosen for this task, talked about their teams' chances in the Sourian Football League, and jumped at the sight of any winged creature, from blackbird to dragonfly.

As the moon crept above the trees, bathing the clearing in a cool silver light, Alistair wished he could shift position to avoid the sharp branch scratching at his leg, but he didn't dare make any movement that might draw the attention of the guards to their hiding spot. Now that the first rush of fear had passed, he was feeling more impatient and uncomfortable than frightened. Something tickled his nose and he brushed at it in irritation; it floated to the ground. Curious, he picked it up. It was a feather. Where had that come from? There'd been no sign of birds in the trees surrounding them. He glanced up but couldn't see anything in the shadows above.

He handed the feather to Tibby, who was next to him. Her eyes widened, and she passed it to Slippers. Slippers looked around Tibby to Alistair, who shrugged and pointed into the treetops. Slippers tilted her head back and gazed searchingly but didn't appear to find anything. As the voices of the guards droned on, though, she continued to hold the feather, stroking it absentmindedly and occasionally lifting her head to peer into the shadows above.

After what seemed like an eternity, Gravelly said in a bored tone, "This is a waste of time, there's nothing here."

"But the sarge said—" began Squeaky.

"I don't care what the sarge said. He was probably just trying to get rid of us so there'd be more cheesecake for him."

"Cheesecake?" Yawning Voice sounded alert now.

"That's what they were serving in the mess for dessert tonight," said Gravelly casually.

"Do you mean to tell me I've been sitting out here eating field rations while the sarge is eating my share of cheesecake?" Deep Voice demanded.

"Of all the low, mean acts," snarled Yawning Voice, standing up. "I'm going back to the mess to get my share of cheesecake."

"Me too," said Deep Voice, springing to his feet

Gravelly, who had egged them on, rose and stretched and said, "Well, if you really think so . . ."

As they crashed through the trees and back up the hillside, Alistair could just hear Squeaky protesting, "But the sarge . . ." as the voices retreated.

When the voices had been swallowed up by the night, the four mice in the bushes stood, stretching their limbs and brushing twigs from their fur, and walked into the center of the clearing.

"Oswald?" Slippers called, and Alistair's heart soared in symphony with the movement of the giant bird who swooped down to join them.

The owl looked bedraggled, Alistair thought, his

feathers ruffled and patchy, but his hooded eyes gleamed with something akin to pleasure as he regarded the four mice.

"We haven't got time to stand around talking," he said gruffly. "Tobias needs you back. Glad to see you're all here."

"We're glad to see you, Os." Slippers ran her hand briefly along the owl's wing.

"Let's not risk anymore separations," Oswald proposed. "It'll mean a slower flight, but I will carry the four of you together."

"Are you sure, Os?" Feast asked, concerned. "That's a heavy load."

The owl simply inclined his head.

Tibby Rose moved over to stand close to Slippers Pink, who had her eyes closed and her face screwed up as if she was concentrating fiercely on something very important. It reminded Alistair of the expression Alex sometimes wore when Uncle Ebenezer asked him whether he'd prefer a chocolate and blue cheese brownie or a strawberry and Parmesan muffin in his school lunchbox— though he suspected Slippers was thinking of air sickness rather than cakes.

Feast Thompson pulled Alistair into position so they were standing side by side, rucksacks securely over their shoulders. Alistair noticed that Feast had crossed his arms over his body so that each hand touched the opposite shoulder, and he did the same.

Oswald lifted off the ground to hover above them, and

carefully closed each talon around a pair of mice in a tight grip. Minutes later, they were airborne, the darkened landscape, moonlit, passing beneath them in a blur of black and white.

He couldn't have said how long their journey took, but Alistair noticed that the beat of the owl's wings, which had once seemed so strong and sure, seemed tremulous, subject to every eddy and whim of the wind.

At last, though, they began to descend, and as the school on the hilltop above Stetson came into view Alistair finally allowed himself to anticipate the joyous reunion with his family. For the first time since he entered the prison cell on Atticus Island and found that his parents were not in it, he felt happiness welling up inside him.

When the owl had set his passengers on the ground and released his grip, Alistair asked, "Do you think they'll be in the cafeteria, Tib, or back at the dormitory?"

But before his friend could answer Flanagan appeared from the shadows.

"I'm afraid your family will have to wait," the dark gray mouse said. "Tobias wants to see you straight away. Oswald, you're to wait here. You're still needed."

Before any of them could protest, Flanagan was ushering them toward the school office. They passed several mice along the way, but there was no time to stop and talk as Flanagan hurried them up the steps, down the corridor and into the principal's office, where Tobias, looking more weary than ever, was waiting.

"Tobias, please," Slippers began, as soon as the door

closed behind them, "can't the debrief wait till morning? Or at least let Alistair and Tibby Rose go find their family." She glanced at Alistair and lowered her voice. "The mission to rescue Emmeline and Rebus did not go well."

"I'm sorry to hear it," Tobias said gravely, and his expression was indeed sorrowful. "And yes, the debrief can wait—but this can't: Alistair, Tibby Rose, I have another mission for you, and you need to leave immediately."

Alistair stared at the older mouse in disbelief. "Another mission? But we just got back! Can't I at least see—"

"There's no time," said the marmalade mouse harshly. "It's urgent."

"Tobias, they're exhausted, Alistair has had a terrible shock . . . and there's the leak. We were almost caught in a Sourian trap: they knew exactly where we'd be and why. Surely no one should be sent on any missions until—"

But Tobias cut her off too.

"We have no choice, Slippers. Zanzibar himself has ordered it. Slippers, Feast, I need to speak to Alistair and Tibby alone, if you don't mind."

But no sooner had Slippers Pink and Feast Thompson left the room and been swept away by Flanagan than Tobias was on his feet, urging Alistair and Tibby Rose out into the corridor.

"I have here a letter for you to deliver," he explained rapidly, handing Alistair an envelope as they strode outside and down toward the oval. "Oswald will tell you more when you get to your destination."

It was all happening so fast Alistair's head was spinning. He and Tibby Rose had made it back to Stetson, only to be sent off on another mission immediately? By themselves? And on Zanzibar's orders? He had a thousand questions, but as he watched Tobias whisper instructions to Oswald, he didn't dare ask any of them. As the owl tilted his great head quizzically, Alistair turned to Tibby, who looked as mystified and apprehensive as he felt.

Then Tobias turned to nod at them curtly, the owl enclosed them in his vicelike grip, and they were airborne once more.

As they soared above the school, Alistair caught sight of Tobias. To his surprise, the marmalade mouse wasn't walking back to his office. He appeared to be heading toward the road—at a run.

22

Songbird

Grouch?! If Alice could have gasped without inhaling a mouthful of lace handkerchief she would have. Why on earth was Solomon Honker planning to take the balloon to the capital of Souris? His next words surprised her even more.

"Sophia," said Solomon Honker. "You're looking as lovely as ever."

As Sophia stroked her whiskers vainly, Alice and Alex exchanged a wide-eyed look, then gaped at their teacher. The realization filled Alice with a dark, cold dread: Solomon Honker was Songbird.

"Hello, Horace. Feeling chipper, are you?"

The coal-black mouse regarded the rusty-orange and white one glumly. "Hello, Solomon. Couldn't be better."

"So, four passengers then? I'll crank up the inflator fan." As the balloon began to fill, Sophia explained to her captives, "Solomon taught me everything I know about spycraft—which, as I'm sure you'll agree, is a lot."

"Now, Sophia, you're being too modest, as usual," chided Solomon Honker. "I dare say I learned one or two things from you. You always were my best pupil. And you've captured the brats, I see."

"Yes," said Sophia, looking at Alice and Alex almost fondly. "I found them at the palace in Cornoliana. It was quite serendipitous meeting them the way we did. We had some unfinished business."

Alice had a sudden image of the flash of a knife blade and struggled against her bonds.

His eye must have been caught by the movement, for Solomon said, "Wriggly, aren't they? I'm going to secure them to the basket so they don't get any ideas about throwing themselves overboard when we take off."

He hefted Alex over his shoulder like a sack of potatoes, while Horace lifted Alice, and the two captives were soon tied to the inside of the basket.

And then they were lifting off, the balloon almost brushing the tips of the cypress trees at the edge of the field. The last traces of red and orange to the west, the dying embers of a fiery sunset, told Alice that they were headed east—to Souris.

For a while Sophia seemed content just to lean over the edge of the basket, watching the darkening landscape go by, while Horace, who didn't like heights, huddled at the bottom of the basket looking queasy. When Sophia finally tired of the view, she turned to face her fellow passengers.

"So what have you been up to lately, Solomon?" asked

Sophia above the hiss of the burner.

"Oh, this and that," said Solomon vaguely.

"I understand," said Sophia. "Can't tell, eh?"

Solomon smiled. "You know how it is. What about you?"

Sophia smiled mysteriously. "This and that," she echoed. Then, with a small smirk of triumph, "Let's just say we've got Zanzibar exactly where we want him."

"Is that so?" Solomon let out an admiring whistle. "How did you manage that?"

But Sophia just tapped the side of her elegant nose in a knowing way. "Why don't you tell us what you're doing with this balloon?"

"I found out about the rendezvous and decided to do the meet-and-greet myself," Solomon explained.

"Ah," said Sophia, "so you've been talking to Songbird too."

"That's right," said Solomon with a wink.

Alice was puzzled. If Solomon had been talking to Songbird, that must mean he wasn't Songbird himself. So someone else in FIG must be the traitor, not Solomon Honker. Or, rather, it meant there was another traitor, she amended glumly. For Solomon Honker was most definitely a traitor too.

She looked over at her brother, who was watching Solomon Honker with a murderous expression. She knew how he felt; to think that the mouse Tobias had entrusted to run their undercover operation was himself a Sourian spy! And now they were on their way to Grouch, where they'd be thrown in Queen Eugenia's dungeon, no doubt. She remembered the mouse in the dungeon of the Cornoliana palace and wondered if she and Alex too would become pawns in the Sourians' treacherous plans. But how valuable could they really be? They had only just joined FIG; they didn't know any secrets. And yet if they were included on the list of the heirs of Cornolius . . .

As a gust of cool sweet air filled her nostrils, Alice realized they must be flying over the Winns. How much farther to Grouch? she wondered. Her musings were interrupted by a cry of disbelief.

"What? It can't be possible!" shouted Solomon Honker. "Sophia, Horace! Quick! Over here!"

As the Sourian spies rushed to the other side of the basket it rocked wildly.

No! thought Alice, remembering Claudia's warnings about destabilizing the basket. We'll tip. . . .

And then her feet were in the air and her head was facing the ground as the basket was upended. There seemed to be legs and arms scrabbling everywhere and cries of alarm, and from her upside-down position Alice saw two bodies hurtling down—or was it up?—toward the river.

When the basket was righted, only Alice, Alex, and Solomon Honker remained, and they seemed to have changed direction.

"Good riddance to bad rubbish," remarked the rusty-orange and white mouse, peering over the edge to the dark gleam of water below.

He swiftly untied Alice and Alex.

"Sorry if I gave you a fright there," he said.

Alice stared at him in astonishment, trying to make sense of her confused thoughts. She opened her mouth to speak, then remembered it was full of cotton. She pulled the handkerchief from her dry mouth, swallowed and licked her lips, then said, "So you're not a Sourian agent?"

"Nope."

Alex was massaging his wrists where the rope had cut into them. He looked bewildered. "But Sophia and Horace thought you were Sourian."

"Long story," said Solomon Honker, "but I'm FIG through and through."

"And you're not Songbird?"

"I am not—but I'd love to know who's been singing our secrets to the Sourians. When Claudia told me about your encounter with the dirigible it sounded like a premeditated attack, and I began to wonder how the Sourians could have known. It seems clear now that they have a source in FIG—the one they call Songbird. And you've heard the name before, I gather? Was this at the palace?"

Alice and Alex described the conversation they'd overheard in General Ashwover's office.

"Queen Eugenia is moving to Cornoliana," Alice recalled. "They were talking about it being the capital of Greater Gerander—and they're going to take over Shetlock too!"

"Ah." Solomon nodded wearily. "So that's what they're up to: the reunification of Greater Gerander. That makes sense of the troop buildup on the borders." He ran a hand over his face. "It looks like we've got our work cut out for us indeed if we're going to stop them. I just wish I knew who Songbird was and what else he or she has been telling the Sourians. . . . "

"They had a message Songbird had sent them," said Alice. "It was a list of the heirs of the House of Cornolius and where to find them."

Solomon's fatigue was replaced with an alert expression. "Is that right?"

Alex nodded. "Yeah. I guess they're using it like a hit list, so they can bump off anyone else who might fight Queen Eugenia for the throne."

A hit list . . . The fur on Alice's neck prickled. And they were on it. She recalled the conversation in General Ashwover's office, and Horace saying, "You mean they all have to be killed?" and Sophia replying, "It would be best if Queen Eugenia's was the only claim to the throne of Greater Gerander."

Alice swallowed at the memory of that silvery voice. "What do you think has happened to Sophia and Horace?" she asked.

Solomon raised his eyebrows. "They went straight into the river," he said. "They'll have hauled themselves to the bank by now, and if I know Sophia she'll be spitting with rage. You know, I almost feel sorry for Horace sometimes. It can't be easy working with Sophia." He shrugged. "Not that I'll have to worry about ever being in that position. I rather suspect I've just blown my cover."

"Did you really teach Sophia?" Alice demanded.

"Oh yes," said Solomon calmly. "I've worked for years as a Sourian spymaster. And I was telling the truth when I said I'd learned from her in return—she taught me the art of double-crossing, for one thing."

"You're a Sourian spymaster?!" Alex was staring at the rusty-orange and white mouse with a mixture of revulsion and fascination.

"I grew up in Souris," Solomon explained. "Spent my entire childhood in a Sourian boarding school. Despite my heritage," he indicated his rusty-colored lower half, "I thought of myself as completely Sourian."

"Didn't you get teased at school, though?" Alice asked, thinking of how much hatred was directed at ginger fur by those Sourians she had met.

"On the contrary," said Solomon. "I always did exceptionally well at school, and was marked out very early on as someone who had the potential to be of great use. I worked as a spy for many years before I defected to FIG. Though I must have neglected to tell the Sourians I defected, come to think of it."

"Wow!" exclaimed Alex. "So that makes you like a double agent."

Solomon Honker was amused. "I suppose I am."

"But is this the real you?" Alice asked slowly.

"What do you mean?" said Solomon with a sidelong glance.

Alice struggled to put her thoughts into words. "To be a double agent, you're always playing a part—like when you were being the stern teacher with us."

"One mouse in his time plays many parts," said Solomon softly. "Shakespeare," he explained, in answer to Alice's questioning look. "And it's true, I was playing a part when I was teaching you, but that was for your own good. If there's one thing I know, it's that a spy can never afford to get too comfortable. You need to have your wits about you at all times."

"Who else knows you're a double agent?" Alice asked, curious.

"Zanzibar, of course. Tobias and Flanagan. Slippers Pink and Feast Thompson have some idea. I don't think they quite trust me. . . ." He smiled ruefully.

"But you're not the only double agent, are you?" Alex pointed out. "You're a Sourian spy who's really a member of FIG, but Songbird is a member of FIG who's really spying for the Sourians."

"You're quite right," said Solomon. "Tobias mentioned his suspicion that we had a leak, but I don't think he realized quite how serious the situation is. If Sophia thinks Songbird is in a position to betray Zanzibar . . ." Solomon shook his head sadly. "That's as serious as it gets. Poor Tobias has a lot to deal with. And I'm afraid he's been rather distracted lately. Flanagan says he's missing his son."

Missing his son . . . And then a thought pierced Alice like an arrow. He has a son about our age, Alistair had told them. He showed us a photo of him and he looked just like Tobias, Tibby had said. Tobias, who had fur the color of orange marmalade. . . . There was a mouse about their age in the palace dungeon in Cornoliana. An orangey mouse, Alex had said. Songbird's son, according to Sophia.

"He's not just missing his son—his son is missing!" Alice burst out as the pieces fell into place. "It's Tobias—he's Songbird!" As the words left her lips she clapped a hand to her mouth, aware of how treacherous she must sound. For surely it couldn't be Tobias. He was the head of FIG in Zanzibar's absence. He was Zanzibar's own cousin!

But Solomon didn't seem to find her outburst offensive. He merely said, "Explain."

In a rush, Alice told him about the boy in the dungeon, Songbird's son—Tobias's son, she now realized.

Solomon looked grave, but he didn't contradict her conclusion. "Very good," he remarked, and for a moment Alice was reminded of the classroom back in Stetson. Then, with a grim set to his lips, he looked up at the balloon. "If only this thing could go faster," he muttered. "We've got no time to lose. If Tobias is Songbird, then Sophia was right: the Sourians will recapture Zanzibar."

Alice's heart sank as she thought of all the secrets Tobias must know—all the secrets he must have told the Sourians. And then, with a sinking feeling so bottomless and immense that it was like falling into a deep black pit, Lester's words were ringing ominously in her mind: the brat with the scarf may be within reach.

"And Alistair," she croaked. "Tobias was helping the Sourians to set a trap for Alistair."

Solomon looked at her sharply. "He betrayed Alistair too?" And then, to himself, he said quietly, "He really would destroy us all."

The balloon sailed steadily through the night air, and with every hour that passed Alice grew more anxious. Alistair was heading into a trap. . . . The Sourians were probably on their way to Zanzibar's hiding place. . . . Everything FIG was fighting for had been betrayed and no one knew it but them! The wait was unbearable, but at long last they were descending into the clearing below the school, Solomon was switching off the balloon's burner, and they were pushing through the branches of the narrow path and running up the hill toward the school.

"Go find your aunt and uncle and see if they've heard anything about your brother," Solomon ordered. "I'm going to find Tobias." And then he sprinted up the road into the night.

"Where do you think they'll be?" Alice panted. "Back at the dorm?"

"Let's try the cafeteria," said Alex. "It's on the way."

They burst into the cafeteria and almost immediately Alex was saying, "There they are!"

"Uncle Ebenezer! Aunt Beezer!" Alice called as she and Alex ran toward the long table where their aunt and uncle sat nursing mugs of tea. "Alistair . . ." She was breathing so hard she could barely get the words out.

"My dears!"

Ebenezer sprang from his seat and held out his arms, his whole face glowing with pleasure.

But Beezer must have caught something in the expressions of her nephew and niece, because she too sprang up, looking serious. "What is it?" she asked. "What's wrong?"

"Are Alistair and Tibby Rose back from their mission yet?" Alex demanded.

"They are!" said Ebenezer happily. "Someone saw Oswald fly in not long ago, and apparently Alistair and Tibby Rose were with him, along with Slippers Pink and Feast Thompson."

Alice flopped onto the nearest bench, the adrenaline suddenly drained from her limbs, too weak with relief to speak.

Alex sagged against the table. "That's brilliant news. Where are they now?"

"They must be debriefing with Tobias. I expect they'll be here any moment."

Tobias! Alice stiffened, but her uncle was saying, "Oh, look, here come Slippers Pink and Feast Thompson now. Alistair and Tibby Rose can't be far behind. Slippers, Feast, over here!" Uncle Ebenezer called. "Alice and Alex have just arrived home safely from their mission and are eager to see their brother—we all are. Are Alistair and Tibby Rose coming?"

Slippers Pink shook her head. "Alistair and Tibby Rose have been sent on another urgent mission, but Feast and I weren't required." She looked faintly troubled.

Alice gasped. "No! We have to stop them. Quickly!"

Thankfully, the urgency of her tone was enough to send

everyone rushing toward Tobias's office without asking for explanations.

On the way they met Solomon striding rapidly toward them.

Alex said, "Tobias?"

Solomon replied, "He's gone."

"What about Alistair and Tibby Rose?" Alice's voice came out high and scared. "Were they there?"

Solomon shook his head gravely, and Alice fell to her knees, overcome by a wave of despair. They were too late.

It was a solemn group that gathered around a table in the cafeteria to work out what to do next.

After Alice and Alex had explained everything to Uncle Ebenezer, Aunt Beezer, Feast Thompson, and Slippers Pink, Solomon said, "So let's presume that Tobias has sent Alistair and Tibby Rose to Zanzibar's hiding place, and will then alert the Queen's Guards."

"A logical proposition," Aunt Beezer agreed.

"But where is Zanzibar's hiding place?" Uncle Ebenezer asked. "Maybe we can reach Zanzibar first."

"Tobias said that it was a place known only to him and Zanzibar," Slippers Pink said thoughtfully. "I had the impression that it was somewhere they knew from when they were children."

"Is there anyone else who might know?" Solomon prompted.

Feast Thompson snapped his fingers. "There is one person," he said. "Though I don't know where he is right..." His words trailed away and a look of astonishment appeared on his face.

"Zanzibar's hiding place?" said a voice behind Alice. "That's too easy. Ask me another one."

Turning, Alice saw a tall mouse with—she blinked and looked again. No, she hadn't imagined it: his fur was midnight blue, except for one arm and leg, which were a swirl of different colors.

"Timmy the Winns!" said Slippers Pink, laughing in disbelief. "Just when we need you the most, here you are. You're not some kind of mirage, are you?" She had risen from her seat and was hurrying around the table to where the midnight blue mouse stood.

"No more than usual," he said, opening his arms to embrace the almond mouse. "So, it's Zanzibar's hiding place you're wanting? I know it, right enough, but I have to tell you, only a matter of life or death could persuade me to reveal it."

"It is a matter of life or death!" Alice burst out.

Timmy the Winns gave her a shrewd look, then dropped to the bench beside her. "Explain it to me, little sister," he said, "and then we'll see."

So Alice did, finishing with: "And if we don't hurry, the Sourians will get there before we do."

"If they haven't already," Alex added gloomily.

Timmy the Winns was already on his feet. "Okay, how are we going to get there?"

"Where?" several voices chorused.

"The source of the Winns," said Timmy. "Our grandparents' cottage."

"Your grandparents?" asked Alice, puzzled. "You mean yours and Zanzibar's?"

"That's right," said Timmy the Winns. "Zanzibar is my brother. Z and me and our sister used to spend our summers with our grandparents by the Winns. Tobias would come too occasionally."

"That must be the cottage we saw near the spring," Slippers exclaimed to Feast. "It's a long way from here though," she said worriedly.

"We can take the balloon," Solomon said immediately.

"Aye, that'll serve well," said Timmy. "Let's go then."

"You have to let us come," Alice begged.

"I've rescued my brother before," Alex added matter-of-factly (if not quite factually).

Solomon looked unsure but Timmy the Winns said, "Ah, come on, Sol."

"All right!" said Alex, but Uncle Ebenezer shook his head.

"No," he said. "You two stay here."

Alice had never seen her easygoing uncle look so determined. "First Oswald comes back all battered and bloodied having been attacked by eagles, telling us he'd dropped Alistair and Tibby Rose somewhere on the Sourian side of the Crankens. Then Claudia comes back with the story of the dirigible's attack. We thought we'd lost all of you! Well, as far as I'm concerned, that's it—I'm not letting you out of my sight again." He crossed his arms stubbornly.

Alice shot her aunt an appealing look.

Beezer asked, "So how big is this balloon of yours, Solomon?"

Solomon gave a resigned smile. "Big enough."

And so it was decided: Alice and Alex and their aunt and uncle would accompany Solomon and Timmy to the source of the Winns.

Alice just hoped they'd get there before the Sourians did.

23

Betrayed

"But, Oswald, we've just come from here," Alistair said, when the owl had released them. "This is the source of the Winns."

"I know where we are," said Oswald sniffily, glaring down at Alistair over his hooked beak. "Better than you it seems." He raised one feathered wing to indicate the path. "You go that way. I'll meet you back here after sunset tomorrow."

"I don't understand," said Alistair. "Where are we going? Who's the letter for?"

The owl looked at him steadily. "Zanzibar, of course."

"Zanzibar?" Alistair repeated incredulously, hearing Tibby Rose gasp behind him. "Wait . . ."

But the owl was already beating his wings, rising steadily toward the treetops.

Alistair turned to Tibby Rose. "What do we do now?"

Tibby shrugged. "Follow the path, I guess. Perhaps Zanzibar's waiting for us farther along."

It was hard to make out the path in the dark, so Alistair focused on the sound of the stream, gurgling through the rocks and rushing over the stony bed. This sound, too, was a song of the Winns, he realized.

It was only when they rounded the bend to see the stone cottage nestled in the hollow that Alistair understood that this was their destination. Tibby Rose put a hand on his wrist, and they stopped and gazed at the silent cottage. As before, there was no sign of life. No light flickered in the window, not even a solitary candle, and no one moved within.

"I suppose we should knock on the door," Tibby murmured, and she led the way up the path to the front door. After a glance at Alistair, she lifted her hand and rapped on the wooden door. The sound echoed loudly. Alistair listened for any movement on the other side of the door, but there was none. Perhaps they had been wrong, and this wasn't Zanzibar's hiding place.

Tibby had just lifted her hand to knock a second time when the door was opened. A tall mouse stood in the doorway. His fur, Alistair noted, was not so much ginger as the color of burnished gold, rich and glowing in the moonlight, as if it had caught the sun's dying rays.

Gazing down at the two young mice on his doorstep, the golden mouse looked puzzled. "Who—" he began in a deep voice. He tilted his head to one side and frowned slightly. "What are you—" He stopped again.

Alistair stepped forward. "I'm Alistair," he said. "And this is my friend Tibby Rose. We're sorry to disturb you, sir, but Tobias sent us with an urgent message for you." He held out the sealed letter. Zanzibar took it absently, but made no move to open it.

"Alistair," he repeated. "And Tibby Rose." He looked slightly dazed. Alistair supposed it must be startling to find two young mice landing unexpectedly on your doorstep when you were in hiding. Though wasn't he expecting them? Tobias had said that Zanzibar had ordered the mission, hadn't he?

Zanzibar shook his head suddenly, as if his thoughts had been far away. "Come in." He laughed, a deep rumble in his chest, and stood aside so Tibby and Alistair could enter the cottage. "You caught me unawares, as you can probably tell." He looked left and right before shutting the door.

"It's rather dark in here, I'm afraid," Zanzibar said, "and it can get quite cold at night, but it's better than the Cranken prison."

They were standing in a dim parlor. Zanzibar gestured for Alistair and Tibby to sit on the sofa while he himself sank into an easy chair.

"So what is Tobias up to, I wonder?" He stared down at the sealed message in his hand. Alistair thought he looked more apprehensive than curious, as if he already knew its contents. He tapped the letter on his knee thoughtfully, then said, "Tell me what you have been doing, the pair of you."

Alistair felt himself starting to choke up at the memory of their failed mission to rescue his parents, so Tibby briefly outlined their journey to Atticus Island, and what they had found there.

Zanzibar gave a heavy sigh, and Alistair raised his head. "Do you know my parents?" he asked curiously.

"I know them very well," said Zanzibar. "Very well. In fact—" But he was interrupted by an urgent pounding at the door. A look of concern flashed across his face, and he raised a questioning eyebrow at the two young mice on the sofa. "Did you tell anyone you were coming here?" he asked in a whisper. "Anyone at all?"

Alistair and Tibby shook their heads, but Alistair's heart was knocking in his ribcage. Could they have been followed? But there had been no one at the spring, he was sure of it.

Zanzibar put his finger to his lips then rose silently and padded toward the door.

"Zanzibar!" a thin high voice cried. "Zanzibar, I know you're in there. You have to let me in. I'm trying to save you." The owner of the voice began to pound at the door again.

Zanzibar hesitated, then flung the door open.

Alistair cried out in shock and Tibby screamed at the flash of red as a Queen's Guard burst into the room.

Zanzibar took several steps backward and flung out his arms to shield Alistair and Tibby Rose, but the Queen's Guard raised both hands into the air and they saw that he was unarmed.

"I'm not here to hurt you—I'm trying to save you," the young guard repeated. He was breathing hard, as if he had run a long distance. "You've been betrayed. There's a regiment of guards on the way," he panted. "They're coming from over the mountain." He pointed toward the spring. "Now—tonight. Not far behind." Unexpectedly, he dropped to his knees at Zanzibar's feet and bowed his head. "My mother is Gerandan," he said. "I never told anyone. But I couldn't let them recapture you. I snuck away as soon as I heard what they were planning."

Zanzibar placed his hand on the young guard's head, then helped him to his feet. "Thank you for your good deed," he said. "Now you should return to your post quickly, before you are missed."

The guard nodded once, then, still breathing hard, turned and bolted up the hill toward the spring.

"And we have no time to lose," Zanzibar told Alistair and Tibby Rose. He ushered them toward the door, and pulled it shut behind him.

"We know somewhere to hide," said Alistair. "This way." He stumbled a bit in the dark, until the fresh cool scent of the river calmed his frayed nerves, and he let the gurgle of the Winns guide him along the path. As he ran his mind was racing. Zanzibar betrayed? He could scarcely believe it. Yet Tobias must have known his cousin was in danger— that was why he'd sent the message. If only Zanzibar had opened it earlier they would have had more time.

He could hear Tibby's light steps and short quick breaths behind him, and the heavier tread of Zanzibar behind her.

Would he be able to find the cleft in the rock without the sun's last rays to illuminate the place? The doubt had barely flashed through his mind when his feet seemed to stop of their own accord.

"This way," he said, and darted toward the cleft in the

rock and squeezed through the hole into the cavern. Hurrying to the niche in the wall he took a candle and lit it, then led the way to the alcove in which he had found the map of the secret paths which matched the design on his scarf.

Without uttering a word, Zanzibar beckoned Alistair closer, then unsealed the letter he still carried and began to read it by candlelight, his expression grave. When he had finished he refolded it and, clutching the letter in one hand, placed the fingertips of the other to his forehead. Several long seconds passed in which he didn't move or speak.

Finally, Alistair, who was burning with curiosity, asked, "Did he say who betrayed you?"

Zanzibar dropped the hand from his forehead and looked at Alistair with a face full of sorrow and pain. "He did."

Tibby made a small noise and clapped her hand over her mouth.

Alistair waited expectantly for a name, but instead Zanzibar said, "Sometimes leadership demands more of an individual than they can bear. How could Tobias choose between his child and his country? It is too much to ask. A decision no one should have to make."

Suddenly Alistair understood. He did, Zanzibar had said. The golden mouse hadn't meant that Tobias had revealed the name of the traitor—he meant that Tobias himself had been the traitor! Alistair thought of Tobias's kind eyes and a feeling of utter despair washed over him. If they couldn't trust Tobias . . . It was hopeless, he saw. FIG could never win.

"Tobias betrayed us?" Tibby Rose sounded distressed, as if she couldn't bear for it to be true.

"The Sourians kidnapped his son." Zanzibar's voice was bitter. "They gave Tobias a choice. What a choice . . ." Then his voice became urgent. "Does Tobias know about this place?"

"No," said Alistair. "He knew about my scarf, and that we were going to look for the secret paths, but when we returned from our mission he didn't ask a single thing about it. And then he rushed us off so quickly we never had time to tell him." Now that he thought about it, it was odd that Tobias hadn't wanted to know the whereabouts of the secret paths. Surely the Sourians would have been grateful for the information.

As if he knew what Alistair was thinking, Zanzibar said, "I'm glad to hear it. If Tobias truly had the heart of a traitor, he would have wanted that knowledge for the Sourians."

Yet it was Tobias who had sent him on the fruitless quest to find his parents, Tobias who had told Keaters where to find him, Alistair realized, feeling the slow burn of rage rising in his chest.

"But he is a traitor," Tibby Rose was insisting. "He told the Sourians where you were hiding."

"He gave them what they asked for," Zanzibar agreed. "But no more than that. And he sent you to me, knowing you could lead me to safety."

Then Alistair remembered Keaters's reaction when he'd learned that Slippers Pink had accompanied Alistair to the island. Keaters hadn't been expecting that. Had Tobias intended for Slippers and Feast to protect him?

Zanzibar continued, "And don't forget, Tibby Rose, it is the Sourians who are in the wrong here, not Tobias. They threatened to harm the most precious thing he has in the world: his child. To have to choose between the needs of your country and the life of your child . . . Some sacrifices are just too great."

To Alistair's surprise there was no anger in Zanzibar's voice as he spoke of his cousin's betrayal—only a deep sadness and . . . understanding, perhaps?

Alistair thought about his parents; they must have known when they went on their mission that they risked sacrificing their freedom—and perhaps even their lives. And what about his own mission? If he was honest with himself, he had wanted to find the secret paths so he could use them to free his parents; he had thought more of freeing his parents than freeing Gerander. So could he blame Tobias, really? Wouldn't he have made the same choice if he were in Tobias's place? It was like what Slippers had said about the difference between thinking with your head and not your heart. It troubled him, though, how ready he was to put his own needs, the needs of his heart, ahead of FIG. Maybe the members of FIG just weren't ruthless enough to defeat the Sourians. But if the members of FIG were ruthless, would they be the kind of mice he would want to fight alongside? Surely a good heart was important too? He was about to ask Zanzibar what he thought, when there was the sound of footsteps.

The three mice froze.

"The tunnel," Alistair said in a strangled voice. "There's someone in the tunnel."

"They're coming for us," squeaked Tibby Rose in alarm, as a murmur of voices reached them.

Alistair just caught the look of concern on Zanzibar's face before the golden mouse blew out the candle. And then they were enveloped in darkness. Alistair could feel Tibby Rose trembling beside him and he felt panic catch at his breathing as his heart pounded in time with the approaching footsteps.

Maybe they won't look in the alcove, he told himself hopefully, when the footsteps grew louder, then stopped. As candlelight filled the room he heard a scream of terror from the doorway and then the candlestick was dropped. The light was extinguished and Alistair jumped up, dragging Tibby with him, thinking he would try to run for it. Then there was the scrape of a match and the hiss of flame and the room was filled with steady light once more. Alistair had just noted with despair that the exit was blocked when someone said, "It's you! Oh, it really is you!"

The voice was soft, sweet, and a bit breathless. Her soft brown fur was matted, and she was heartbreakingly thin, but her voice was just the same.

"Mom!" Alistair cried. "Mom!" And then he was in her arms and he couldn't speak anymore.

24

The Heirs of Cornolius

When Alistair finally lifted his head from his mother's shoulder he saw his father, white fur dirty, his whiskers creased in his same old smile, and he thought his heart would overflow with gladness.

As Alistair hugged his father, Emmeline looked over to where Zanzibar stood with his hand on Tibby Rose's shoulder.

"Zan! I can't believe it's really you!" She flung herself at the tall golden mouse, and he caught her in his arms and swung her around, laughing.

"It's really me, sis," he said.

"Sis!" Alistair exclaimed. "Do you mean—Mom, is Zanzibar your brother?"

"That's right," said Emmeline.

"But that means . . . he's my uncle!"

Emmeline looked at her brother. "Didn't you tell—?"

He gave a brief shake of his head.

Alistair could hardly believe it—here were his parents, alive, and Zanzibar was his uncle! Surrounded by family, he felt a sudden pang as he remembered Tibby Rose. She was standing against the wall, looking happy but a bit alone.

"Tib," he said, "come over here and meet—"

But Emmeline was already rushing forward, her hands outstretched. "Tibby Rose," she cried in her low, sweet voice. "Is it really you? Oh, my dear, look how you've grown. Oh!" She pulled Tibby into a tight hug.

Alistair was astounded. "You know Tibby Rose?"

"Well, she was only a baby the last time I saw her," Emmeline said, "but I'd know her anywhere." She held Tibby Rose's face in her hands and looked into her eyes. "Your parents were very dear to me, Tibby Rose. I loved your mother like a sister." She gave Tibby another squeeze.

Tibby looked overwhelmed but very, very pleased, Alistair thought.

Emmeline's expression turned serious. "But Nelson and Harriet—they haven't . . . ?"

Tibby must have guessed what she was thinking for she cried, "Oh no! They're fine. It's just that Alistair fell on my head and then . . ." She shrugged. "It's kind of a long story."

"We have four years of stories to catch up on, don't we, Em?" Rebus stood behind his wife with a hand on each of her shoulders. She leaned back against his chest and for the first time Alistair noticed how frail and tired she looked.

Zanzibar must have noticed too, for he said, "Let's rest here awhile before we move on."

"I thought we could go to our grandparents' cottage," Emmeline said to Zanzibar.

Her brother shook his head. "I'm afraid it's not safe there anymore, Em. The Queen's Guards are probably there right now looking for us."

Emmeline shivered. "Not there then. I never want to see another red coat in my life."

"Where will we go?" Tibby Rose asked.

"To Stetson," Zanzibar decided. "I'm through with hiding. FIG needs me to lead, not hide. How to get there is the question. . . . " He tapped his chin with his finger.

"Oswald—" Alistair began, then realized that to retrace their steps toward the source of the Winns would surely mean encountering Queen's Guards.

"We'll have to head south," said Zanzibar, "and see if we can find a way across the Winns. Then we can try to cross the border into Shetlock."

It sounded terribly risky to Alistair, but he couldn't think of another way. He looked at his parents, both so tired and weak. Would they be able to survive such a journey?

"Could we use the tunnels?" Rebus suggested.

Alistair and his mother looked at each other. "No, the tunnels don't run that far south," said Emmeline. "And there are no tunnels to the east of the Winns."

"There are other paths in the east, though," Tibby Rose

pointed out. "We met an old mouse who knew them, but she couldn't tell us about them because they could only be passed down through her family. Do you think those other paths are on the map?" She jumped up to study the map painted on the wall of the alcove.

"They are on the map," Emmeline said. "But I don't know how to read them. My grandmother only taught me about the tunnels."

Alistair walked over to stand beside Tibby Rose, his eyes scanning the picture in the flickering candlelight. His eyes traced the long main tunnel running alongside the northern part of the Winns, and the network of smaller tunnels leading west. To the east of the Winns was a web of green, with no sign of the curved brown arches which indicated the presence of a tunnel.

He sighed. "We can at least use the tunnel to travel some of the way south," he said, running his finger down the blue stripe of the Winns. "Maybe there'll be a place where—" Alistair stopped. "Tibby, look at this."

Tibby peered at the blue stripe where Alistair was pointing. "It looks like a thin green line," she said. "A line across the river." She turned to Alistair, her eyes wide. "Do you think it could be a bridge?"

"It's possible," said Alistair. "Let's see if Mom knows anything about it." He was about to call to his mother to come see, but then had a better idea. He unwrapped the scarf from around his neck and carried it to her.

"I remember knitting this scarf," Emmeline said softly as Alistair laid it on her lap. For a moment Alistair himself could see the dancing flames in the fireplace of the cottage of honey-colored stone where he and Alice and Alex had passed the first eight years of their lives, and Emmeline knitting beside it. "And it brought you here." She seemed both happy and sad.

"Mom," said Alistair, "do you know anything about this green line here across the Winns?"

Emmeline bent her head to look. "I've wondered about that line," she said. "I asked my grandmother about it, but she didn't know what it meant. I've always thought it might be a mistake, a slip of the artist's brush." She glanced up at the painting on the wall.

"It could be a bridge, though," Tibby said.

"It could be, I suppose," said Emmeline, her voice doubtful. "But it's such a thin little line." She traced the delicate stitch on the scarf with her finger.

"Since we were planning to head south anyway, let's leave the tunnel at that point and investigate," Zanzibar decided.

As they passed back through the tunnel he and Tibby had traveled so recently with Slippers Pink and Feast Thompson, Alistair recalled their return from Atticus Island. He had been expecting to travel from Cobb back to the north of Gerander with his parents and, despite his joy at being reunited with them now, this journey through the tunnel still reminded him of the heavy heart with which he had last trod this earthen floor. Now, when he had least expected it, he and Tibby were traveling south through the tunnel with Emmeline and Rebus—and the famous

Zanzibar! He smiled to himself as he pictured the look on Alice and Alex's faces at their triumphant return. Though there were many dangers between them and a triumphant return, of course.

"We went to Atticus Island to find you," Alistair told his parents. "But you weren't there."

"All the prisoners were moved off the island about a week ago," Rebus explained. "We were being moved to the Crankens." He related how a sympathetic guard had helped them to slip away from the convoy of guards and prisoners one night, and Emmeline had used her knowledge of the secret tunnels to find an entrance.

Zanizbar looked thoughtful at this. "Another sympathetic guard," he murmured. "Perhaps the tide is turning. . . ."

"We should take this," Tibby, who had memorized the map, interrupted as they neared a smaller tunnel branching off to the left. A few meters down the path, the smaller tunnel ended at a ladder.

Zanzibar climbed the ladder first to check that it was safe, then at his signal one by one they clambered up to join him. They were standing under a thick canopy of trees. Alistair could tell by the pale sky it was dawn. After the close earthy atmosphere of the tunnel, it was a relief to breathe the clear cool air of the trees and river.

There was no bridge. Alistair had barely had time to register this fact when a gentle breeze set the leaves of the trees rustling. And then he heard it: a faint whistle, almost like a sigh.

"Tibby, listen!"

"That sounds like Althea," Tibby said, looking around as if expecting to see the elderly mouse with curly gray fur.

"It's not Althea," Alistair told her. "It's the trees—just like she described."

They both cocked their heads to listen to the peculiar fluting sigh. Glancing at the others, Alistair saw that his mother had her head cocked too.

"What is that strange sound?" she was asking. "Can anyone else hear it? It sounds like the trees are whistling."

Rebus and Zanzibar shook their heads, but Tibby Rose said, "I can," and Alistair said, "Me too. Althea, the old mouse from the east who we met in the tunnel, told us about the whistling. She said not everyone can hear it though."

Tibby looked thoughtful. "You know how the rustling reeds play the Winns's north song? Maybe this is like the Winns's east song."

"The sound was like a song to Althea," Alistair recalled. "Remember how she taught me to whistle like that when you were dancing?" He pursed his lips and began the sequence of inhalations and exhalations that sounded remarkably like the sighing whistle of the trees.

"That's it," said Tibby. She began to move her feet, hesitantly at first, then more confidently, until she had traced out a pattern in the earth.

"And she said something about the murmur of the Winns below helping her to find her way home. I thought

312

that was funny actually—the bit about the Winns below, like she was walking on water." He stopped suddenly, struck by a thought. "Or walking above it." He tilted his head back to look into the canopy. In a gust of whistling breeze he thought for a moment he saw a fine web of branches intertwined. The way they wove together seemed familiar somehow.

He glanced down at the pattern Tibby's dancing feet had made, then looked skyward again.

"It's the trees!" he said. "She was walking in the trees! The branches have woven together to make a path."

He pointed into the canopy, and when the breeze parted the leaves the woven path of branches was briefly visible once more.

"And the green lines on the map show the secret paths through the trees," said Tibby. "And you can find them by the whistling sound. Yes, it all makes sense!"

Zanzibar was watching their exchange with a pleased look on his face.

"What a clever pair," he said. He turned to Emmeline and Rebus. "You've raised him well. You must be very proud."

"We are," said Emmeline quietly. "Though a lot of the credit belongs to Ebenezer and Beezer. I think Tibby's parents would be very proud too."

"Indeed they would," said Zanzibar solemnly.

It seemed to Alistair that Tibby Rose's pink-tinted fur looked more pink than usual, and he could feel a blush heating his own neck and face. "We still have to find a way up there," he pointed out, to change the subject. "I can't imagine old Althea climbing trees with her walking stick."

Tibby began walking slowly through the trees lining the river, scrutinizing their upper branches closely. She paused by one tree for several seconds and Alistair looked at her inquiringly.

"Have you found something?"

She circled the trunk, looking up into the tree's leaves, then shook her head.

"No," she said uncertainly. "But the whistling sound is really strong. Come listen."

Alistair joined her beneath the large spreading branches. "Wow," he said. "That's almost piercing. I wonder what's so special about this tree." He put his hand to the bark and tapped it lightly, then started in surprise when he felt it give beneath his touch. "What . . . ?" He pushed at the trunk more forcefully, and gasped as with a slow creak a section of the trunk swung inward. "It's a door!" He stuck his head into the tree's dark interior, and by the light streaming in through the door could see a set of wooden stairs cut into the wood. "With a staircase."

Alistair ran up the steps till he came to another door. He opened it and climbed out onto a path of braided branches high above the ground. He turned to see the expectant face of Tibby Rose, and nodded. Then, with the murmur of the Winns below, he began to walk above the river toward the thick mass of treetops on the other side.

Only a few minutes later he was hurrying down a spiral staircase inside a tree on the east side of the river.

He pushed open the door at the base of the trunk and stepped out to find himself at the edge of a broad meadow stretching toward a series of rolling hills. Long grass was interspersed with wildflowers that filled the air with the scent of honey. The sun hadn't yet risen, but the few clouds in the pale mauve sky were tinged with pink and gold. It was an exquisite dawn and, as Tibby Rose, his parents and Zanzibar joined him, Alistair couldn't help but feel that he was at the threshold of something more than just a new day. Everything would be different now, he sensed.

They gazed in silence for several minutes, then Zanzibar remarked, "I get so used to thinking of our country as a pawn in a political game that sometimes I forget how beautiful it is."

Alistair was just about to ask which direction they should walk in when Tibby said, "What's that?" She was pointing into the sky.

"Dirigible," said Rebus immediately. "The Sourians have been using airships to patrol the borders."

"I don't think so," said Zanzibar. "It's the wrong shape. It looks more like a hot-air balloon."

"Whoever it is, do you think they've seen us?" asked Emmeline. She sounded worried.

"Yes!" said Alistair. "Look—they're waving." And he ran into the long grass, waving his own arms above his head, his heart lifting into the air with the blue balloon, for he had recognized its passengers.

Then the balloon's basket was skidding along the

ground and two familiar mice tumbled from it and raced across the meadow.

"Oh, my children!" Emmeline's face lit up as Alex and Alice threw themselves at her and she gathered them into her arms.

Alistair came up behind his brother and sister and flung an arm around each of them, and Rebus wrapped his long arms around the whole lot of them.

They stayed like that for some time, then his mother lifted her head and exclaimed, "Timmy!" Alistair saw that his mother was laughing as well as crying. "Look at you! What have you done to your fur? It's all blue!"

Alistair turned to see Timmy the Winns loping across the grass toward them.

The midnight blue mouse winked at Alistair. "See the trouble I get into without my big sister to look out for me?"

Big sister? "You mean . . . you're Mom's brother too?"

Timmy the Winns gave Emmeline a quick glance then said, "I surely am, little brother—or should I say nephew. And what names are you two going by these days?"

"Alistair," said Alistair, "and Tibby Rose." He blushed, remembering how he and Tibby Rose had given Timmy the Winns false names when they had encountered him in Souris. They hadn't known who to trust in those days. All the same, Timmy had seemed to know them. . . .

"You knew who we were all along," he said accusingly.

Timmy just raised his eyebrows and gave Alistair an enigmatic smile.

"Hang on," Alice said, "if Timmy is Zanzibar's brother,

and Mom is Zanzibar's sister, then you three are the heirs of Cornolius—and me, Alex, and Alistair are too: we're the next generation."

"What do you mean?" Alistair asked.

"We were working undercover at the palace in Cornoliana," his sister explained, "when—"

"You were what?" Alistair felt his jaw drop in astonishment.

"It's a long story," Alice said. "The point is, Queen Eugenia has this hit list. She wants to kill off anyone else who has a claim to the throne of Cornolius so she can reunite Greater Gerander and rule without opposition."

"I get it," said Alistair. So that was why Tobias had betrayed him, why Keaters had planned to leave him to die on Atticus Island. Because as Zanizbar's nephew he was an heir to the throne. . . .

"And if anything happens to Zanzibar, Mom, or Timmy, I could be the king of Gerander," said Alex.

Alice pulled his whiskers. "Or I might be the queen," she said.

"Whatever," said Alex, rubbing his cheek. "But I'm right, aren't I, Solomon?"

"Yes, Your Highness," Solomon joked. "I guess I'd better pilot this thing carefully seeing as I have the whole Gerandan royal family aboard."

After much jostling and stepping on tails they all managed to squeeze into the basket. Alistair couldn't believe that all the people he loved were finally together in one place.

"Is everyone ready?" asked Solomon over the happy hubbub.

"Yes!" they all chorused.

"I just have one question," Tibby Rose piped up as Solomon started the burner and the balloon drifted skyward.

"What's that, Tibby?" Zanzibar asked, resting a hand on her shoulder fondly.

Tibby put her hands on her hips and looked from Uncle Ebenezer to Rebus and back again. "What was the mozzarella doing in the icy crevasse?!"

Rebus, who had one arm around the shoulders of Alice and the other around Alex, looked startled for a moment, and then began to laugh. Soon everyone joined in, even those who had never heard Uncle Ebenezer's stories before (or maybe they had, Alistair realized), seemingly struck by the absurdity of Tibby Rose's question.

As Rebus and Uncle Ebenezer argued good-naturedly about precisely who had fainted in terror and who had bravely scaled the sheer icy wall of the crevasse—for Rebus seemed to have an entirely contrary recollection of the adventure—Alistair turned to stare at the silver gleam of the Winns. He remembered when he had first heard of it, as Timmy had sung of his love for Gerander's mighty river:

> *"Wherever the Winns takes me, that's where I'll be,*
> *For me and the Winns will always flow free."*

He felt his happiness dim a fraction as he thought of the setbacks FIG had suffered in their efforts to free Gerander, and of the new challenges they faced if Queen Eugenia really meant to reunite Greater Gerander; that would mean Shetlock, too, was in danger. He thought of what Alice had said: he was an heir of Cornolius. So like Zanzibar, like his mother and Timmy the Winns, he had a responsibility to his country that ran deeper than his family ties. He must learn to think with his head as well as his heart, then, he realized; he would have to put the good of all Gerander ahead of his own needs.

He would do it, he vowed. He would do whatever it took to ensure that the Winns ran free again.

Acknowledgments

For doing what they do so well I would like to thank David Francis, Tegan Morrison, Lydia Papandrea, Mel Maxwell, Kate O'Donnell, Priscilla Nielsen, Barbara Mobbs, and Helen Glad. And thanks to David and Rhonda Legge, for sharing their scary story!

FRANCES WATTS worked as an editor for ten years before writing her best-selling picture book *Kisses for Daddy* (illustrated by David Legge). Other books include the award-winning *Parsley Rabbit's Book about Books*; *Captain Crabclaw's Crew* (both illustrated by David Legge); *A Rat in a Stripy Sock* (illustrated by David Francis); and *Goodnight, Mice!* (illustrated by Judy Watson). Frances has also written a series of chapter books about two unlikely superheroes, *Extraordinary Ernie and Marvellous Maud* (illustrated by Judy Watson). Her books have been published in 20 countries. Frances lives in Sydney and divides her time between writing and editing.

www.franceswatts.com

Also in The Song of the Winns trilogy: